Taken to Kor
Xiveri Mates Book 5

D1714287

Elizabeth Stephens

Contents

What happened previously...

Mathilda, once leader of the human colony, has been exiled to Kor for her crimes. Her last act before exile was to give Kor's pirate ruler, Rhorkanterannu, a human with access to coordinates leading to a lost human satellite.

The human escaped with help from Deena, Mathilda's granddaughter — and *prisoner* for the past rotation. Deena was offered up to Rhorkanterannu as well, but he refused her, citing her as "defective." That didn't stop Deena from stealing away on his ship.

Busting out of Mathilda's prison, she squirreled herself away on Rhorkanterannu's ship, freed the human captive, and took off in an escape pod.

The only problem? Deena only knows one set of coordinates and they lead to the lost human satellite. She has no idea what she'll find there, only that it has to be better than being taken by Rhork and his horde of brutal Niahhorru pirates.

Right?

Pronunciation Guide & Glossary

Bo'Raku (*boh - rah - kooh*)
Title of the former ruler of the Drakesh planet, Cxrian. The title of Bo'Raku is passed from one Cxrian ruler to the next. The Bo'Raku with the slave named Pogar was responsible for establishing The Hunt on the human moon colony. He also led an unsuccessful invasion on Nobu, which was stopped by Nobu's Okkari or Va'Raku with the slave name Kinan. Pogar was then exiled to Kor. His son with the slave name Peixal, became the new Bo'Raku and continued the practice of the Hunt until it was abolished by the Raku and Rakukanna of Voraxia.

Centare (*cent-are-ay*)
No in Meero, the most common trading language; primary language of the Niahhorru

Eshmiri (*esh-meer-ee*)
Second largest group of space pirates; known for their short, stocky builds, laughter-like language, and fighting pits on the asteroid Evernor

Kor (*kohr*)
Trading city located in the grey zone between Quadrants 4 and 5; ruled by the Niahhorru species commonly referred to as space pirates; their leader is Rhorkanterannu

Krisxox (*chris - zawcks*)
Voraxia's chief battle strategist

Ontte (*aunt-tay*)
Yes in Meero, the most common trading language; primary language of the Niahhorru

Oosa *(ooh-sah)*
Species of Quadrant Eight; ruled by Reoran; large blob-like figures that illuminate from within whenever speaking or expressing emotion; extremely difficult to kill

Raku *(rah - kooh)*
Overarching ruler of the Voraxian federation and its seven planets; based on, and ruler of, its principle planet, Voraxia

Rakukanna *(rah - kooh - kah - nah)*
Mate of the Raku

Shrov *(shrohv)*
Common Meero curse

Va'Raku *(va - rah - kooh)*
Ruler of the Voraxian planet, Nobu; referred to as Okkari on Nobu

Va'Rakukanna *(va - rah - kooh - kah - nah)*
Mate of Va'Raku; referred to as Xhea on Nobu

Voraxia *(voh - racks - ee - uh)*
Chief planet of the Voraxian Federation; base of the Raku; characterized by expansive werro woodlands and a sandy forest floor

Yamar *(yeam-are)*
Yamar is a precursor to yeeyar, is a static non-biological power source, and is the common communication/translation tool of the Eshmiri Reavers

Yeeyar *(yeeh-yare)*

Yeeyar is an advanced power-source used by the Niahhorru pirates of Kor; it is a biological organism that can be melded with other static metals and glasses to create spaceships, payment discs and Niahhorru communication tokens

To Euhania,
the matriarch who united my family
more than blood ever could.

We miss you.

One half rotation, or two hundred solars, previous...

/

Deena

"Hello?"

"Interesting."

That's the reply. The voice is as dark as it is chilling and that chill has nothing at all to do with the frigid temperature down here in Mathilda's dungeon and everything to do with that impish yet svelte intonation. He didn't expect me, and I know who he is. He doesn't know who I am yet, and he has no reason to. I'm nobody.

But he's curious.

I know I should take the little bead I found out of my ear, but I don't. I'm too starved for any sort of human interaction at all to care. Well, human or…otherwise.

"Um…hi."

"Hmm," he says and it's almost a sigh. For as gruesome as he's known to be, he sure has a voice that's satin-laced sin. *Not sin, but another S word. Rhymes with decks.* I wince at the thought, but knowing it's wrong does nothing to help the next thought that comes to me. *I want to hear him say something else.* "You know who I am."

What? How does he know that? Can he read my mind through this thing! Shit! I don't know the technology. This is the first time I've ever opened up the communication channel. What if he knows what I'm thinking and he knows that I stole this and what if he tells Mathilda and I get caught?

I laugh at that. It's more like a snort. What could she do to me that she hasn't done already? Kill me?

Well, she could do that.

"So um…" I clear my throat because my voice is all gravelly and hoarse. "How do you figure that?"

"You have this device and I can read its identifier. I know who once owned it since I gave it to her, but you aren't her and, since you haven't asked me who I am, I have to assume that you know already who I am and that you stole it. Now, why don't you identify yourself so that we can make this conversation a little less one-sided?"

He sounds so at ease, like nothing in the world could unsettle him. Like he's planned all this. Like he's seen every eventuality and in every scenario, he comes out on top.

I swallow hard and stare a hole through the ceiling. I'm lying flat on my cot, but my mouth is dry, so I sit up and grab the bottle of water Mathilda slipped into my cell last night. She hasn't been by since and it's been a full solar. I guess she assumed that, with the weight I'm carrying, the one meal she gave me would be enough.

"I um…" am stuttering again. I can't figure out what to say. I only half expected this to work since I have no idea what I'm doing and only acquired this device ten solars ago. Or has it been twelve? More? Who knows. Down here in this cage, time is irrelevant. "I don't think you need my name."

"Fine. Then tell me what you want."

"I um…"

"Um… I'm beginning to think this is a word of some significance in your language because it doesn't translate to mine. Either that, or you didn't expect your communication to be received and now you're completely stumped."

Shit. He *can* read my mind. I touch my ear as I chug what's left in my water bottle. Water dribbles down my chin. I wipe it off with the back of my hand and cross one arm over my stomach.

I should take the earpiece out and smash it into shards, but I don't do that either. Partly because I'm not sure I'll be able to smash it, but mostly because if I do, this will be the end of my lifeline. The last being I might have a chance to talk to except for Mathilda. *And I'd rather skin her than make conversation.* Only that isn't true, is it? I'm too terrified of her to do anything.

"Yeah, you're right," I confess.

He doesn't respond right away and I find that kind of funny. I chuckle. "What? Are you stumped now?"

"A little."

I don't answer. I don't know what to say. "I…"

"What are you looking at right now?"

The question is unexpected. Unexpected, but smart.

I look through the clear walls of my cell at the rows and rows of food my *grandmother* has been hiding down here from the rest of the colony. From me. Breaking the lock and coming down here for the first time to discover all this marked my undoing. That was when she locked me up. She couldn't have me spilling the beans and I would have because the colony hasn't seen beans in rotations. People are starving topside and my grandmother has been hoarding supplies away for herself this whole time. And that's among the least troublesome crimes that conniving creature has been committing. *No, not creature. Another C-word. One that rhymes with runt.*

I could tell him that I'm looking at rows of vegetables growing underneath solar lights, but then he'd know right away where I am and I don't know what he knows yet. Maybe he's the one that gave her all of this. Maybe he's on her side. Maybe he already told her that I have her device and that I'm speaking to him when I shouldn't be. Maybe they're in cahoots. Cahoots. That's a funny word. I always thought so. *Rhymes with... actually, I don't know what it rhymes with... Wait. What are we talking about?*

"Water." My voice breaks. I clear my throat.

"Water," he repeats, just as rough, just as smooth. I didn't know a voice could be both. "Interesting. Is this water for drinking or water for swimming?"

"There's water for swimming?"

Again, he hesitates. "There is. Vast quantities of it."

Incredible. I don't even know how to picture it. "Really? Where? Is it in big tanks?"

"Many different places. Not in tanks, at least, not the kind I'm speaking of. This kind appears in nature, but not on little moons like yours."

I swallow. So he knows where I am, but not who I am. That computes. "You...have you...um..."

"I've decided I don't like this *um* word. Use another."

My lips quirk. I'm smiling. Wow. When was the last time I smiled? I frown then, unable to remember it. "Well, mister, I'm not the best conversationalist. I don't exactly get a lot of practice."

"Is that so?" He grumbles, voice sounding a lot like a growl. *There's that word again. Starts with an S and sounds an awful lot like specks.*

I reach for my water bottle. It's empty, flecks of water clinging to the inside of it but refusing to pool. Dang it. I don't know when I'll get another. I glance at the bucket in the corner. The two buckets. One for pee one for…everything else. If Mathilda doesn't come back soon, I guess I'll have to go with bucket number one. *Pee rhymes with yipee!*

"No. I don't talk to many people."

"Humans," he answers. "You don't talk to many humans."

"Right."

"But you are human."

"And you're not."

"Centare," he answers. "I'm not."

"Centare," I repeat. "What language is that?"

"Meero. The language of the Niahhorru."

I swallow hard, thoughts firing too fast to capture them all. I blurt out the most random one. "Will you teach me?"

He laughs. *Laughs.* It sounds strange because it isn't translated, so it's just his raw voice. It sounds like overlapping notes, all tangled together but easy to listen to. It's soothing. My shoulders relax down my back. I close my eyes, just listening to his laugh repeat itself, like he's speaking through a tunnel and I'm the only one at the other end. It's nice. Even if he is the enemy. Because everyone is an enemy. I don't know one person that's actually good. Maybe my mom. She was good, at least from what I can remember. But maybe I'm remembering wrong. I was just a kid when she was taken from me. My dad, even though he had the same dark skin most colony people do, succumbed to the sun plague just after I was born. I never knew him.

"I only have a mutinous planet of pirates to manage, but of course, I have no problem taking time out of my busy solars to teach you Meero."

"Okay, good," I say, refusing to rise to his sarcasm.

He doesn't speak for a while and I fully expect him to recant his obviously fake offer, but so far he hasn't done anything expected. *I don't know what I expected.* He laughs that laugh that's so beautiful it hurts. I'm still coming down from the high and I miss whatever he says next.

"What?"

"I said, you will have to give me something to call you by."

I chew on my bottom lip, gnawing it to shreds. "Deena," I finally answer.

"Deena," he repeats in his strange brogue. I like the way it sounds when he speaks it. Like he's savoring it.

"And...what's your name?" I stutter.

"Deena, you already know my name. I suspect, you already know quite a bit about me."

"You're trying to steal women."

"I'm trying to save a species."

"It's still stealing. You tried to take Miari and Svera."

"Perhaps that is only because I hadn't met you first."

My chest tightens. I imagine him wanting me. I shouldn't want that, but I do. I'd be willing to do a lot for a little attention at the moment. It's only been a few solars since I've been stuck in this cell, but it feels like a lifetime.

"Rhorkanneteru," I whisper.

He laughs again, this time a little shorter. "Rhorkanterannu."

"Rhorkanterannu," I repeat, then huff. "It's too long."

"All Niahhorru have long names. At least, all Niahhorru of worth."

"I still say it's too long. You could make it shorter. Just the end part, or the beginning."

"What would you call me then?"

I reach for my water bottle again, then again, lower my hand. I cross my arms over my chest and lie back on my bed, staring up at the ceiling, imagining it a lunar sky full of stars. "How about Rhork?"

There's a long silence after I say that. Then, "Interesting."

And that is the first time I ever met Rhork.

Two hundred solars later, or now...

2

Deena

My whole body is jittery. It has been since I boarded the Niahhorru battle transporter, helped rescue Svera and managed to escape. Now, I'm in the escape pod staring blankly at the control pad built into the armrest of one of the four chairs in this tiny little thing.

I got it to jump space, like Krisxox told me too. That was good advice. Without it, I'm pretty sure I'd have been caught right away. But now the control pad is flashing at me in bright blue, asking me for coordinates to my destination because I'm apparently low on energy, or fuel or whatever thing powers this pod. That's what I think the blue blinking light means, anyway.

Coordinates.

My mind goes completely and utterly blank.

And then I start to laugh. I laugh long and hard and so crazily, I'm forced to remember every single time Mathilda, my dearest grandmother, told me that I was insane. Mental. Mad. A madwoman. A lunatic. I feel it, then. I feel all of it.

Because I don't know the coordinates to take me back to the human colony. I don't know *any* coordinates except for the ones Rhork wants more than anything else in the universe.

I gnaw on my bottom lip, tearing it to pieces as my fingers hover over the controls. Finally, the warning signs get louder and I fidget in my chair. What are my options? I could sit here and die, or I could go there and try to find the humans. Maybe start a new freaking life.

Yeah. A new life. That'd be good.

At least, it can't be any worse than the one I just left.

My fingers are jerky and hesitant as I input the coordinates I *do* know. The only ones I know because they're the only ones ever given to me. Svera told me to use them only if I was in a bind, but right now I'm in a pretty massive bind, so I throw them in and strap myself into the control chair and brace as the ship jolts, changing sectors again and returning me back to the grey zone between Quadrants Four and Five, not too far from where I disembarked the Niahhorru mothership in the first place.

I'm headed to the satellite that Rhork's been trying to get to all along. *That's* why he took Svera and not me. It has nothing to do with the fact that I'm defective. He just wanted the coordinates…

The dusty colony sand swirls around my ankles and sticks to the sweat on my skin. I'm sweating everywhere. I have been since Mathilda dragged me out of that basement and brought me here to watch this deal go down with Rhork. She's going to give him Svera, the human advisor to the moon colony.

Svera has the coordinates that Rhork wants.

Mathilda needs Svera out of the picture because Svera knows things she shouldn't. She knows what Mathilda did to the colony women. She knows she's been killing them and selling their babies to the exiled scum called Bo'Raku — Pogar. That's what I heard her say his true name was. And his son, Peixal, is the one who took over the position of Bo'Raku and continued the awful practice of the Hunt. At least, until he met Kiki...

But Rhork knows me. We've been talking for almost half a rotation now — that's two hundred solars! He's taught me how to speak Meero almost fluently. He's described to me galaxies much farther away than this one. He's told me about water. About oceans. He'll listen to me. Right? He's made me laugh.

I've made him laugh.

He likes me.

"Rhork, please," I beg, the goons on my arms holding me back as I try to propel myself towards him and the black and clear ship looming like a monstrosity behind him. A Niahhorru pirate ship, in the flesh. It's the most beautiful thing I've ever seen. Except maybe for Rhork himself... "I'm asking you. I'm telling you. I'll do the shekurr. Take me instead."

The ritual doesn't exactly appeal to me. Having sex with a dozen or more Niahhorru pirates at once — for them, an honor — for most humans, a horror in the making. But I'd do it if it meant I got to have Rhork to myself just once.

My cheeks burn with the thought. And then they burn for another reason entirely when Mathilda strides up to me and gives my right cheek a good whack.

My head spins and I get dizzy for a moment, letting my weight fall onto the guys holding me. Human guys working for Mathilda. Cowards. I hate them. When I look up, Rhork has his weapon pointed at Mathilda like he's got every intention of pulling the trigger. My heart beats harder. Is he...could he be...upset that she hit me? My insides squeak at the thought.

It makes me want her to hit me again, just so I can see his reaction. Nobody's ever cared about me before. Nobody.

"Those who harm females in my presence tend to lead very short, painful lives," he whispers, his teeth flashing in the harsh sunlight.

Mathilda simpers, "Rhorkanterannu, your Grace…"

Ooohhh. Big mistake. Pirates are pirates. Pirates look down on kings.

As Rhork tells her as much, Mathilda makes her way forward, palms upturned, arms outstretched. She apologizes like the slithery snake that she is, and then she says something that I should have expected, but didn't.

She tells him I'm a virgin and that I'm available, for the right price.

I'm your granddaughter.

I don't know why those are the words that come to me first, but they are, and because the second thought that strikes like a viper is that Mathilda killed her own daughter — my mother — so why should she give a shit about the blood that runs between us? I manage to use the second thought to trap the first thought behind the gate of my teeth. Instead, I just glare at her while heat ravages my cheeks and tears build in my eyes. Not sad tears, of course. But pissed as shit tears. I decide then and there that it would please me to see this woman die.

At least, it should *please me.*

She's my family. And she just tried to sell me.

And then my hatred for my grandmother evaporates like smoke in the face of something far more dreadful. After a lengthy pause, Rhork says, "Centare. I don't want her."

I choke. Gag. Everything I thought I knew comes crumbling to the ground around me. Everything. *Because Mathilda's hatred and her impish ire and her malice are all things I know as well as the dark brown lines crisscrossing over my palm. But Rhork has shown me nothing but kindness since I've known him and this is the fall.*

I start to fall.

The blow Rhork just struck has only grazed the surface. He isn't finished with me yet. The blade in my gut twists and, if it weren't for the goons holding my arms, I'd have brought my hands up to try to staunch the flow of emotions from the wound, from my shredded and torn chest.

"She is defective," Rhork says and I know he means my leg. It's twisted from that time that I was six and Mathilda broke it so I wouldn't have to participate in the Hunt. I loved Mathilda then. She hurt me, but I loved her. Just like Rhork. Only he didn't break my leg, he cut both my legs out from under me.

Because I'm insane to love monstrous things.

Never again.

"I could not even give her away at the slave auction. Release her. She is not even worth the ebo it would take to keep her fed."

Mathilda laughs and orders her goons to release me. I break free and flip them off and as I look back at Rhork it's with a knowing that he's just as bad as her. I run off into the desert, but when I have to decide between going back to the colony and telling everyone what happened or doing something more reckless, I take the crazier of the two decisions.

I climb over the pile of rocks and sneak onto Rhork's ship, using the token in my ear to guide my entry. Defective? I'll show him defective when I ruin all of his plans and free the human he took instead of me.

He should have taken me.

Yes. He should have taken me.

I stare down at my leg. It isn't obvious in the jeans I'm wearing that it's all scarred, but underneath I know what I look like. Worse than the scars that wrap around my leg like coiled snakes though, is the fact that the bone didn't heal right, so my foot is angled out to the side unnaturally. It gives me a limp when I walk, but that's never stopped me.

I frown.

I don't know why it bothers me so much to be called that by him and I sigh, shake my head, put it out of my thoughts. He's just as bad as Mathilda and the things…the horrible things he was getting ready to do to Svera…He would have taken her in shekurr if I hadn't stopped him.

My muscles all firm up at the thought and I get up, out of my seat, and pace around the small escape pod. I locate weapons stashed in a cubby in the middle of the floor and quickly scan through them. I find a sword and pull it out, slash it around a few times aimlessly. I've never held a sword before.

I chuck it aside and duel an imaginary opponent with a spear. At least, I thought it was a spear until it started vibrating at one end and a giant bolt fired out of the other. I scream and drop it back into the cubby as the bolt clinks uselessly off of the impenetrable wall of the pod instead of exploding it open and launching me into space.

That was close. Hehe.

I'm not stupid enough to try any of the blasters, or the glowing purple balls that sit in a glass case. Eventually, I get bored of the weapons and try some of the other floor panels. Eventually, one of them springs open.

"Food!" I shriek with glee at the sight of the tubes of black liquid and the clear packages wrapped around a brown mushy substance.

Since the packages look kind of like someone pooped into bags, I go for the tubes first.

"Aguheaaaeeey!" I choke and have a hard time recovering my breath. The taste is like someone beat a fish to death with a bag of garbage and then liquified both with battery acid. It tastes sour and sweet and like sick all at the same time. *Not sick, another S-word. Rhymes with spit.*

The taste claws up the back of my throat and enters my brain and I immediately chuck the black liquid away and opt instead for a bag of crap. "Huh." Tastes like peppermint. A little like melon. It'll do.

I eat three more of the bags of poop and look down at my stomach when I'm finished. I feel full and right now, in just a tee shirt that stopped fitting me a hundred solars ago, it shows. I frown again. My stomach is full and my breasts are even fuller. Monster jugs, they sit heavy on my chest and sometimes, even make my back hurt. One would think that my giant bottom would have balanced out the weight, but I guess it just doesn't work that way.

Too bad.

I didn't always used to look like this. Just…after Mathilda put me in the basement. Food was the only thing I had to occupy my time. I didn't realize that I'd gain weight. Nobody on the colony has ever gained enough weight to get round, so it didn't even occur to me that I might.

As I walk around the eerily transparent edge of the escape pod, I drop my hand from my stomach and force myself to concentrate instead on the vastness and magnificence of space. Faraway stars blink like beacons to massive ships, calling them home. Though, in a way, I guess planets are kind of like ships transporting millions of people through the enormity of the universe. I smile at that, feeling my cheeks redden for no reason at all.

I press my palm to the edge of the pod and whatever black material that periodically flares up over the transparency appears beneath my fingertips, like it's trying to communicate.

"What are you trying to say, little buddy?" I ask it, but the black material that looks like inky fabric just darts away and doesn't answer me. *Rude.*

I grin, used to things not responding, so I just shrug and continue to count the comets and shooting stars I spy. "Eight...nine...eleven...thirty-three..." The shooting stars are hard to make out because the asteroids are starting to bunch together, closing in around the escape pod like reaching hands, making me wonder if they even are asteroids.

They're big blocks of black and brown rock, some the size of this escape pod or smaller, but most, huge, hungry, hulking things. Despite their size, the escape pod maneuvers around them easily and I wonder how it knows to avoid the space debris and universe junk. Sensors? Sight? Is this thing alive? Can it see? Can it feel?

"If you can feel me, sorry for throwing around your weapons." I hold up my hands as I stare around at the transparent walls and the space beyond them. Cautiously, I return all the weapons to their cache while humming a song I made up.

"Do you like music?" I ask the pod.

Crazy person! Yeah, maybe. But since I figured out how to disable my communicator, I know that I'm back to where I started. Alone. *Alone in the emptiness of space. Except, is space empty, really? Maybe it's full. Think of all the life floating through it. Me, just a solitary little pinpoint among the trillions. What's bigger than trillions? Gazillions? What's bigger than that? Gabajillions?*

"Oh right, you don't speak Human." *Duh.* "Do you like music?" I ask the pod again in Meero.

It still doesn't respond. "Humph. Maybe you just don't have experience with music. I can fix that."

I open my mouth and sing the silence a song I wrote in Meero, "Droganeene nene erro, wa da rogar tre hodona." I'm belting the words out now. It's a song about a plant. Lacking some er…inspiration when I was down in that cell under my sweet old gramma's house, I only thought up songs about the things directly in front of me.

"If you lift your green leaves up to the sun," or in the basement plants' case, the sun lamps mounted above them — but who's really factchecking? "Then you'll grow big and strong…Ahh!" I scream as the entire escape pod lurches to an alarming stop.

My whole body sails, arms pinwheeling in the air. I'm headed straight for the clear wall on my left and, because it's clear, I'm caught off guard when I hit it. Luckily, I managed to bring my arm around to cover my head. Unluckily, I hit my elbow against the clear and black surface.

"Augh!" I writhe in a funny sort of agony as my funny bone sends jitters all up and down my left side. "You stupid shroving wall!" I kick my feet on the floor, hoping to dispel the sensation when a hard voice cuts into the quiet, just like it did that very first time...

"You nosey little cretin!" She hits me so hard my lower lip splits and I taste blood the moment I hit the floor. The carpet is hard and scratchy under my palms, but there's something smooth among the threads, something soft. I wrap my fist around it at the same time that my grandmother *wraps my locs up in her fist and lifts me up by them. She's stronger than she looks as she drags me, kicking and shrieking, down the hall, down the stairs into the basement.*

I've been down here before. I broke the lock. That's what started this whole mess.

I'm so dazed I don't realize where I am or where I'm going until I'm on the floor and a door is sealed before me. It's glass, or something like glass. Something harder because it doesn't break — I spend the next few solars trying. Realizing it's pointless on the ninth solar, I eventually turn to the little device. I try to use it in all kinds of weird ways and eventually make it work on accident. I'm sleeping with it underneath my pillow when I first hear the static. I listen closer...and closer... and closer...and then the thing crawls *into my ear canal.*

I scream when it lodges itself deep inside my head and I try to shake it out. But then I hear something. I think I do anyway. It sounds like someone speaking very far away. It sounds like a man's voice. A male's anyway, because I know it can't be human. I think about how wonderful it would be to actually talk to someone and then all at once, the connection sharpens, becoming clear. All other sounds drown out and I'm left listening to someone who I know can hear me.

"Hello?" I say.

A momentary silence.

"Interesting."

The same voice jolts me into action now. "Deena, are you alright?"

"Shrov!" I jerk at the unexpected sound. Cursing in Meero, I quickly scratch the communicator out of my ear. I stare at it in my palm, completely and totally agog. Agog. I always thought that word was dumb. Like somebody meant to exclaim, *"I'm a frog!"* but mispronounced it.

"Holy shit!" I curse again in Human at the little silver bead — it's a Niahhorru token and allows me to communicate with any other Niahhorru token. Ships are made out of the same material, allowing me to control this one without use of the pad built into the armrest. Or at least, it did, but I…I was sure I disabled it.

"You're not real!" I shout at the bead only to be rewarded when *laughter* echoes all around me. *It's coming from the ship! It* is *alive! And it didn't even compliment me on my singing. Alive and* rude.

I glance around at the emptiness beyond the walls. Planets, stars, asteroids, all listlessly floating by, minding their own business. And me, an intruder among them, listening to laughter that can't be real. *Maybe, I* am *crazy.* I'm less mad about the fact that I might be clinical than I am about the fact that, if I am nutso crazytown, that means Mathilda was right about something.

But then the voice says, "You didn't think you'd get rid of me that easily, did you Deena?"

"Shrov! How did you…" My jaw works. I amble from my knees onto my feet and shake my fist at the ceiling. "I disabled my token!"

He breathes out very slowly and makes a clicking sound. "Deena, that isn't possible."

"You…you told me it was possible." I'm suddenly mortified. All those times I thought I had privacy and he was listening? "You taught me the command to disable it…" I can remember it now…

Humming to myself, Rhork's voice crackles into the space. "Can you keep up singing like this the entire solar?"

I chirp. And then I burst out laughing. "Shrov. I forgot you were listening. Isn't there a way to turn this thing off?"

"You never answered my question. And it's tengay, *not* tenjay."

"Shrov." I repeat the word he says for listening, *then add, "Do you mean to tell me you don't like my singing?" I gasp and immediately start to belt out the words to another song I made up. This one a much jauntier tune than the last. That one was about unrequited love.*

A charged roar zings through the line. "You have got to know that singing louder doesn't improve the quality of the pitch."

I laugh and immediately stifle it. Like I always do.

"I hate when you do that," he says, voice low and, I imagine, a little bit sadder than it was. Maybe not sad, *but at least a little more melancholic.*

My tone drops to match his, or maybe just because I don't want Mathilda to hear me through the walls or the ceiling or the pipes or wherever. I'm lucky that she thinks I'm a madwoman because it's already been a couple times now that she's caught me talking out loud to Rhork, though she obviously thought that I was talking only to myself.

"Do what?"

"Sensor yourself. You stop yourself from laughing." We both get quiet then. Questions go unasked. Their answers go unvoiced. Then he snorts and even that sounds rehearsed, far more syrupy than it should be. Syrupy, no. Another S-word,

yes. This one rhymes with eventual. *"You don't stop yourself from singing though."*

"If you wanted me to stop singing, all you'd have to do is turn off the dongle."

"Dongle?" He repeats the Human word I used and hearing him speak in Human gives me the willies.

"You speak Human weird."

"You speak Meero weird, but I'm at least polite enough not to tell you."

"Centare," I laugh, stifling it again. *"You correct me all the time."*

He doesn't laugh with me like I thought he might. Instead, he sighs, *"I hate it when you do that."* I don't answer. I just wait. I don't have anything to say. I mean, what would I say? That my sweet, runt of a grandma might come down here if she hears me and take him away? That I would hate that? That it might...that it might break me? Nah. I can't say any of that.

I'm humming again without realizing it. At least, until Rhork clears his throat. *"You can turn off the communicator by issuing the silence command."*

"What's that?"

"Just say the word in Meero with meaning, followed by the command Tak.*"*

"Tak?"

"Ontte."

"What does that mean?"

"It means immediately."

"Severennu tak." A visceral, jarring sort of silence emanates from the other end of the communicator so suddenly it makes my stomach plummet. *"Rhork?"* I try after a beat of that silence. *"Rhork,"* I say again. I'm sitting up, pacing my little cell now. Back and forth. Panic building. *"Rhork!*

Rhork." No. No no no Nono. I sent him away. I don't know how to get him back. I don't know how. I don't know... "Severennu tak. Severennu tak," I shout a little louder when it doesn't work the first time. But I'm telling it to be silent. What's the opposite of silent? Loud? Speak? I shout both words in Meero. Then I remember. "Teoranka tak."

"Back so soon, Deena?"

The breath I exhale shakes my whole body. Tears wet my eyelashes. I lean my forehead against the glass partition separating me from the world. From everything. Everything but the one thing I get to keep, because it's the only thing Mathilda hasn't taken from me. And I almost lost it.

"Deena?" Is that concern? No. I'm not stupid enough to believe he'd worry about me. I've only known him a few solars. A dozen. Holy crud. Not a dozen. More like eighty. Maybe a hundred. Have I really been down here that long? My chin starts to do this annoying trembling thing that makes me feel like I'm two feet tall.

"Deena!" He barks so loud I jump and that jumping makes me bang my head.

"Ow. Yeah. I mean ontte." I rub my forehead with the heel of my hand, which makes the bump already rising there hurt worse.

"You don't sound...well."

I laugh but it's a sticky laugh, full of saliva and snot. I sniff. "I'm fine. All good. No biggie." Not like my heart is about to launch out of my chest on a rocket ship with no fuel and no destination.

"You do not sound well."

"You already said that."

"And you did..."

"I just think I'm going to take another break now."

"Deena," he growls.

"Which one was the command to turn...turn it back on?" My voice strangles on the word. He hears it. He has to.

"Deena..."

"Was it teoranka or heverenoya?" The words for speak and loud, respectively.

Silence.

"Which...which one, Rhork?" I rub my face roughly.

"Teoranka," he finally says.

"Thank...thank you."

"Deena..."

"Severennu tak." The communication between us empties out, like a jug turned over. Spilled, maybe.

I jerkily start to hum to myself, but it's only so I don't blurt out the command to end the silence...

Silence. I wait with my lungs in my mouth for his answer. *Everything* depends on it. Everything. "I lied."

He. Lied.

He lied to me. *Lied. Lied rhymes with tied, rhymes with tried, rhymes with cried.* Cried. He...he heard me cry. Not once. Not twice. A dozen times. A gabajillion. And he...heard...*everything.*

I open my mouth, but I don't dare answer. I have two options. Only two. I know already that he knows all gabajillion times I cried and did...uhm...other things, too, thinking that he wasn't there and that I could keep the microphone in my head in place without him hearing me. All he needed to tell me was that I could take it out and he wouldn't be able to hear...but he *wanted* to hear. He *wanted* to shame me. So, that leaves me with just the two options, then.

I can scream at him about what a psycho sicko tormented weirdo freak he is — but I knew that from the beginning, so really, who's the dummy here? Me, or

Rhorkanterannu — aka, the *bad guy?* Everyone knew he was the villain. Everyone. *But he was all that I had.*

He still is.

So that leaves me with option two. Make a bad joke and pretend like I don't care. Like he's nothing to me. Or like I'm nothing. Like we're both big fat nothings. *Nothing, rhymes with fluffing. Or bluffing. Strange, that the words look nothing alike.* "So you liked my singing that much, huh?"

But I keep forgetting — *how can I keep shroving forgetting!* — Rhork is a villain. Instead of meeting my joke with one of his own, he sounds super, annoyingly serious when he says, "I liked listening to you when you thought I wasn't listening. It felt like listening in on secrets not meant for me."

"That's because they *weren't* meant for you," I snarl back before I can stop the heat in my chest from climbing into my throat.

"Don't worry, Deena. I gave you your privacy when it counted."

"Like when? Did you at least let me take *a dump* in peace?" I don't know the word for *to crap* in Meero, so I shout that bit in Human and hope that the translator takes care of the rest.

Rhork makes a laughing-sighing sort of sound. "Centare, I did not listen to you *void.*"

"Or piss?"

"I removed my communicator when I heard the telltale signs of pissing, but I can't say I didn't hear some of it. But pissing and shitting, that's not what you're really curious about, is it? You want to know if I heard you...*singing.*" He says the word with such savory inflection, I know he's talking about something else. I *know* what he's talking about. "And ontte, Deena. I heard you *sing*. Sometimes, I even heard you *sing* for me."

My fingers curl around my communicator. I don't need it at all now that I can talk to him directly through the ship. Knowing that, my impulse is to toss the thing across the pod in a fit of embarrassed rage, but given my propensity to hurt myself on nothing at all, I shove it into the pocket of my pants instead. Men's jeans that belonged to my dad, they barely stay up on my hips — wouldn't, if I hadn't fixed them with a power cable.

"You're a bastard!" I screech.

His reply is, as ever, calm. It makes me want to pull out every one of my locs at the root. "Centare, I'm a pirate. We have no bastards because every child that is born is ferociously loved."

"You!" I howl and my shoulders are so tense by my ears and my face is so twisted in rage that, for a moment, I think I might actually pass out. *Calm, Deena. Get your shit together! Shit rhymes with pit. That's what my stomach feels like right now. Rhymes with spit. That's what I'd do in his stupid face if I could see it. Calm. Stay fucking calm!*

"Get out of my escape pod!" My voice comes out ten times louder than I meant for it to, rising in a chaotic crescendo. *No, another C-word. Rhymes with hazy.*

"*Your* escape pod?" Comes the omnipresent reply. The thing I hate most about it? I don't know where to look.

I shout up at the ceiling. "Yeah! *My* escape pod." I thump my chest. "I'm escaping in it, aren't I?"

"I believe that pod and its contents belong to me."

I hate the shimmery, slippery way he speaks. Hate it only because it affects me. I've heard that voice in the dark, late in the lunar, when I'm all alone. I've let its shivers wrack and wreck me. Let it get under my skin, into my bones. I've even *sung* to it when I thought he wasn't listening. *But he heard everything.* Everything. That word makes me want to purge. *Rhymes with urge.* Or vomit. *Rhymes with dawgonnit.* I'm so angry I could just burst!

Stay fucking calm!

"Well." I open my mouth to fake a yawn and choke on it. Then curse. The rage comes back all over again when Rhork chuckles. "Well, you can have it back when you catch me!" I shake my fists up at the image of Rhork hanging there in the ceiling laughing at me. I've...I've only seen him once with my own eyes and it was every bit as shocking and arousing as I always thought it would be.

If only I could divorce the four-armed, spine-spiked alien from his personality, which is one hundred percent *yuck. Rhymes with duck. Rhymes with ffff...*oh dear.

"Make no mistake in thinking I won't."

I flush again for no reason at all. "Big talk from a guy who has no idea where I am."

"Tell me and I'll know."

"Cute. Anyone ever called you cute before?"

"Centare, they have not."

"Well, I think you're positively adorable. Big bad pirate wandering space totally lost trying to find a little ole' defective human. Just darling, really."

Silence. I think I hear him grumbling words to someone else, but they're all indistinct until he says, "Tell me where you are and I will punish you less."

I laugh at that. It isn't genuine so much as it is loud. I flip my hair up and down, the tips of my long locs spanking me in between the shoulder blades as I stand back up. I totter as I do, catching myself on one of the chairs. "You know, you're not very good at this. Don't you know bribery comes before threats?"

"Is that what Mathilda taught you?"

"Centare," I shudder. "Mathilda went straight for punishment. But that's not a step available to you right now, because you aren't here."

He doesn't answer again, not right away. It makes me angry to hear his voice but only because I hate how I wait...just wait...*Need. He knew...the whole time he knew how much I needed. He had the whole universe at his fingertips. I had him and nothing else.*

"Got nothing to say to that, cutie pie?" The pod lurches before he can answer and I fall to my knees, banging them hard on the floor.

"Sit down before you kill yourself on accident," Rhork hisses.

"Can you see me!" I shout, voice still just as loud as it was before. I clear my throat and try again. "CAN YOU SEE ME!" Nope. Not any better.

"If I could see you, don't you think I'd be asking you for something else?" I don't know what he means but the tenor of his voice coupled with the sudden lurch of the pod makes me stumble again. "Deena! Sit down."

"You ain't the boss of me," I shout even as I amble awkwardly with my twisted leg over to the chair with the control pad. Grabbing hold of the arm rests, I yank myself up into the seat and pull up the star map plotting our trajectory — *my trajectory, remember? Rhork isn't here.* That's right. He *isn't* here. Maybe he never even was. Maybe, this whole time, he's just been a figment of my imagination because I well and truly am a psycho. I frown at that. And then my cross-eyed confusion manages to uncross itself enough to make sense of the blinking dots and bright squiggly lines. My jaw drops. *I'm almost there. At the heart of this asteroid field, I'll be there. The first to reach the other humans hiding in their satellite in a hundred rotations. Maybe more.*

"Buckle yourself in."

"Centare," I pout, but Rhork still exhales deeply the moment I've got the belt fastened, making me want to shout CAN YOU SEE ME all over again.

"Fine," he sputters, sounding momentarily *deeply* exhausted. I should know, I've had almost an entire rotation to study his voice's many shades and tones. It almost makes me feel sorry for him. Then I remember Svera, how she looked when I saw her on a slab waiting for Rhork to come and...*force* her. *I didn't think he was capable of that.* Even though I knew that really all beings in this universe are truly terrible, I somehow thought he wasn't.

Ha. Who am I kidding? He was *all* I had. He *had* to be the best, the most beautiful.

I won't waste any regrets on him though. *No, he's just as wretched as everybody else and anything good I ever saw in him is just a product of my loneliness.*

"Fine, what?"

"Fine. I will bribe you."

"Sweet. Whatcha got, Rhorky bear?"

He growls, hating the condescending nicknames I've given him over the solars. This one he hates more than most. "If you tell me your coordinates, stay there and wait for me to come pick you up, I will not make you perform shekurr for my brothers."

"Oh wow. This is quite a bribe. Just picturing it now...sigh...*not* having to shove thirty monster cocks inside me all at once. How lovely."

"Don't make me do this the hard way, Deena," he says and his voice does get deeper, and yes, it does make my toes curl against the cold floor. I'm not wearing shoes. *Why would grandmother dearest give me shoes? That would make it easier to run.*

"Back to threats are we? So fast? Let me see... the things I'd rather do than do shekurr with you and your brothers." I lift one hand and start to make a list. "I'd rather impale myself on an asteroid, throw myself out of an airlock, drink a hundred more of those nasty black tube drinks. You know what? Instead of thirty cocks all at once, I'd rather grow a cock out of each of my eyes."

Silence. "That is a wholly disturbing image."

I smile and kick my feet in the chair, having a jolly good time. "Ontte, well so is the image of me with you and all your brothers."

"How about just me?"

My smile falls. My feet still, toes barely touching the floor and only if I edge as far forward in my seat as I can without falling off of it. "What?"

"Does this image also disturb you?" He breathes and his voice is doing that damning, twisted thing it does for me. It dances in the dark, like some kind of sultry strip tease. I'm not...used to boys talking to me like that.

But he's a monster. I'm defective. And I haven't had access to boys in rotations. I'm just messed up. I know that...I know it. But in the moment, it's hard to remember it.

"Of course," I finally choke, but my voice cracks and I know that he hears it when he chuffs out light laughter. "It doesn't matter anyway." My fingers tense around the arms of my chair. I feel my face getting all hot and am glad he can't see me. *Not just because of my blush, but because I'm me.* "You're not going to catch me and even if you do, I'm not going down without a fight." Or flight. Right now, flight seems like the better option of the two.

"Interesting..." I hate it when he does that. It's like he's figuring something out. "You mentioned asteroids. I know that you aren't going to your human colony. The nearest asteroid field is too far for you to be on course here. And, given the amount of fuel in your pod, there are only three available routes for you to take. I've moved transporters into all three locations, but imagine my surprise when all three turned up empty-handed. So where did you go? Hm?

"I'm beginning to think, little Deena, that Svera gave you something very precious before she and her mate took off."

He's speaking, but I can't hear him. All I can do is blink. And then a few breaths later, blink again. My jaw opens and my tongue flails uselessly inside my mouth. I grip the arms of my chair and try to push myself up only for the seatbelt to yank me back.

"Gugg," I yowl.

"Deena, tell me," he says, but I just shake my head because my little escape pod has just rounded the curved edge of one moon-sized asteroid and sitting directly in front of me is a satellite.

The satellite.

Shadowed by the asteroids behind it, it's illuminated only by very distant starlight — and the light of my bright little pod. The asteroids seem to be locked in its orbit and rotate around it very slowly. I start to follow the path they take in my little bright beacon and draw nearer and nearer as it comes closer and closer…

"Deena. Did Svera give you the coordinates?"

"What coordinates?" I mumble, unstrapping myself from my seat and rising with complete and total awe. I approach the view pane and press both palms against it. Unlike the glass case my *loving gramma* kept me in, against the view pane, my breath does not fog.

Balesilha.

That's the word printed in huge block letters across the satellite's rounded surface. A magnificent thing, the satellite is structured in three components — two huge sections on either end that look like slowly rotating wheels and, between them, one huge sphere linked to them by enormous tube-like bridges. The wheels are both silver and gleaming, shining like they were just built yesterday. The ball however, is inert and patchy, covered in black and a sort of rust color that looks eerily like dried blood.

Some bits of it, I see as I draw closer, appear mossy green. *Like vegetables after they've been left out too long.* I remember because one of my many protests was to deny all the food Mathilda gave me. I let the food spoil and, eventually, the meat and the vegetables grew these funny, fuzzy white and green spots. They also smelled so bad, I threw up. Looking at the sphere now and its coloring makes me remember that food and get all queasy. *Rot.* The word comes to me. *The color of rot.* And that's where my escape pod is headed.

"Deena, come back to me," his hard voice snaps and I jerk to attention, preparing for my little pod to dock. Preparing to meet the new humans! Oh my gosh, what will they be like? What will they think of me? I glance down at my clothes, my bare feet, the stains and smudges on my tee shirt. I sniff my armpits and make a face. Well, I guess my stank can't be helped at this point.

I tighten a few of my locs with my fingers as I jump eagerly from foot-to-foot. I refuse to answer Rhork as he speaks, whispering more orders to somebody. I'm getting close...super close! The giant sphere looks positively jumbo sized now as I approach it and we lock onto a port with a hiss.

"Deena!" Rhork curses. He almost never does. "Deena, you can't do this. This is my escape pod. You are *mine.*" I don't know how he figures that, but it sounds pretty stupid from where I'm standing staring up at the ceiling, watching the black matter that makes up some of the ship part to reveal a rot-colored portal that's sealed shut.

The black matter slides down all syrupy and slow to form a single post with hand and foot rungs sticking out of either side of it. Cool. A ladder. I grab on and start climbing up. "'Preciate your company these past solars, Rhork, but I'm off now. Don't expect to hear from me anytime soon. Or ever."

I should throw the little token in my pocket out and leave it behind in the escape pod so he can't find me...

I should do this.

"Deena," he says and I *hate* the way he says my name only because I hate him and I actually like the way he says my name, and I shouldn't, don't, wish I didn't. "I'll take you to the ocean." The velvet chords act like oil on the rungs. I slip and trip and fall back onto the floor below. I curse and massage my butt.

Rhork curses and says, "I will take you to the ocean, Deena. I have a place. One for you and only you. Where I've never taken anyone."

"Liar."

"I'm not…"

"Don't!" I rise with a huff and grab hold of the ladder again.

"Deena."

"I said *don't.*"

My foot slips from the rung it's on and my arms shake with the effort it takes to hold up the rest of my body. *Crap. I'm real out of shape…* I wonder if that's what Rhork meant when he called me defective, not my leg. I glance down at my jeans-covered right leg and frown. It's kind of hard to walk up the ladder with my foot bent out like this, but it doesn't stop me. It hurts sometimes, yeah, but it hardly ever slows me down.

"I will take you to this place, Deena. It's yours already…"

"Nah," I say even though my heart does this annoying funny thing. It clenches. The ocean. *How many times has his melodic voice described it to me? How many times?* "I'd rather take my chances with the humans than trust you again."

"Deena, you don't even know if you can breathe the air on this satellite."

That stalls me with my hand on the top rung. I hesitate.

"You open that latch, you could die."

"Hmm," I say in forced imitation of his usual flippant tenor. "Well, if you don't want me to die, I suggest you tell me how to figure out if there's breathable air."

Silence. "Centare."

"Naturally." I reach up and feel around on the portal. Its gritty surface flakes off on my fingertips, staining them a sickly green. *Rot. The color's called rot.* It's not wet, but it's so cold it feels wet. It doesn't feel like anything I've ever touched. Like a bunch of wet sand got freeze-dried and melted. It stings.

"Deena," he barks. "What's natural is a desire to live. Don't you have one?"

"Ontte. A big one." I snort at the joke, but he doesn't get it. "But to do that, I've got to take a risk and right now the choices are you and your brothers' thirty cocks or the nice people on this satellite who are going to welcome me with open arms and breathable oxygen."

"You're bluffing. You wouldn't be so stupid to enter a ship without even checking the oxygen levels."

"Bluffing rhymes with nothing." Aha! Take that!

"Deena! I'm not playing one of your rhyming games! Check the shroving control panel."

I hesitate. "The one on the chair?"

"There is only the one."

I amble back down and check the armrest on the control chair. There is a purple light blinking and, when I press on it, a panel in the floor opens up between the two chairs across from me. I go to it and see a strange contraption.

"Take the yellow hook and loop it around your ear." His voice is sober. Deadly. *Sad.*

I do what he says and am surprised when it *moves*. Given the status of the token, I guess I shouldn't be *that* surprised when it suddenly swells and elongates, the yellow end hooking around my ear while the other end slides over my cheek, across my upper lip and then hooking over my other ear. A soft breathing sound echoes louder than it should and I jump again and glance over my left shoulder. It sounds like Rhork is here, standing over me.

"Oxygen will flow freely, no matter the atmosphere in the satellite, but it will not flow indefinitely. You have twelve solars. Possibly more depending on how calm you manage to remain. Less, if you panic."

"Thanks, Rhorky bear," I tease, hoping to elicit some kind of reaction from him. I don't like this voice, this tone. I've never heard it before. It sounds like...I don't know what it sounds like. Like he just watched his childhood pet beaten to death in front of him.

"Take a weapon with you. You do not know what you will find. The humans may be just as hospitable as those on the home world you came from."

I frown at that, anger making my shoulder jerk. "There are good ones!" Wow. That sounds lame, even to me. *Good. It should rhyme with blood, but it doesn't.*

I open up the weapons' cache and take out one of the more human-sized daggers. The length of my calf, it doesn't look too fancy — *or likely to kill me* — so I shove it into my belt loop, sheathed. While I'm rooting around, I also steal another pack of brown goop — just in case — and a glowing ball with a hand hold that looks like a lantern. I shove it into my back pocket, too. Then I climb back up the ladder.

It takes me a long while to figure out the mechanism to open the latch on the other ship. It's so... ancient. No scanners or vein readers or weird syrupy black stuff. Just an old fashioned hand grip that I have to twist, twist, twist, then push in.

I'm sweating a little with the effort it takes to lift the mechanism up, but eventually, its gritty surface gives and it unlocks. How old-fashioned. *Hissssss.* The doors peel apart in the center and cold, *cold* air gusts down onto me, sliding through all my clothes. Darkness finds me next and I find immediate use for the light in my back pocket. I strap it to my wrist, now.

Shining my light all around, I'm greeted by normal looking walls and a ceiling up above. White and a little green, but overall, sleek and well-preserved. I notice that it gets a little harder to breathe — especially when I take in air through my mouth — so I concentrate on taking easy breaths through my nose, thankful for the contraption.

Why did he help me?

"Thanks Rhork. This oxygen thing is coming in handy already."

He doesn't answer.

"Rhork?"

I hear shuffling and a sigh that immediately soothes my panic. "Goodbye, Deena. I hope that these humans give you everything you deserve."

There's an emptiness after he speaks that makes me wonder if he's still there. I'm too afraid to ask, though, because I don't want him to be gone. I don't want him to leave me. Not again. Not like that one time he left me behind when I wanted to be kidnapped by him. When I wanted that more than anything.

Maybe that's why I'm not as mad as I should be that he listened in to everything that ever happened to me over this past half a rotation.

I'm terrified to be alone.

Because loneliness is my only real friend.

Even Rhork lies to me.

"Rhork, I..." I bite my bottom lip to stop myself from saying the pathetic words I want to say. *I'll miss you.* Because I do miss him. He thinks I'm disgusting and I'm obsessed with him. I close my eyes and turn forward towards the rot-colored walls, determination steeling my resolve. Then, without another thought to Rhork, I climb up into the dark.

3

Deena

"Humans? It's safe! I'm me! I'm one of you! You can come out now. Want to hear my song about plants? It's in Meero, but it kind of translates." I shouted it in the first hall. Now, thirty endless hallways later, I'm whispering it.

I thought I'd find someone sooner than this and I'm starting to worry that I might *not* find anyone at all. Maybe they didn't survive. Maybe...maybe they're all corpses waiting to be found. Maybe they managed to escape. Yeah, maybe they escaped and found a world with vast oceans and beautiful moons hanging like colored lights in the sky. Maybe they have a thriving community somewhere safe in the cosmos where Rhork and the exiled Bo'Raku, Pogar, and Mathilda can't find them. *Where no one can find them. Because they're corpses.*

I wince and cling to thoughts of beautiful planets full of blue water twinkling like jewels, because the idea that I'm going to round the next corner and find a pile of bodies or bones makes me sweat. I'm sweating a lot. Too much. I've been using the goop to mark my path, but I'm running out. What if I can't find my way back to the pod? That thought bothers me until I remember why I'm even here at all.

I have nowhere else to go.

There are no other coordinates in my head and the pod can't fly around until I find some place that's nice and safe — it was running out of energy, whatever substance powers it — *or maybe because nowhere's nice and safe for a human in this great gruesome galaxy...*

"Lift your green leaves and stretch onto your toes. Bend like the wind, tracing the patterns it blows..." I sing softly to myself, first in Human then repeating the words in Meero. My voice doesn't echo. I feel like it should echo but it doesn't.

There's no wind either. Like everything is holding its breath. My feet don't even anchor to the ground like they should. I feel halfway weightless. I'm still out of breath, but my bad leg doesn't drag as much.

I stop walking-floating in the middle of a hallway so dark, I can't see anything outside of the ambient glow of my lantern. It illuminates quite a bit. Maybe twenty paces in any direction. Standing still like I am, I take a few deep, calming breaths. They don't help. What helps is reaching my hand into my right pocket and fingering the token I've still got there. *I'm not alone. No, that's not important. What's important is the knowledge that I won't die here.*

I *won't* die here.

If there aren't any living humans, then it makes sense to just tell Rhork the coordinates. If I do that, then he'll come get me, I'll perform shekurr for him and his brothers and it'll suck but not as much as it'll suck dying of dehydration on a ship full of corpses. *Corpse rhymes with...*

"Hello?" My voice warbles. There's movement up ahead. No...there's *light.*

I don't know how to turn the lantern off on my wrist, so I cover its shine with my opposite hand and, sure enough, there's a subtle blue glow emanating from the distant end of the hallway. From here, it looks as distant as starlight, but equidistant from me and that light there's something that can only be described as *pale* in the middle of the corridor, huddled in front of the next intersection.

"Hell...hello?" I ask it.

The thing moves abruptly, shifting over the floor towards me. I jump and my heart rate starts to accelerate. I remove my hand from my wrist, allowing light to filter into the space so I can get a sense of what the shit that thing is, but the moment the light touches it, the thing screeches and disappears. *That wasn't a human screech. That wasn't a person.*

Nope. Uh-uh. *No.* FTS, my favorite Human expression. Fuck. This. Shit.

The thing was white against the black walls and floor and it was crawling. What the shit could it have been? It looked like a rug being pulled around the corner. Was it some kind of like...sentient bacteria? Rhork once told me about creatures called *Oosa.* They're apparently gelatinous blob beings that like to have sex with everything. Maybe they made it onto this satellite. I can deal with a nymphomaniac blob.

I exhale, smile shakily and shrug. *Still better than cocks for eye sockets.*

I take a step forward, after the blob, when suddenly the light at the end of the tunnel shifts. I glance up and I can see a figure silhouetted against the blue glow. This one's standing, which is already a better start than that crawling rug.

I cover my lantern again and take a few quicker steps towards it, passing the intersection, which is empty. No Oosa or rugs in sight.

I cling to the wall as I move. It's covered in that weird grit that's everywhere. Under my feet, on the ceilings, getting into the cracks between my toes. They curl, not wanting to touch the substance. I don't like this. I don't like any part of it and the farther towards the light I walk, the less I like it, which is already not at all.

Not at all. Not at all notatall. Sounds like *not a ball*. Ball rhymes with drawl. That's what I wish I were hearing right now. Rhork's calming drawl in my ear, telling me that he'll take me to the ocean, show me sand that's not like colony sand but that's soft and forms a thing called a beach. All I have to do is shekurr in exchange. Shekurr? Eh. It might not be so bad. Just thirty cocks. I don't even have to grow them out of my eye sockets or anything.

"Holy…" That's all I manage to say as I finally get close enough to the light to see it clearly. Nothing else shifts in front of it, so I can see what's causing it. What's behind it. What it illuminates. "Oh my shroving shrov…" If only Svera could see this. The little human with more prayer rugs than sense would flip a lid.

I hasten towards it, elbows dropping to my sides as I break out into a sprint. Well, a shuffling, awkward sprint that makes my lungs catch as I take in air from the tube underneath my nostrils. Did I mention I'm out of shape?

I wheeze as I slow down, a stitch spearing my left side. It feels like a clawed hand reached out of the darkness to latch onto my ribs. I take shallow breaths, but that doesn't seem to have any effect on my pounding pulse. The T-intersection leaves me feeling exposed as I step into it, out of the hall and into the violence of the blue light. Dark, empty hallway stretches off to my either side. These three blue cages block my path from the front.

"I…" I want to tell the beings trapped in the light that I'll help them, but they can't hear me trapped in cages that look like they'll need a crowbar and a blowtorch to get into. Or a hammer.

Steel wraps around the sides of each case, but a thick glass panel in the front reveals bodies that are each one hundred percent human. I shake my head, reach my hand towards one of the glass panels then quickly snatch it back, afraid. "What are y'all doing here?"

I glance to the left and to the right, but I don't see anything. Just more hallway that ends in black as soon as it can escape the grip of these luminous crates, which far outshine my torch. I turn back to the human beings.

All three of them seem totally frozen even though it looks like there's liquid underneath the glass. They seem to be frozen by it, instead of swimming in it. Grey clothes stick to every bit of their skin and, even though all three of them are bald and have no hair I can still clearly tell that two of them are men and one's a woman. Tubes feed into their backs and their mouths are distended in shapeless Os. It looks freaky. Like they're screaming with their eyes open.

I rap my knuckles on the glass. It clonks loudly, but doesn't echo. "How do I get you out of here?" How do *I* get out of here? That's the answer I really want, but the former seems more plausible. Then what? I have less poop-bars for myself? Maybe, instead of sharing, I can squirrel away the bars and just give them all the black juice. As much as they can drink!

My mouth is too dry to laugh, so I swallow over and over while I search the floor-to-ceiling length tubes for some sort of control panel, but the glass ends in metal and the metal stretches all the way around to the sides and around the sides…wait a jiffy! The tanks…they kind of wobble… It's like there's something behind the tanks. Maybe…

My fingers search the place where the edge of one tank meets the wall behind it — or *not* wall. What if this isn't a wall at all, but a hall? Heh. See what I did there?

I finger the seam where the tank meets the wall and suddenly, the tank jerks forward, almost as if it were being tugged from the front by an invisible thread. *Or pushed.* A splash of darkness confirms my theory. I lurch back, eyeing the tank like it's gonna bite me. It's wobbling dangerously…oh my shrov! Is it…is it going to? No no no nonononon. Shrov!

I squeal and run down the hall away from the tank just as it starts to totter…and then fall…and then crash! Smash smash smash. That's the sound of the tank hitting the ground. Bing bang bash. That's the sound of my pulse driving me to the brink of insanity and back.

Because the thing hits the ground and the blue light goes out and all that's left is my wrist torch, which is dinky by comparison. From where I am, its farthest rays only barely reach the glass-covered intersection, but I can still see…I can still see them when they come. White blobs. Carpets. They come crawling by the handful. No. By the dozens.

These aren't Oosa, like the sex maniac blobs Rhork described to me. These things have backs and arms and legs, heads and faces. But they don't have faces like humans have faces. They have faces like humans have faces if humans had faces that had been partially erased.

Where eyes should be, there's just a well for eye sockets covered by skin. Where ears should be there are huge holes covered in twitchy flaps. Where a nose should be are only flat slits. Where a mouth should be is a mouth and from the mouth come screams that wreck me.

No nonononononnno. No. Nope. Nope! I'm out. Out out out. FUCK THIS SHIT!

The carpets with the clawed hands and the mouths that scream dive out of the hallway and descend on the shattered tanks. They push the other two over and all twenty of them start working in frightening coordination to turn the tanks over and rip through the glass panels. They pull the bodies — *the shaking, shivering bodies...the people...no nononononono!* — out of the tanks and onto the glass and blue goo-covered floor, and those people? The ones in the tanks? They're breathing.

No. They aren't breathing, but they're tr*ying* to. The man that they have now in their grip is gasping for breath, chest convulsing. His dark skin is the same color as mine and I swear I imagine him looking at me as the first of the carpet-people shoves its hand through his stomach, pulls his intestines out through his belly button and starts to feast.

Fear catapults me to my feet. I turn and start to run. I think of Svera. She'd have probably thrown herself into the fray and tried to fight them with her damn Tri-God beads. But I'm no saint like Svera.

I want to *live.*

I'm not going to fight thirty carpets with razor blades for mouths and screams that make me wanna poo my pants. Another shriek goes off like a siren — more than one — and I know that it's coming after me. One of them. At *least* one. Tears jerk into my lungs and try to drown me, but drowning means stopping and I can't stop because I'm *not* going to die here. Not like this. *Not without seeing the ocean.*

Shekurr. Yeah. Shekurr sounds real good. Just thirty cocks. No big deal, right? What was I even fucking worried about? If Rhork wants, I'll even grow them out of my shroving eye sockets!

The sound of pounding behind me gets louder and I don't know where I am. I marked my path and I lost it just as fast. I pass the mouth of an open tunnel and a carpet person lunges at me and I scream. I scream a bloodcurdling scream. I scream and it takes *all of me* to scream.

I throw my hands out at it and it shrieks and recoils away from me, but not like it's afraid. No. Not afraid. How could it be afraid of me when I'm alone and it has friends by the bloodthirsty dozen? It screams like it's *hurt.* It lifts its arms to ward away the threat, but what… what is the shroving threat? I don't have anything on me except for the man pants I'm wearing, my too small tee shirt and…

Ohhh…

The light. That's all I've got on me right now. That must be what's freaking these things out. I wave my wrist around wildly and jump at it like a bug. "Take that!" I shriek, spotting another one behind it. Another thing. A skeleton with white, translucent skin stretched too thin over its frame.

There's scuttering behind me. I turn around and there's another one of those things and it's about three feet away.

"Fuck! Ahhhhh!"

I don't think. There's just moving, running, getting away. I fly down hallway after hallway, seeing the things sometimes, but not always. They're everywhere, burrowed in deep like sand mites in the sheets back in our squat, adobe colony homes, back before Mathilda upgraded me to a high-tech cage underground. A cage underground sounds pretty good right about now.

I'm running practically blind. The torch on my wrist only shows me the world right before I step into it. I can't look around. I can't find any goop. I don't see anymore tanks. I can't find the escape pod. I don't think these things are Oosa and I don't really care. I just need to stop running. I need a place where I can take a breath. I can't…my lungs…they catch…*keep running*. No, I need to hide. I need to hide.

There!

A grate in one wall practically shouts my name. I turn to it and yank my dagger out of my back pocket, nearly splitting my face open with it when I jerkily free it from its sheath. I whittle the dagger around the edges of the grate and pull it free. I hear things moving around all behind me — so shroving many of them! — but when I glance around, waving my wrist torch wildly, I don't see anyone. Any*thing*.

I get the grate open but I'm shaking so badly it's a miracle that I don't bang it around on the green-grit covered floor below. I bite my lower lip so hard I think it might be bleeding. Shit. I am bleeding. I lick my bottom lip and taste metal. It helps ground me which, at this stage, I don't know that I appreciate. Without the taste of copper and salt zinging through my mouth, I might have convinced myself that this was just an oxygen-deprived hallucination and that I've gone insane. Maybe even, that I was insane from the start.

I hear another loud wail from the hallway behind me and the grate falls from my fingers and lands hard on the rotten tiles below. My shoulders are jerking like I'm doing a dance never seen on the colony before. This one is *all* shoulders.

I start to laugh.

I start to sob.

I start to sweat even though I'm freezing freaking cold. I've never been so cold. Not even when Mathilda used to turn the cooling system way up and take away my blankets just to torture me.

I wave my wrist around in the cubicle of darkness in front of me. It's a duct. Maybe for air. Well, not air because this place doesn't seem to carry enough oxygen, if any at all. And it's gross in there. Covered in an even thicker layer of the rot that's all over the halls. So thick that it's entirely changed the shape of the duct. What was, I assume, once a rectangle or a square is now a rugged, misshapen series of sharp edges and knobby lumps.

"What is this shit..." I moan, then sniffle. What is this shit? I hate it! I hate all of this! I hate hate hate hate hate...Svera! Shroving, Svera! Why'd she send me here? I'd rather be back in that box with my dear, darling grandmother watching over me.

As I smash my body into the duct and pull the grate back into position, using the dagger to try to wedge it in there tight and prevent anything from following me, I start to laugh with no sound. Crying and laughing tastes the same in silence.

The duct isn't bigger than I am and an immediate claustrophobia sets in as I crawl. I crawl until my arms and legs give out, until the crying-laughing gets so intense my whole body shudders with it, like I'm vomiting but my body's got nothing to give up but the packages I was munching on and I have no desire to find myself covered in barf that looks like shit.

I collapse.

My hand is shaking so badly it takes me a dozen tries to reach into my pocket. Where is it? Where is it! I almost pass out. I think I might have passed out in my panic, but only for a breath. I'm not breathing. I drag air into my lungs in wretched gulps, then cover my mouth with my hand to keep it quiet. I hold my light under my chin and look down the length of my body…down.

And there it is.

A pale shadow of a person with a mouth that screams and hands that catch. It's crouching just out of range of my torchlight. All I can see are its fingertips shuffling back and forth. And then it releases a terrible squeal and charges forward, sounding like it's in pain. It grabs every part of my body, but its fingers slide uselessly over my pants. I have the dagger in my hand and lurch up, banging the shit out of my forehead on the top of the duct.

It clings to my clothing, trying to tear it and succeeding.

My head clears of the butterflies that knocking my noggin made appear and I fuel all the strength in my entire body into my left arm. I stab.

I stab and stab and stab until the thing goes limp on top of me and blood fills my mouth that tastes metallic and salty and a lot like the blood that I tasted earlier on my lip. Wait a second…it tastes like my blood. My *human* blood. *The blood tastes human…*

I'm woozy under the thing's crushing weight. I don't know if this particular carpet is male or female or if it's even still alive. I'm sure it can't be with as many times as I stabbed it, but I can't stab it again. My arms aren't working right.

I close my eyes and turn away from the smell of it. It doesn't smell like *anything* and that frightens me weirdly more than the taste of its blood. It should smell like something, but it doesn't. It's just a weird wet weight on top of my body, its head resting on my boobs, its torso pressing down on my bare stomach. It ripped through my shirt like it was nothing.

My fingers are in my pocket and I find the token this time with surety. I pull it out and shove it into my ear and I pray to the Tri-God that my mother so devoutly worshipped and that I never believed in that Rhork has not forsaken me.

Rhorkanterannu rhymes with *I'll do anything you need me to if you just get me the fuck out of here.*

4
Rhork

Nothing. It's all that runs through my mind.

Deena would likely try to rhyme the word with something. I heard her rhyme inconsequential words together when she thought I was not listening to her all the time.

But I was always listening to her, wanting to shout at her that her rhymes made no sense, wanting to tell her that I was coming for her as soon as I determined how I could keep her all to myself.

And now I've lost her.

I laugh wickedly to myself. It is a laugh that the pirates on board this ship know not to question. They don't speak to me, but continue shouting and bickering among themselves as they scour the star maps for signs of the escape pod. It could be anywhere.

I lost it.

That's twice now that I've let a human female slip from my grasp. The first time, I should not have underestimated the power of bonded Voraxian males to their Xiveri mates. I did, and my crew paid the price. We lost a dozen good males that day and at least a dozen wretched ones. And now I let a little human female with a husky voice that has come to replace my own conscience make off in my escape pod and I did not catch her before she jumped.

The escape pod that carried Svera and her mate away, I expected to jump. But I did not expect Deena to know how to do this. Svera's mate must have taught her how miraculously in whatever brief moments they shared together. I wanted Svera and her mate to get away.

I would not dare confess this to my crew, but I knew what they were planning. I could hear into their pod, every gory and salacious detail. I heard as they were picked up by Eshmiri reavers. I know that they will face their trial on Evernor. And I know that Svera's male will fight and win for her because I now know not to underestimate a bonded Voraxian male to his woman.

One female for *one* male.

One male for *one* female.

Mates. And there are only two of them.

That is how the Voraxians work. That is how the humans work. It is a conundrum I have been mulling over for half a rotation. Since I first heard her *sing* for me when she thought I could not hear her. Since I heard her breathlessly whisper my name when she thought she was alone. Since she first called me *Rhorky bear.* Of all the nicknames she has for me, this is my favorite one.

I left her behind and allowed her to board my ship and then escape it all because I was afraid of wanting and being unable to keep her for myself. I did not want her for shekurr because I wanted her for my own private ritual. And now neither I nor any of my brothers will have her.

Though perhaps this is best.

Now, she will be free to start her own life with her own kind, provided that she finds them in that mysterious and elusive satellite and that they take her in and treat her better than her kin did on her colony, that honorless, deceitful female. Deena will find a new family, one worthy of her. She may even find a male…

Centare. I will not think of that.

"Set course for Kor," I say to no one in particular. The pirates who need tokens have them, however, and they all hear me. The mothership can hear me too, though it takes the coordination of more than one token operating in sync to guide it. It is too big a construct for less than that.

Herannathon is closest to me. Or maybe he's just the one with the courage to approach me now when I'm like this. He kicks my boot. "No one blames you for the females escaping. None of us sensed them on board." *I did.*

I nod but say nothing.

"The human, Svera," he says. "You believe they will survive their trial at Evernor?" He sounds worried. I understand his pain. If she dies, that is on us.

I cringe and quickly redirect my thoughts to my token, firing through a list of backchannel communiqués that are all my own and not for my brothers, *just as Deena should have been.* Finding the one I'm looking for, I will my yeeyar token to break through the rotations' old Yamar technology Ashmara carries on her person, always.

Yamar is a precursor to yeeyar and still has strong defenses, making it harder to hack than the pitiful biogenetic life drives worn by Voraxians, but it is not strong enough to rebuff the yeeyar's current.

I have no desire to speak with the Eshmiri pirate, but do now out of necessity. She is a half-human psychopath at her worst and a reluctant ally at her best. She's tried to rob me so many times, it's caused me and the pirates on board my ship to develop a strange affection for her.

I've known her for a rotation — less time than the discovery of the humans by the Voraxians and Drakesh. Then, I'd thought the race to be a pitiful, miserable creation whose sole purpose was for the Drakesh to torment. Then, I met Ashmara. An Eshmiri reaver, I stopped her third attempt to rob us and actually managed to patch through to her yamar for the first time.

I saw images of her for the first time, too. I saw that she is half human and I understood something that has shaped every decision I've made since. Humans can breed with other species. Humans can make hybrids. Humans had the potential to save the dwindling Niahhorru pirate species. Back then, knowing this was enough.

Now, nothing is enough.

I thought any human female would do to make Niahhorru hybrids. Maybe, any human will do, but now, I want more. I want a hybrid made by one female and one female *only*. And I let her slip through my fingers. All twenty of them, rendered simultaneously clumsy.

"Ashmara," I bark as soon as I hear the familiar static on her end of the line. That, and her Eshmiri reavers laughter in the background.

"Shrov!" She curses. There's a loud bang, and then more laughing and shouting mixed together. "Rhorkanterannu, you shroving shitting pirate! You can't just break into my yamar! It's private."

"It's useless. If you'd let me upgrade you, I would."

"Ha. At what price? Want me to lie back and do that shekurr dance with you boys? I wouldn't mind at all actually, but I know you're not interested in getting your hands dirty with a female of my caliber."

I snort. "Cute. You always were a charmer. I'm here for something else."

"Whatever it is, I'm sure you can handle it. Disrupt my yamar again when you have something worth stealing."

"I don't have time for this. There's a human in the Evernor pits. A female. She is not a warrior. Do with that information what you will."

I break the connection without chancing Ashmara's response. Then I lean back in my seat and flick my gaze up at Herannathon. He's still there watching me. "Ashmara?"

I nod.

"You think she'll go for Svera?"

"I'm sure of it. On my honor." Because Ashmara has a certain code of honor all her own.

Ashmara fights for the defenseless, freeing slaves and releasing prisoners. She's made quite a name for herself and her actions have garnered her much attention. Perhaps, too much. It's known that she has a Sky bounty hunter chasing her. More than one, perhaps. Soon one of them will catch up with her. I pity whoever the Sky masters choose to send.

"You sure you want to turn back? We can keep looking for her."

Her. Because there is only one that matters.

I grunt, remaining silent. "Centare. I'm sure of nothing." I look up at him and he watches me with a frown. Does he know that she's my lifeline and that that line has been severed? I think so. I didn't make any real effort to hide it from anyone but her.

He shrugs and huffs out of one corner of his mouth. "Suit yourself. You heard the pirate," he shouts at the three dozen pirates working the walls covered in controls. "Let's get back to mother." The joke earns him a few chuckles, a few bawdy laughs, more than a few lewd comments about the pleasures waiting for us back on Kor.

There are houses for pleasure. Any and all kinds.

But females capable of bearing Niahhorru kits? Centare, these are a rare find.

And I lost her.

I can feel the ship beneath me gathering power as she prepares to warp, but before she can, a soft voice whimpers into reality and for a moment, I wonder if I haven't lost the tenuous grip I have on my thoughts. Instead, I hear *her* and she says, "Te...te...te...teoranka tak."

A shiver moves up my spine and lifts me onto my feet. I twist at the wrong moment, like a youngling whose hiannru tines are hardening for the first time and they aren't yet fully conscious of them, and get stuck in the command chair. I wrench free and find Herannathon watching me with a small smile curling his mouth. I wave him off with a growl, then hold up one hand.

"Wait," I tell him, then turn and stalk across the command center until I reach the view pane. The black yeeyar condenses over my palm before shooting off again, refusing to remain static — its only fallible property.

In the quiet, I whisper her name. "Deena?" There is no answer. "Deena, can you hear me?"

I can't determine what I'm hearing — scrabbling or static or heavy breathing?

"Deena?"

And then a gut-wrenching moan and her voice shoots into my brain so loud it hurts me down to the soles of my feet. "I'll fuck you," she gasps and it doesn't sound like her. This voice is deep and scratchy, starved. *Desperate.* "I'll fuck everybody...every...body in Kor. I'll fuck you...thirty...cocks...all the pirates in the whole shroving galaxy." She's sobbing and it breaks every piece of me.

"Eye sockets," she squeals, voice twisting out of the back of her throat in a pitch so high only beasts could understand it. There's a pounding, like a fist, then she sobs harder, "Just come get me. Rhorky bear, please. Please..."

"Deena — " My voice breaks. I rub my face roughly. I start to pace. The chilling temperature of the bridge drops even further. I watch as my typically-bawdy crew quiets. Wandering hands still. Eyes follow my every move. Bodies edge away from me, framing the perimeter of the asymmetrically shaped room.

There are no hard edges, only fluid angles shaped by the will of the yeeyar. I stomp across every one of them, moving awkwardly, brutally. I grab hold of the back of one chair and grip it with all four of my arms. I squeeze and the metal bends beneath my fists.

"Coordinates," I manage to say, though my voice is thick and Deena is screaming. Crying screaming shrieking breathing way too shroving hard. I need her to calm the shrov down! I need her to explain to me in clear detail what is happening to her and where she is but I know she's not capable of that, not with the tortured way she's freaking out.

"I'll do you and…I'll do Herannathon…Gerannu…Erobu…I'll fuck…your whole shroving…crew!"

"Deena!" I roar and I'm not sure I've ever screamed like I'm screaming now. But it's hard to control my pitch when all of my organs are liquifying and pouring out through my mouth. "Deena, tell me the shroving coordinates!"

"You just want…the other human women…not…defective…"

"Deena!"

She does that screaming squeal again and I pull my right elbows back and send them flying. The chair crumbles inward in front of me. "Promise me you'll come get me, Rhork!" She shouts.

"I swear! Just tell me the coordinates!"

"Quad…quad 0, star system 3-4-8-8-8-8-0-9-0-2, position…position…"

"What is the position, Deena?" My fingers are shaking as they hover over the control panel. It is an enormous thing, spread entirely across one wall. My crew shoves each other to get out of my way fast enough.

"Position 62…you'll…see an asteroid field. I'm in the middle…Balesilha…covered in…rot…" She breaks into sobs again and when they start to peter out, a horrible urge to destroy something sits on my chest like a fat shroving opponent and I can't get out from under it. I sink into one of the command chairs, brace one elbow on my knee and cover my eyes with one hand.

I can feel the movement of the ship accelerating beneath me and my crew murmuring as the transporter jumps, moving us back into the grey zone. We're far from Kor, but not even a location pinned outside of the eight known quadrants would keep me from going for her now. I use my lower left hand to rub my mouth. It's dry and I'm hot and I want to strangle her.

"I think...I'm running...out of air." Her voice is quieter than it was, but no calmer, jerking with every second word.

My gut is shroving fire. I've...I've never felt like this. "You aren't running out of air. You have twelve solars' worth in the oxygenator."

"Then why...why can't I breathe?" There's a banging, like warped metal popping into or out of shape. Where is she? *Where are you, Deena? What happened with the humans on the ship? What have they done to you?*

"You're panicking. If you calmed down, you'd be able to breathe."

"You're an asshole." She bursts into tears and it's a messy, gasping sound punctuated by curses and pleas to a god I know she does not worship. It is Mathilda's god. Those pleas, more than anything, are what make my plates all lift and shift over my chest. For her to pray to Mathilda's god now means that she is facing death.

How did I let this happen? I run one hand over my skull, fingering the raised ridges that the humans do not seem to have. Their skulls are round, smooth and tineless. At least, I assume they are beneath all that hair. Breakable.

I stand abruptly and turn. Herannathon is there holding a tube of black fil out to me. I bat it out of his hand, not because I don't want it, but because I want to hear it shatter. He seems to expect this and holds out a second which I take and devour. "We're nearing the asteroid field. It'll take us some time to navigate, given our size, but we should be to her within a quarter solar."

"Use the cannons. We'll make it to her faster if we blow the asteroids apart."

I turn and approach the view pane again and focus on the next pained breath she takes. It's shallower than the last, no less agitated. I need to calm her down. To distract her from whatever is happening to her. Immediately, I know how and I start to sing words to a song I memorized a long time ago.

"Droganeene nene erro, wa da rogar tre hodona." It's a terrible song, really. Talks about a plant. I could have imagined that it was metaphorical for something else had I not also heard her sing songs about lights and cups and buckets and all of her eating utensils.

The effect is immediate.

Embarrassment.

It's not an emotion I feel often, but when I do, I feel it radiate through every inch of me. My crew is watching me with interest now and most are openly laughing. No doubt, they've never heard a pirate sing before, let alone the captain of his ship. My chest warms and my plates lift to release some of the heat — a telltale sign. Several pirates mock me. Herannathon shakes his head and beams.

I ignore them and turn to the view pane, beyond which I can see the asteroid belt up ahead. The first bits of debris have already started to close in around us, clunking uselessly off of the ship without damaging the yeeyar or the shields.

I sing about her plant reaching for the light, soaking up the water from the basin below it, feeding and twisting and dancing to its delight until eventually I hear her fractured murmur, "Droganeene nene...erro...wa da rogar...tre hodona." She sings with me and the tension in my shoulders releases a hair, just enough for me to be able to move less painfully. We finish the song together, our pitches wildly out of tune with one another, and then there is silence between us that's even more pronounced than the song had been.

"Deena, can you breathe?"

"Centare," she answers after a moment.

My fists clench. All four. I want to punch the view pane, but don't. "You're speaking more easily. Why can't you breathe?" She makes a strange gulping sound. "What is that?"

"Hic-cup," she stutters in Human.

"*Hick-Cup?*" I say, repeating her Human word.

"Hiccup."

"What is that?"

"I don't...know." She does the gulping sound again. It sounds like it hurts.

"It sounds painful."

"The hiccups...don't hurt...it's...him that hurts." Her voice twists at the end, getting all high pitched in a way that makes me cringe.

"Him?" My heart is pounding so hard it's all I can hear. I scan my gaze around at my crew — males I've known for a dozen rotations, since my birth — and right now they all look like enemies. "Who is *him*, Deena?"

"One of the carpet...carpets." She coughs. "I can't get him — it — off of me."

I rub my face. Pace. My ridges rise and shift, releasing heat. "Get us there faster," I say to Herannathon as I pass him before switching my concentration back to Deena. With this silent command, I will my token back on. Because I lied to her. The command to shut it down is not a verbal command, but a mental one.

"This...*person* on top of you." Herannathon makes a shocked face as he hears the words I say. Several other pirates do, too. Altogether, they look enraged and I feel the ship lurch as the males wearing tokens activate the cannons and fire at the incoming asteroid that would take too long to maneuver around. We'll go through them. All the males on board this ship are fighting for her now.

"Is he alive?"

"Centare," she whisper-squawks.

"How did he die?"

"I stabbed him with this dagger I found in the escape pod." She must mean sword because there are no daggers in the escape pod. "I...I killed him."

"Good. I'm proud of you."

She sniffles and it sounds wet and angry. "You are?" Her voice is shaky, but hopeful. It makes me smile.

It breaks my heart.

"Ontte, Deena. I am proud of you."

There's shuffling again. More of that popping metal sound. More of her strange swallows. More sniffles. But her breath...it seems to come a little easier and I'll take it if that's all I can get for now.

"Deena, who attacked you? One of the human males?" The asteroids are crowding in around my ship and our cannon fire is causing chaos. Huge chunks of asteroids bounce off of our shields, scraping the yeeyar, which is a delicate substance. Each time it sustains damage, I can feel the yeeyar's ire in my token, needling my brain like a splinter. Tevbarannos asks me if we should keep going at our current speed. He urges me to slow down.

I shake my head. "Keep going."

"I don't know what it is," Deena says. "Please don't make me look." More scrambling again, then she heaves out a breath. It sounds like relief.

"Did you get him off of you?"

"Ontte."

"Good. You need to look at him now. Tell me what he is so I know how to kill him." How to make him suffer.

"Centare, Rhork," she bellows. "I can't look."

"You can."

"I'm going to shit myself."

"Then do it. Just tell me what you see." There's a long silence in which I can hear her silent and weighty debate. Then she gasps.

"Did you shit yourself?"

A bolt of laughter is swallowed by one of those painful-sounding Hick-cups. "Centare," she whispers.

"Good. Now, what do you see, Deena?"

"I...I don't know. There's so much blood. But he... he doesn't have eyes. They have claws, but not like the Voraxians do. No clothes. He...shouldn't be hard for you to kill. I think it's just the numbers." She makes a sound like a controlled scream then inhales a gasping, shuddering breath. "There were so many of them."

"How did you avoid detection?"

"The light," she breathes. "The light hurts them."

A spasm makes my neck contort. I bend it until it cracks. "It's dark? There's no light?"

"Centare. Just...just in the cells."

"Cells?"

"Not cells. They're..." she says a word in Human that translates to *tanks*.

"Tanks."

"Ontte. There are humans in tanks. They...the creatures that look like carpets..." She drops her pitch so low I strain to hear it. "They *eat* them."

Shock. Disgust. Pain. Rage. Ontte, rage. Emotion consumes me like vitriol, endlessly whispering, *you lost her.* "That's what this male wanted to do to you?"

"Probably," she says, still whispering.

"It is a good thing you killed him, then."

She snorts, sniffles, doesn't answer.

Gerannu approaches me holding an oxygenator and a multi-range fusion blaster. The same kind that disabled the Voraxians' holoshields. It can tear through anything. Most easily, these creatures frightening Deena.

I turn to Gerannu. "As soon as we recover Deena, I will need you to tap into whatever technology this satellite uses and bridge our yeeyar through to it."

"Create a bridge? For what purpose?" He smooths his three free hands over his scarred plates. Capable of withstanding the bite of claws and most blades, we will have no trouble with these creatures, whatever they are. With four arms, silver plates covering almost every visible inch of our bodies and sharp grey spears shooting out of our spines, we are war made flesh.

"We need light on the satellite. Whatever creatures currently inhabit it are injured by it." I pitch my voice loud to those on the bridge and open communication with the entire ship so that my voice can be heard by every pirate.

"All pirates on the bridge and in the lower galley will board the satellite with me. I want Gerannu and his team to patch our yeeyar through to whatever tokens they have on their ship so that we're able to light it up on my command but *only* on my command. First, we'll need to find and secure Deena. We'll do this in the darkness. I don't want any excuse for the creatures to feel threatened by her or for her to get caught in the crossfire. We'll fight on their terms until we find her, then we'll scorch them out, rescue the humans in the tanks they're being kept in, and bring them on board."

"Humans in tanks?" One of the males asks.

I nod. "It would seem that there are humans on board. For now, they're being eaten by whatever creatures exist on this satellite. We will not let whatever of them remain fall to such a fate."

"Especially not Deena," Herannathon says.

I meet his gaze, wondering what it is that he's thinking behind the skein covering his eyes. He seems to read or see something that I'd rather hide. "Especially not Deena," I confirm, tone low with menace.

He tips his head forward and looks away, distracted by the male talking excitedly at his side. Everyone is excited. The pirates here, the pirates back on Kor, males and females alike. The promise of humans has always excited us, but now, the promise of battle keeps those emotions high and rising. Cheers and bickering prevail. Gerannu grins at me and nods in a way that irks me because it looks dangerously like a bow.

"Can't wait for that command. Anything harming Deena and her humans will answer to us."

"And you're sure you'll be able to tap into their controls?"

"As sure as I can shoot the eye out of a Voraxian battle cruiser." Which he can, because I've seen him do it.

"They are likely using ancient technology that hasn't been accessed for some time. Hundreds of rotations, potentially."

He considers, cocks his head. "If I can get into the network that powers their lights — even if it's a physical one — then I can bridge our yeeyar through. She's more than strong enough to power their satellite, at least for a short time."

"A physical one?" I say, latching onto the part of his explanation that I did not understand.

"Ontte. If this satellite is as old as we believe it to be, then it may rely on physical wires and cables to bring energy to and across their systems. The energy likely emanates from a single centrally located power source. My only concern is that we may have to enter with you to reach such a power source if the yeeyar isn't able to travel their cables to reach it herself."

I make a face. "Are you joking with me? This sounds entirely made up."

"Wish I was. The Eshmiri still lay physical lines for everything except for their cloaking devices. That's almost the only thing they've upgraded over the past fifty rotations."

"Shroving Eshmiri." I shake my head and strap my arm cannon to the sling that dangles from my hiannru spines. "If you need more pirates to get you in, then take them."

"Rhorkanterannu!" Erobu shouts across the deck. The wall in front of him is covered in controls, but he's pointing with both of his right arms towards the view pane. "We're here."

I turn and see the enormous satellite looming up like a solitary star in the center of its own private universe and remember what Deena said, that funny word she used. *Rot.* Ontte. A universe that has rotted from within. And Deena's hidden herself away in its heart.

"Rhork...Rhork where are you?" As she crosses my thoughts, her voice cracks into my token.

"I'm here."

She exhales a shaky breath. "Don't leave me."

"I never have," I say. My answer stalls me. It must stall her, too, because she makes a soft sound.

Why did I say that? I could have told her that I won't or wouldn't. Why did I tell her that horrible *embarrassing* truth?

"I..." But her softness switches to sharpness at the turn of a hat. "Did he just..." Scrabbling, scrambling.

"Deena, what is it?"

"I thought I just saw him twitch."

My heart rapidly powers down. My mind hallucinates Deena's death. I can see it clearly now — now that I'm mere moments from being able to touch her for the very first time, even though it's been two hundred rotations of imagining just what that would feel like. *The first time I touch her will not be to recover her corpse!*

"Deena, get out of there!"

"I can't! Don't you think I would if I could? I don't have anywhere to go."

"Get your sword and stab him again, this time in the eye socket and then again in the throat."

Gerannu comes to me and hands me a lunar shield. I press the token to my temple and the shield stretches to cover the top half of my face. I lower the protective skein that covers my eyes beneath it, but I don't turn the lunar shield on just yet. To do so now in this brightly lit chamber would be painful. I move out of the command center first and onto the ramps that will take me to the closest docking port. I can hear dozens of boots pounding just at my back.

"I...my dagger...the tip is broken."

I stagger. Ice slides down my spine. I struggle to catch my breath. Two arms reach out and grab me to keep me upright, but I don't know who they belong to. I can't see their faces. I can't see any faces except for one that I've only seen once but that I imagine I've carried with me for a lifetime.

"Deena, listen to me," I bark, using my austere tone to command her attention. "Did the dagger you used have glass on one side, metal on the other?"

"And a metal handle, yeah."

"Shrov! Deena get the shrov out of there!"

"Wh...what?"

"That wasn't a shroving dagger!" I start forward again at a run, shouting over my shoulder as I move, "Get us to that shroving satellite!" The yeeyar responds and I'm nearly knocked off my feet when the ship hurtles forward. "Deena, are you moving away from the thing?"

"Ontte, but I can't move that fast. It's too small in here."

"Where are you?"

"A vent or an air duct or something."

"Deena, hear me now." I lick my lips, debating the merits of telling her lies. *Centare, lies will not serve her now.* And she is stronger than she looks. "That was not a dagger. That was a needle."

"A needle! A needle? It's huge!"

"Huge for *you*. For us, it's a perfectly acceptable size and that doesn't matter. What matters is what's in it." I press my palms to one outer wall of the ship and the yeeyar does what I need it to. It shifts so I can see through the exterior of the ship and watch the smooth curve of the satellite, stained by the misery of time, as it draws closer, closer…close enough to touch.

A blinking beacon sits on its lowest curve. *Deena.* Her escape pod. That must be where she docked.

"Can we get any closer to where she breached?" I ask Erobu, still at the controls.

"I'm looking for a closer port but I…centare. Got nothing. We'll have to breach here."

"Shrov!" I curse and the sound echoes throughout the vastness of my ship. I feel the temperature drop, but it is nothing compared to the chill rampaging through me.

"What?" Deena shouts through my token. "What… what's in it?" Her voice is jerking again with panic and I can hear the awkward way she drags her body through whatever tunnel she's in.

"It's a stimulant." I don't know if I should tell her more. I don't know if I should have even told her that.

"But…but he was…but he was bleeding. I stabbed him."

"Centare. You *injected* him."

"But he looked *dead!*" Her voice cracks and in those cracks, I can hear her sobs fighting for voice just under the surface. More metal pops and bends. I crack all twenty of my knuckles.

I press one hand to my chest while two others remove the cannon mounted to my back. Herannathon appears on my left. "We're almost there, Rhorkanterannu. We're almost to her."

"We're not close enough."

"Rhork?" Deena whimpers.

"I'm here. Are you clear of the thing?"

"I rounded a corner, so I can't see him anymore. But...but...what was in the syringe?"

I cringe, hating to answer and fighting to find honor. I do, but I have to scrape the bottom of the barrel for it. "Adrenaline mixed with a potent healing agent. It's for use in extreme emergencies. I've only used it twice — once, when my ship crashed and I had to drag myself eight solars through the Egamion desert and then again in battle against a Lemoran fleet. It's extremely potent. The user will look dead for as long as it takes for the healing agent to kick in, then comes the adrenaline and those things are proportioned to Niahhorru sizes. If you've given it to a creature any smaller than a Niahhorru, it will make him crazed when he wakes." Lethal. "You need to get away from him. Brave the others, but get away from this one."

Her breathing picks up. She's panting now. I can hear her fiddling with something while I bounce on the balls of my feet, watching the satellite come closer. So close. And then it touches down. Gerannu is first to stroke the yeeyar walls of the ship. With our shared command, the exterior of our ship peels back to reveal a portal covered in a sickly green crust. I reach for the substance first, batting Gerannu's hands out of the way, but I can't find the token reader.

"Get the shrov out of my way, Rhorkanterannu." Gerannu pushes me off, reaches into a small depression in the hard, static material and pulls a hand-lever. I frown. "I told you. Everything here is manual."

Shrov.

"Everyone got their oxygen?" He shouts over his shoulder. Without waiting for an answer, he starts to pull on the grit-encrusted handle while the yeeyar forms a protective barrier around the full length of the ramp, thus shielding the rest of the ship from the satellite's atmosphere.

Frost blows out of the satellite like breath over a candle. Grumbled assent and a few curses chase me into the darkness. I'm running before I even land.

"Rhorkanterannu! Your pirates aren't even all on board yet!" Herannathon shouts. Even though there's a disparaging note in his tone, he keeps pace with me.

"I'm not stopping." I switch communication to Deena, who I can hear thumping around through the token. She has not turned off communication on her side. She doesn't know how. "Deena, what are you doing?"

"I'm...getting...this...pole...uughh!" A banging sound is followed by a pained curse.

"Deena!"

"It's attached to another grate that leads down... down another tunnel. I think this might be how this one got in. Ahh — there! Ugh. Ugh."

"What the shrov are you doing? Are you out of the tunnel?"

"Centare, I'm trying but...there isn't an exit. I haven't...found...it's just darkness." Her voice tilts up at the end, entering that trembling, too-high-to-be-human treble. It's a tone she never used before, not even when she was with Mathilda.

I understand something quite important. *This* is Deena's fear. And even though I thought I had, I've never heard her afraid before.

And then she sniffles and sucks in a sharp breath. "I'm going to have to fight."

"Deena..." But I never get a chance to finish that thought as something falls onto my head.

"Rhorkanterannu!" A voice behind me shouts, but Herannathon has already killed it by the time I dislodge it from my tines and shoulders and place it under the ray of my cannon.

"Seven shrovs." Herannathon moves forward and kicks the thing. As it flops lamely over the floor, I understand why Deena called it a carpet creature. "Is it a warat?" He says, referring to the creatures of the sand plains of Norath, a beautiful place populated by some of the Quadrants' most hideous beings.

"Warats have eight limbs — these only have four — and warats have exoskeletons. I don't think so."

"We should take stock. Wait for Quintenanrret to tell us what it is before we continue. They may have defenses we can't see."

I nod, but without feeling, because my own urge to stop and inspect the creature is tempered by the sound of Deena shuffling on the other end of the token. She's breathing harder than she was before and my heart is beating harder as if there's a direct link between her panic and my pulse. *Such a bridge shouldn't exist, but it does.*

"We can't. She…" I cough, clear my throat. "I can't spare the time. We'll have to proceed blind." As she did. My fearsome Deena with silk ropes for hair and the crystalline waters of a beach she has never been to glistening in her eyes.

Herannathon looks up at me, his silver eyes luminous beneath the glow of his lunar shield. He meets my gaze, stunned at first, maybe confused. Then the protective skein covering his eyes lifts and he really *looks* at me. I don't know what he sees, but it's enough.

"Let's go," he agrees.

He darts off before I do and I quickly fall in line at his left wing while more of my pirates V out behind us. And as we charge down the halls, more and more of the flimsy, wriggling creatures start to appear.

They lunge at first, charging Herannathon in the lead. He picks them off with his short-range blaster while I clean up any that he might have missed with my cannon set to its weakest frequency. They are easy to kill, but I know what Deena meant because for every one I kill, ten more crop up like weeds.

And then they start to shriek.

"Aghhh!" I roar. In front of me, Herannathon drops to one knee. I hear the unmistakable thud of more bodies hitting the floor behind me, my pirates shroving incapacitated by the sound. And there's only one sound that has such an effect on Niahhorru males.

"They're female!" Tevbarannos shouts behind me.

Not all might have been, but some *had* to be female. The high-pitched vocals screaming in pain. It's a sound that can wound a pirate. One of the only things that can.

"Gerannu, we need a scrambler!" I roar as I collapse to one arm on the floor. I feel the weight of a body slamming into my back. It impales itself immediately, but the scream it emits is enough to keep me grounded.

"Auuuurrraghhh!" I shout to try to drown the sound out. It drives an anvil through my skull, breaks each of my bones, makes me want...makes me want... "Deena!"

"Rhork?" She mewls. "Rhorky porky...please... please talk to me."

I want to laugh. I do laugh as I peel the creature caught on my hiannru tines off of me and toss the wet, weighted body onto the floor at the same time that another attacks me from the side. I see it coming and grab it around the throat before it can unleash its battle cry — before *she* can unleash *her* battle cry.

I smash her skull against the ground, crushing it easily. My fingers sink through hard bone, wet, fleshy skin and then the hot, sticky matter beneath both. Red ink leaks across the floor and I'm captivated by a strange thought.

A memory of blood. The color had been so strange to see. A violent, terrible red that glistened with voracity. Human blood is the only blood that shares this color, of all the creatures I've ever encountered in this galaxy.

A lull in the screaming is what I need to be able to rise to my feet, even as unease tangles my thoughts and scrapes its bloody nails across my chest. More creatures wail — but in a deeper pitch — and I look up in time to be able to swing my cannon around and fire at the things leaping at me, jaws distended, tongues lavishly long and a bright, unnatural pink. I fire my cannon three times, rendering six of them dead.

Breathing picking up, I try to marshal it. She doesn't need to know about this weakness. She doesn't need to know that these creatures might have more in common with her than she thinks. She doesn't need to know that this battle is more challenging than we'd hoped. I want her to have no reason to think I would ever fail her.

"We're fine," I answer, reopening communication between us. "Just worry about yourself. Are you out of the vent yet?"

"Still...working on it."

"Keep working on it. And Deena?"

"Yeah?"

"You might hear a loud sound echoing through my token soon. Don't panic. It's a scrambler and will help us fight. I'll still be able to hear you over the sound."

"Oh. Okay, but..." She sniffs. "I really want to get out of here."

"I'm coming for you."

Three turns later and I catch the scent of ebo nut. Crouching down, I spot smears of it on the wall. It's at this point that the scrambler goes live and a harsh white noise blasts through my token. It drowns out the sound of the screeches, but not the sound of Deena's gasp.

"I've found your trail and am following it. I'll be there soon." Up ahead, broken glass floats in thick, viscous puddles on the floor. Metal tanks lay bent and broken among them, like shipwrecks. All that's missing is the storm.

"Rhorkanterannu," Herannathon says. He's stopped at a body by one of the tanks and uses his foot to flip it over. "Look." The body appears to be a human male. With skin like darkness layered over gold and distinct features, it's clear that this male was not one of the creatures. "The tanks were ripped open and this one." He curses and so do the dozen other pirates that crowd into this intersection with us. "This one was female."

A human woman with pale skin and a bald head lays split open in the center of the hall surrounded by her own half eaten entrails and bloody footprints leading away from her down the hall to the right. My heart jerks.

They were chasing her.

The scent of ebo nut is long gone, but I follow the tracks the bloody footprints make to the next hall. Another right. Another left.

"Shrov." Herannathon snarls at my back.

The hall is *filled* with them. Overflowing.

"There are shroving hundreds of them!" He opens fire as vibrations echo through the floors. Standing at the intersection of this hallway, I glance left and I glance right. He's right.

There are hundreds. Centare. There are thousands of them. And they're all descending on us simultaneously.

I need to get Deena. And then we need to set this place ablaze so that it burns like a sun.

5

Deena

"Deena, where are you? What are you doing?"

Run-crawling. That's what I'm calling it anyway. Because there's a pounding in the tunnel behind me that sounds like I'm being chased by a bomb with feet. It's neither timed nor predictable, rattling with an unsyncopated beat that could loosely be classified as *jarring*. Another word would be *soul-killing*.

For reasons passing understanding, I start to scream. Well, I do understand the reasons. They resemble frustration and rage and just…irritation! How did I survive rotations of Mathilda only to end up on a ship of creatures that want to eat me? Do the gods that run this universe really hate me that much?

Problem with screaming at your enemy is when the enemy starts to scream back.

"Blaaaaaaahhhhh!"

And he's close.

Way fucking closer than I thought he was.

And where am I? I'm making progress, but I'm not sure it's the kind of progress I want to be making because I'm nearing another grate and this one looks like it leads out of the ducts and into a corridor full of beings waging war against one another.

Feet are pounding, bodies are falling, carpets are shrieking, orders are being shouted in Meero. It should give me confidence to hear Meero, but it doesn't. It won't until I'm sure that they're winning. And I can't exactly help the cause when all I've got to defend myself with is a metal stick with a jagged end that I snapped off from the tunnel grate that led me here.

"Deena!" The voice comes through my token, but a screech incinerates my response along with whatever reservation I carried about entering the war through the grate. Because that scream is even closer than it was before. In the narrow space, I crane my head around, bending it so hard and far I feel like my neck's about to break. I let out a wild shriek as I see the lunatic rug that's been chasing me just a body's length away from my toes.

"You stupid goddamn carpet!" I bellow, energy sweeping my entire skeleton that makes me feel like I'm caught in the vortex of a tornado.

Rage.

Panic.

Fear.

These all fall. What rises up in their place is the lunatic that I am deep down inside.

Only this time, I don't fear that lunatic. I own her.

The thing screams and starts to claw its way forward, jagged claws sinking deep into the green gunk as it uses the calcified shell surrounding us to drag its way towards me at an impossibly fast rate.

I turn awkwardly around in the impossibly small space until I'm facing it. As I move, blood comes off on my hands and face, smearing the groove-covered tunnel around me. *Grooves made by nails. Not claws, fingernails.* It's alarming, knowing that a little of the blood may be mine — okay, a *lot* of the blood — but it also makes me strangely proud.

"I'm proud of you." That's what he said and maybe I'm a sucker, but he sounded like he meant it. Nobody's ever been proud of me before. And why was he proud? He'd been proud of me before for fighting. For surviving. And I'm not going to let him down now.

I am *not* going to fucking die here.

The hysterics choking me solidify into a solid mass that's impossible to cry through. I can feel it in my arms as I wriggle my way backwards, farther and farther until my feet finally hit the grate. I kick. The thing screams and dives.

I lift the metal staff in my hand and release a battle cry so loud it makes my entire body levitate, "I'M NOT GOING TO FUCKING DIE HERE!"

The screamed reply makes me buck and torches my eardrums, but my arms are steady. No, fuck that shit. My arms aren't steady but what's steady is my will and tenuous dose of pride.

I kick the grate behind me at the same time that the carpet creature opens its ugly mouth and I stab. I shove my makeshift spear forward as hard as I can. My arms are shaking and I nearly poke out my own eye when I draw it back.

Speaking of eyes, I manage to hit it in the eye — where its eye should be. It looks nonplussed by my efforts. Rhork is somewhere in my head shouting my name, but he's gonna have to hold on a hot, shitty second as I bring my arms back and stab it in the other non-eye.

I scream the entire time. "You are a fucking ass hole carpet!"

And, "Carpets are for walking on!"

And, "Carpet rhymes with fuck you!"

The thing is still coming closer, its arms swirling around like a top gone out of control. It looks entirely spineless as it tries to maneuver above me so that it can avoid the strike of my spear, but nah-uh. Fuck that shit!

"Carpets don't eat people!"

I stab at the same time that it releases another deafening shriek. My spear catches its maw and I force it back, but apparently, this thing doesn't want to die, either. Its arms whip around and it manages to reach past my spear to my face. It scratches its claws across my cheek, like it's going for my eye — and I actually *have* eyes! — but I manage to snap my lids shut at the right moment.

"Rhork!" I shout and then I kick the grate behind me, trying to get it open.

"Deena!"

"I can see y'all. I'm in the grate fighting this stupid carpet!"

The token goes dark for a moment and I have the audacity to wonder if he's doing okay — who am I kidding? Is *he* doing okay? Am I doing fucking okay? NO, I'M NOT! — before returning my attention to the blood-hungry bathmat trying to stick its claws into my stomach.

"Carpets don't fucking scream at people!" I shout.

I stab and catch it just below its neck, right where a collar bone would be if it were human. My spear pierces its skin and lodges awkwardly around the bone and, when I push, sinks in deeper.

The thing screams, but unfortunately, I don't seem to be in deep enough to kill it and now my efforts have just brought it closer to me. It slashes for my face again, but I manage to lift my right forearm in time to catch its claws there. Fire rakes over my arm and I kick and this time, I'm rewarded for my efforts when the grate behind me gives.

Hands close in around my ankles. Four of them. I'm flying back over my stomach and suddenly, I'm spilling out of the cubicle of darkness and I know without looking up that it's a Niahhorru body behind me. *Bodies.*

But I don't have time for them right now either, because it's still coming.

I brace both feet on the ground and level my spear at waist-height and when it emerges onto two legs instead of four, I pull back and then shove my spear forward on a scream, "I fucking hate you, carpet!"

I gut the thing, stabbing straight through its center. It folds over my spear, trying to reach me — actually succeeding in scratching my tits, which are out and exposed in just a tattered blue bra.

I roar. "Aaaaaahhhhhhhrrrrrrr!" I level my weight into it and shove it back into the duct, but it holds onto the edges, refusing to go quietly into the dark.

"Rhork, she's here!" I hear someone shout behind me in Meero.

And then the carpet creature I'm locked in a battle to the death with suddenly, finally, explodes. At least his head does. It's there one moment and the next, pop! It slinks down onto the floor in a pile of goo and I withdraw my spear while bodies suddenly close in around me. They're all sharp spines in every direction as they turn to face out, all except for one.

I look up into his face as he lowers the cannon on his arm and our eyes meet — well, I look up at the translucent bright green light shimmering where his eyes should be, and his head tilts down like he's looking at me. His jaw is set and his lips are pressed into a thin line. He looks furious to see me and I've got no clue why, only that my blood is hot and I'm ready for another one.

"Don't they know carpets aren't supposed to fight back!" I shout at him stupidly.

He flinches, like I've slapped him, but the edge of his mouth twitches as his lower left arm stretches towards my face. He pushes a loc draped over my nose up over my head, out of the way. Then he nods at me once. "We can't turn on the lights. There's too much of this rot everywhere. We'll have to kill them all."

I scream, unable to control the volume of my pitch, "Bring it on."

He hands me a weapon strapped to the spikes on his back. In his hand it looks like a little grenade, but it takes me two hands just to lift it. He flips a switch on the side and the whole thing zings and a bright pink flare rips down its right and left sides. "All you have to do is point and press." He steps behind me, positions my hands so that one supports the barrel and the other holds what feels like a crank on the right side. He makes the motion to press the crank forward and then pull a small trigger mounted on the handle.

"Got it. Now where's one of those fuckers?"

His laughter rumbles in my ear and he whispers an order that I can't imagine anyone can hear over the horrible sound of static making it impossible to freaking think, but the warriors immediately comply when he tells them to free me from the protective barrier they've made around me.

The tunnel stretching away from me has only carpets in it. The Niahhorru warriors are all behind us. Perfect. No chance of hitting anything I don't mean to. I fire before Rhork tells me to. The blaster or whatever the shit this is bucks in my arm and would have sent me flying back if he weren't right behind me, acting as a bracing wall.

"You understand the recoil now?" He whispers in my ear and his voice sounds like some dark melody. Not trying to cage me, but trying to *unleash* me.

And he succeeds.

Tears come to my eyes. I feel them on my cheeks. I hear him whisper somewhere in the nightmare filled-darkness, *I'm proud of you,* as together, we fight these monsters. And as we fight, we're no longer a human and a pirate. We're no longer a male and a female. We're just two beings who want to live. Two equals.

And when he glances down at me once and a while, while I shout curses and complaints at the carpets that won't stop coming and won't go away, he smiles.

6

Rhork

Emotion tears through my chest hotter than a swallowed ember and makes me recall a series of moments. When construction of the mothership finally completed and I walked the command deck for the first time. When I was rotations younger and pillaged my first Eshmiri ship successfully, without one lost life. And the first time I heard Deena through my token call me Rhork.

The emotion I feel now fighting next to Deena against this demented horde hits me like the sum of these moments combined and magnified, amplified louder than the scrambler that makes her words almost impossible to make out. Almost.

"Fucking...carpets...people...aren't...for eating!" She launches another round of yeeyar-enhanced ion at the approaching creatures. There are four now where before they came at us in waves of twenty. We are thinning the herd — Deena more effectively and perhaps zealously than most.

I laugh as the bodies fall and Deena lets out a maniacal cackle. I think she might be losing her mind, but I am enjoying this too thoroughly to pull her back from the edge of whatever precipice she's standing on. Because I understand the bloodlust. I understand the fever of battle. I understand the rage and the madness of it. And I'm far, far too selfish to give this up. Because never in the life of a Niahhorru pirate has he had the fortune of fighting a battle alongside a female. Let alone the female that he loves.

I love her.

It's clear even though the terminology is new to me. Niahhorru pirates don't have such a concept, but I have heard of it before. In Quadrant Two, the Lemoran thrive on it. The Voraxians have their Xiveri Mates, which is a close comparison, I think, though I wouldn't know.

The Lemoran, like the Voraxians and the humans, also only have one mate.

I always thought that such a concept would create a hindrance to the act of procreation and, since the Niahhorru numbers have been in such decline over the past dozen rotations, procreation and keeping our species alive was all I could think about. But shrov if I care now. Because this female firing rounds like a madwoman into the darkness at beings that tried unsuccessfully to eat her alive is the female I love, that I will mate with, and that I will die to protect even if no kits ever come from it.

Funny, that I thought I cared for my crew in a way that looked like this elusive *love*. But I didn't know love, because I didn't know Deena yet.

As I contemplate this phenomenon and casually clean up any carpet creatures that dare escape Deena's firepower and draw too close to her, I notice that the sound of the scrambler is dimming. Eventually, all I hear are a few errant blasts behind me and the much louder trill of Deena having the time of her life.

"Carpet, take that! You stupid bathmat! I hate you! I hate rugs! You ate those people! I never want to see another rug in my life!"

I will have to avoid taking her into the room of human memorabilia then. That room aboard the ship is full of carpets. I laugh quietly to myself and suddenly the end of Deena's weapon is swinging towards me.

"Shrov!" I jump back.

A violent roar cuts between us as Erobu tackles Deena, nearly knocking her to the ground. I see red as I advance, deftly grabbing Deena by the arm to keep her upright while my two left arms grab Erobu by the shoulder, spin him to face me and clock him in the left eye.

"Shrov! What was that for?" He grabs his eye and staggers back, hitting the wall of Herannathon's chest.

"You touched his female," Herannathon says in a low voice that I hope Deena doesn't hear. I don't need her knowing of my intentions just yet. Not when she's like this.

I snarl at Herannathon in a way that I hope communicates my threat before turning my attention back to Deena. I carefully maneuver the barrel of her blaster away from my stomach. "I think you got them all."

"Get me more!" She shouts up at me. Her lower lip is shaking. I wonder if she knows it. "I want more to shoot at!"

I chuckle. "Enough, Deena."

"Centare!"

"Enough, for now."

"Centare!" She shakes her head and the ropes of her hair fly across her face, sticking to her skin in blood that makes my stomach clench. How much of this blood is her own? "You aren't the boss of me!"

I slip my fingers up into her hair and wrench her head back. I arch over her body, coming low enough to smell the blood on her mouth, even though I have not and will not taste her like this. Not yet. For now, I just need her attention. An end to her rising panic.

"You don't need a boss, Deena. You need an enabler. Someone to let you do anything and everything you've ever wanted and can possibly dream of. You want to find and shoot more carpets? I will find them for you and bring them to your door. But right now, there are no carpets, so either you intend to shoot nothing or you intend to shoot me. The former would be a waste and the latter, I think, a tragedy. But what do you think? Do you want to shoot me, Deena?"

I pull back enough to be able to focus on her face. Her eyes are large and wet and I can see the green of my lunar shield reflected in them like a starburst.

"Lovely," I whisper, shaking my head at the sound. I sound like I don't believe the word myself. I don't. I've never seen anything so lovely as her light.

She doesn't seem to hear me though. I'm in competition with her crashing adrenaline and don't stand a chance. It feels like she's going to fall down, but right when I anticipate the pleasure of catching her, she sucks in a breath quickly and stiffens. She swings her blaster around and I block its path. Carefully, I reposition her grip on it, so she can keep hold of it and point it down. It's clunky in her grip, but her hands are so tight around the holds that I can see the veins swimming across the backs of her hands. The skin around her knuckles is tight and pale. Her shoulders sag with its weight, but I do not take it from her.

"Rhorkanterannu, I think we've got them all for now. Should we head back to the mothership?" Ewanrennaron asks.

I don't look at him as I answer. "There may be more humans trapped in those tanks. We should search the ship. Ewanrennaron, take Deena back to the mothership. I want no less than fifteen pirates accompanying…"

"No." She shakes her head, hair dripping blood as the ropes swing around her shoulders. "Centare, I mean. I wanna stay with you."

I try not to betray how her words move me, but fail. When I straighten and roll my shoulders back, a grin disrupts my features. Just a small one, but it is enough. Herannathon is near and is watching me again, shaking his head. So do several of the other pirates nearby. We all watch as Deena moves her weapon to her right arm so that she can hold my lower right hand with her left one.

The whisper of her skin against mine makes me shiver. It's the first time we've touched and it solidifies the desire running rampant through my chest.

Deena is *mine* even if it means abandoning Kor. Even if it means tearing it down. Even if it means building another empire on another planet.

Her palm is sticky with blood and hotter than mine as we make our way down hallway after deserted hallway. Gerannu and his team meet up with us at a point. He apologizes profusely for not realizing the rot would be enough to cover the lights, which were functional beneath it. I wave him off. Very little, right now, could upset me.

With our larger numbers, I decide that we have the forces needed to keep Deena safe and still break off into smaller groups. We lost none to the carpet creatures in the battle that brought Deena safely back to me, so I don't worry too much about the pirates I send off to explore the rotating units that flank either side of this central globe. Gerannu leads us towards the center of the sphere, where the one power source once originated, though it is long dead by now.

He's chatting away excitedly about whatever elements these former humans might have used and organizes a team to collect samples of the rot. Quintenanrret also departs with a small team, their intention to gather a few of the carpet corpses and take them back to the ship for study. Information is power and these new species — or perhaps, this evolution of an ancient species — is something of note.

I wonder if Deena knows these rugs, as she called them, are humans.

I glance down at her and my swollen heart lurches with an unfathomable kind of desire. I feel it jerk in my core, and then snake lower into my cock, threatening to release it, which would be more than embarrassing. A Niahhorru male leaking seed all over the place would be downright mortifying.

She looks up at me and our eyes meet and I quickly break the connection, while still firming my grip on her palm. I want her to know what I'm too embarrassed to tell her. That she is wanted and desired and perfect and loved.

"Centare." Her whisper is broken and she clears her throat to try again. "Centare," she repeats a little louder, but no less shakily.

"What are you talking about, Deena?"

She shivers, like she's cold. Likely, she is and I frown. I have nothing to give her. "You asked me if I wanted…" Her chest jolts and I stare down at her, shocked by the action.

"What was that?"

"Hiccup."

"And it does not hurt you?"

She shakes her head, then tilts it to the left. "I guess it's a little uncomfortable."

"I'll call the healer."

She laughs and shakes her head. Her laughter is… *off*. It starts as it usually does, husky and damning, but quickly morphs into something lighter and frazzled, something a little manic. Still, even that raucous laughter is a soothing sound. The balm to the satellite's previous screams. I see how the posture and tension within the pirates who can hear her entirely eases. Mine does, too. At least, until her laughter fetters out and she tries to wipe her cheek with her shoulder, having insufficient arms to hold my hand and carry her weapon and wipe her cheeks. So I do it for her.

I smooth my fingers beneath her eyes, trying to be careful with her right cheek. I can see the cuts and they make me proud. She is a warrior, my female. My *mate*. I will have her and she will have me and we will be as the Lemoran and Voraxians are in their strange realms where they share only one mate apiece.

The gesture must startle her, because she looks up at me like I've grown yet a fifth arm straight out of the top of my head. I grin. "What is it?"

"I…" The jerking of her chest nearly takes her off of her feet.

I frown. She laughs wildly.

"I was just saying that it's crazy that I'm covered in cuts and you want to call the doctor to help me handle my hiccups." She does the jerking motion again and I frown harder.

"Are you injured?" I glance down at her body. Bloody and war-ravaged, ontte, but I don't see any disabilities.

She shakes her head and does her *hick cup* again. "Centare. I mean, I don't think so." Another hiccup.

"Do you need me to carry you?" I don't know why I ask her this. It is clear she does not need to be carried.

A frown pulls the edges of her full lips down and she looks away from me with a purpose that I don't understand. Her hand tenses in mine and she might have even gone so far as to try to retract her hand had I not tightened my grip, preventing her.

"My leg is fine."

"Your leg? Is your leg wounded?"

Though elegant when walking over dead bodies, here in this wide empty hallway, she stumbles over nothing at all. "I…"

I catch her with two hands and with a third, attempt to take her gun away from her. She holds onto it like a fist with rigor mortis. "Your leg?" I ask her again.

"You asked to carry me," she says, still refusing to meet my gaze.

"What about your leg? I offered to carry you because your *hick cup* makes you look like you're going to shoot off of your feet and hurtle into the ceiling. I'm offering to ground you rather than have to catch you later." I frown down at her, confused with what she's blabbering about. Perhaps I *should* carry her. It's likely she's never fought in a battle before. Maybe she's too exhausted to walk.

The thought doesn't feel right.

Even if she had never waged war, she did so successfully. To carry her simply because she's tired now would be an insult to any Niahhorru and I don't dare shame her in front of my crew. It would shame me, too. Plus, they already idolize her.

Her lips part as she stares up at me, utterly mute. Like what I've said makes as little sense to her as what she said does to me. Her face scrunches all of a sudden and she shakes her head again, then inhales deeply, squares her shoulders and picks up her pace to match mine more evenly.

I smile. I was right not to think she was too exhausted to walk.

"You asked me before if I wanted to shoot you. Centare. I don't want to shoot you. But I'm not giving you back your blaster thing. It was a gift!" She raises her voice in a warbly shout and yanks on my hand.

Laughter rumbles through and out of me. She shivers again at the sound, like she's cold, but I don't have any cure for her now. On the mothership, I will make sure she has everything she needs. Just as I will for the rest of her life or mine. Whichever ends first.

"Ontte, it was a gift."

She glares up at me and I smile.

"You don't believe me?"

Another shiver. She blinks quickly and tears her gaze from mine. "Ontte. Centare. I don't know. You're too slippery to catch."

"I'm nothing if not honest."

"You've lied to me before."

"This is true. But I will never lie to you again."

"Yeah right."

I will have to do something to convince her, then. On the other hands, she might be right. Perhaps, I will lie to her again. How can I predict the future? So I just nod and smile and say, "Interesting."

She shivers again, this time even more violently, and when she looks up at me, her adrenaline must be crashing fully now because she looks utterly dazed and fully spent. "You...you don't..."

"Rhorkanterannu!" My name reverberates through my token loud enough to steal my attention from Deena.

"What?" I snarl.

Deena jumps and opens her mouth, but I use one hand to point to the token in my ear and a small understanding seems to dawn on her.

"We found more of the tanks in the right unit. Gravity seems to be working a little better here, thanks to the fact that we're rotating, but unfortunately, we also ran into more of the creatures." I freeze at Herannathon's words.

"How many tanks?"

"About fifty of them, but they're empty. Give you one guess what happened to them?"

I snarl, "Kill any creatures you find and keep up the search."

"Search is over. We're heading back to you now."

"Meet us at the core. Gerannu will send you a map now." With the silent commands issued, I check in with Tevbarannos leading the command into the left rotating unit. Again, he confirms the gravity is stronger, but for whatever reason, oxygen levels are even lower there and he and the pirates searching haven't come across humans — of the tank or carpet variety — at all.

"Gerannu, how far are we?" I ask out loud as my token goes silent.

"At the end of this tunnel, we'll find a shaft — perhaps once containing some form of lift. We take that up and we'll be there in four stories."

"Good. Communicate the map to the others. They can meet us there."

Reaching the shaft, Deena watches the pirates begin to climb up around her nervously. "I...I don't think I can do that. I don't know how to climb."

"Well, to start, you'll need to put down your blaster. Pity you don't have more arms with which to carry it. I can see how your impediment would prevent you from climbing easily."

She removes her hand from mine with a jerk and hugs her arms around herself. I do my best not to ogle her exposed chest, which means I fail entirely and stare as much as I like. "Impediment," she mutters. "Don't you mean my defect?"

"Having only two arms is hardly a defect. Voraxians have only two arms and I guarantee you that none would be daunted by such a climb. You should be able to manage this. Look. There's even a ladder here," I say, banging on a series of metal rungs built into the wall inside of the shaft to my left. "But since I desire to feel your body pressed against mine, I won't harass you like I would another pirate, but give you the option of being carried."

I bend in close and brush her blood-stained hair back over her shoulders. I glance down at her chest, those full, ripe breasts even riper than many Niahhorru females'. Utterly compatible with our species. The likeness is extraordinary.

Her mouth is so near to mine and it's parted just enough for me to imagine that she wants to be kissed by me. I stroke her bottom lip with one of my thumbs while two of my arms circle her waist and lift her up. She drops her blaster and I catch it with my fourth arm, affixing it to the sling on my back.

"Careful not to circle your legs all the way around me. I wouldn't want you to get scratched on my tines." I brush my lips over hers as I lift her high against my chest. The act is over so quickly it might have seemed unintentional to the adrenaline-dazed and battle-weary-confused, of which Deena is both.

But make no mistake in thinking that I did not immediately memorize the pressure of her impossibly soft lips against my much harder ones, or the taste of her steeped in blood. *Lovely. Just lovely.*

She seems to have gone spontaneously mute, which is fine, because it leaves more of my mind free to concentrate on the lush feel of her curves pressed against my body. It's so easy just to sink into her. Like she was made for me. Her knees lock against my sides and the insides of her thighs shake as I take the rungs of the ladder in my two upper hands and climb, feeling rather foolish as I approach the climb two-handed, like a human would.

Most of my pirates are long ahead of me, but I don't rush this. So far, there aren't any carpet creatures here and Deena has her hands on my shoulders and is holding onto me in a way that I like far, far too much.

The only trouble is my cock which, the moment I get stimulated enough, will push free of its sheath and begin to weep semen all over the place. Not exactly the first in-person impression I had hoped to make with my mate-who-does-not-know-yet-that-she's-my-mate.

She chews on her bottom lip and I focus on it too hard. I will need to say something to keep my cock under control before it's too late. "Pity for such a perfect lip."

Her body tenses even tighter around mine. She's still shaking. She's still scared. I wonder...is she frightened of me? I don't like that but I'm simultaneously unsure how to fix it. I will need to be careful with her emotions even more so than with her body. "Wh...what?"

"I said, pity for such a perfect lip. You're chewing it raw."

"Oh. Shrov." She keeps her face turned to the side, but it does little to prevent me from watching her openly. We are so close. Eye-level in ways we aren't when we're both standing.

My lower hands have a hold of her full bottom and I make no attempt at all to distance myself from the softness of those curves. I wonder if her squirming and shaking has anything to do with the placement of my hands on her thighs. I tilt my head, watching her as I climb, trying to figure out where the singing fool and the battle-hardened warrior have gone and why they have left me now with this timid version of a female I know to be fearless.

"Is it because you've seen me for the first time and are displeased?" I ask her evenly.

Her gaze flashes to mine and widens in alarm. I can see her clearly. I wonder, with her human eyesight, if she can see me at all in the darkness surrounding us, illuminated only by the muted glow of the torch on her wrist. Its glow makes it more difficult for me to see her through my lunar shield, so I retract it and then lift the protective film that covers my eyes so that I am just as vulnerable now as she is.

Her pulse quickens. I can feel it in her chest, hammering hard through her skin against mine.

I think my pulse may quicken, too.

I want to kiss her. Rut her. Savage her. Wreck her. Move her. Just like I want to be moved.

I feel more exposed than I expected watching her like this in the dimness, where her little light reflects off of the curve of her cheek, making it glow like the sun's reflection off of a moon. She is so beautiful.

"Why...why did you stop climbing?" She says, voice soft and catching, but at least not with those horrible *hick cups* she had previously.

I laugh softly and her heart beats faster, which makes my heart beat faster. "I didn't realize I had. Your beauty prevents me from concentrating on two things at once."

Holding onto the rung above both our heads with just one hand so that I can brush my fingers over her forehead, but she flinches back. "Don't make fun of me."

"Make fun of you?"

"Yeah, I know what I look like. Don't call me that word." Her gaze genuflects and she fidgets like she's trying to get away from me, but has nowhere to go.

My gaze drops inadvertently to her chest as she wriggles and my blood heats. My cock poses its threat and, by will alone, I batter it back mercilessly. I continue climbing as I turn Deena's words over once, and then a second time just to be sure I've understood what she said and moreover, what she meant.

She does not find herself beautiful. Could that be her concern? That she finds herself inadequate relative to me?

"Interesting," I breathe.

"What is?"

"Mathilda's skill with manipulation and psychological torture."

Deena makes a sound that is all but confirmation of my assessment. At least some of her tension deflates as the topic returns to her kinswoman. "You have no idea."

"I would like to."

"To what?"

"Have an idea."

"Don't you already? You were always listening."

"I was, but I could only hear you."

She does not respond to this, but continues to try to look anywhere but at my face. Every so often, however, she steals a glance. I suppose steal isn't the right word. They're all freely given.

I pause again on the rungs and she tenses, as expected. I touch her face again, prepared for her to attempt to retreat. I don't let her, but slip my hand around the back of her neck and hold her still while I lean forward and press my lips to her forehead. She tastes like a fever dream, raw, unrepentant adrenaline crashing like a wave on the rocks. She tastes like war.

Frozen as she is, when I pull back, she doesn't retreat. I tilt her chin up and lick the blood from her bottom lip with my tongue. "I will fix it, Deena."

She gasps and jerks in my arms. I can see her expression in the dark and it's lost. Adrenaline or something more? I'm not sure. But it doesn't matter. "What?"

"I will fix what she broke in you."

"You...you mean my leg?"

I growl, frustrated and my hand tightens in her hair, pulling harder than I wholly mean to. "Deena, I will tell you only once, I have no idea what you're talking about. You will have to show me whatever is wrong with your leg when we are alone..." My hand drops from her neck to the front of her chest. I trace the outline of whatever contraption she wears that cage her breasts, warring with myself on whether or not to tear it off. "...and I have ample time to examine it, along with the rest of you."

"But...you...don't want me for shekurr."

"Centare. I don't. I don't want to share."

She winces, but I tighten my hand around her right breast and she shivers and straightens and releases a little breathy moan. She's breathing hard again and her eyelids are fluttering and the shadow of a fleeting guilt flutters over me. Maybe she is crashing and I'm making things worse by making lewd suggestions and pawing at her like I am. As things stand now, I don't even know if *she* wants *me*, though I'm fairly confident she does.

I'm confident in all things and have confidence enough for us both. One day soon, I will teach her to wield a confidence that is all her own.

"I will teach you," I say, ending the conversation as a voice flutters through my token. Herannathon's. "Rhorkanterannu, you and Deena need to hurry up. You need to see this *now*."

"Teach me what?"

"Everything." I withdraw my palm from her chest and reposition my hands around her bottom, hoisting her up and tighter against me as her grip goes momentarily slack.

"You're not making any sense, Rhork."

I grin at her use of my nickname as I take the rungs two at a time and begin moving faster. Looking up, I can see now that we're the last two left in the shaft and a light filters through the opening in the wall my pirates disappeared through.

"I am making sense. You just aren't hearing me."

She opens her mouth to reply, but at the same time, a screech from above is followed by a pirate's roar. A pale body suddenly sails down the shaft dangerously close to where Deena and I climb. I pull myself over her body, arching to prevent the creature from clawing at her without first impaling itself on my spines. It narrowly misses me. I can feel the air whoosh across my back as it plummets past.

"A little warning next time!" Deena shouts up the shaft. Her words are met with laughter, some of it mine.

A face peers over the edge of the opening and Quintenanrret and another male, Rhegaran, reach down to grab my upper arms and help lift me up. Only when I've got my feet firmly planted beneath me do I set Deena down. I take her hand in mine and weave between the pirates who I think part more for Deena's benefit than they do for mine.

The blue glow gets brighter the farther forward we walk until soon, the short breezeway ends and a universe of light opens up before us. My jaw goes slack. I glance down and see Deena's mouth hanging openly as stupidly as mine is. The males to her left and the males to my right all wear identical expressions.

"It's beautiful, isn't it?" Rhegaran says beside me.

I nod, incapable of responding.

"Beautiful," Quintenanrret answers on Deena's other side. He has tears swimming in his silver eyes. "Don't you think, Deena?"

Deena doesn't look away from what's in front of her. The unimaginable sight. It's more than we could have ever hoped for. It's more than I ever thought I'd find. Deena doesn't look particularly thrilled, nor do I blame her. She reaches her free hand up to her hair and, when I go to firm my grip on her hand, she rips it away. I frown. Her hand that belonged to me for a time reaches up to join its mate in her hair.

She's breathing hard again, only now she's cursing. "I *fucked* up, didn't I?" The word she uses in Human translates loosely to shrov, but a pirate behind us still picks up on it.

"Fuh-huck," he says. Another repeats more closely to the intonation Deena used. "Fuhhk. I like this word. Fuhhk!" And soon they're all shouting it.

Deena's not paying any attention to the rabble behind her, though. She's staring at the tanks lining the circular room, stretching up above our heads ten stories. Cautiously, she enters the room until she's standing in the center of the space, blue light pouring over her, turning her skin unusual colors and making the bright blood splashed all across her chest and arms and face glitter like precious stones.

Her hands are still in her hair as she looks up, up, up, and ever farther up at the tanks holding members of her species. There are not hundreds of them, but thousands. Enough to fill one of Kor's smallest cities. And that's saying a lot. Kor is inhabited by millions.

But I can't keep this many humans on Kor. Correction — I can keep them there, but I can't keep them safe.

A cold trickles through my chest as a dozen warning bells go off in my mind in uncoordinated cacophony.

Fuck, as Deena and these humans would say.

My gaze returns to her and more alarm bells sound. Rage or shock or fear or something else has her shaking even more violently now. She looks like she's going to shatter into a billion pieces and if she does that, I worry about my own ability to collect and reassemble the parts.

"Deena," I say, keeping my voice severe.

Her gaze flicks to me. She sucks in a ragged gasp, and then she says the last words I would have expected her to say to me. "I guess you don't need me for shekurr anymore. I guess you don't need me anymore for anything." Laughter that does not sound like laughter fills the room around us and does not echo.

I reach her and grab both of her wrists with two of my hands, pull them away from her hair, lest she yank it out at the root. "Deena, I needed you the first time I heard your voice, though I didn't know it then. I needed you the first time you called me Rhorky bear. I need you now more than ever."

I don't know if she's listening to me. Her head is swiveling on her neck, gaze seeking salvation, but finding only pirates. And we have never looked like salvation, not to anyone.

"I shouldn't have brought you here, should I?" She tries to twist her wrists out of my grip, but she isn't really trying that hard.

I laugh in a short burst, "And leave these humans to the cannibals aboard this satellite?"

"Shrov." She's sweating, twisting her wrists, blinking uncontrollably. Losing control. Her left knee buckles, but I still have her by the arms and hold her up.

"Deena, look at me."

She looks at me.

"Deena, take a breath."

She inhales once jerkily, and then inhales again.

"Deena, I was not expecting this quantity of humans. I will need your help. You already fought a war for me. Are you really going to fail me now?"

"What?" She shakes her head, looking stricken, looking like she's been struck. "I would never fail you." Her voice warbles. Water wells on her lower eyelids.

I smile and stroke her cheek with my thumb. Her words have just confirmed a previous suspicion.

I love her, ontte, this I knew.

But she also is in love with me, too.

She has no idea about the former, and is even less aware of the latter. But it doesn't matter, because I'll spend however long it takes to convince her. However long she needs.

"Good. Because I need you here with me."

She nods, inhales sloppily, and shudders. Then she straightens and when she blinks, I know that it's me she sees. "I'm with you, Rhork."

I feel my lips jerk up. I want to tell her that she always will be, but I know she's not ready to hear that. So I just think it and out loud, whisper, "Good. Now tell me what to do with these humans."

I release her wrists as she turns around again, as if the answer is written in one of the tanks. When she comes back around to face me she laughs lightly, but it's a real laugh this time. One that swims uncertainly into her eyes and makes her shoulders jump in small pulses. "I have no idea, Rhork."

"Where would you suggest we begin?"

Her face scrunches and when she responds, it's in a question. "Getting the tanks onto your ship, but leaving the people in them until we figure out where they'll live?"

I nod. "Good. That's what I think, too."

"You do?"

"Ontte."

"You aren't going to take the women out to perform shekurr?"

"Rip them out of their tubes and rut them immediately? That's what you think I'm capable of?"

"I..."

I frown in the wake of her silence, then shake my head and chuckle softly, "I suppose I have given you no reason to think otherwise. But centare, Deena. I will not unleash our world onto them until we have a plan. You and me." I advance on her in slow steps and imagine that I can feel her pulse accelerate beneath the thin bones of her chest and all throughout her lush curves.

"Me?"

"Ontte. You."

Another deep breath makes her breasts rise. A dire threat to my cock's already tenuous equilibrium. Luckily, what she says next helps, "Okay. Okay, I can do this. Give me back my blaster. Just in case more of the stupid bathmats show up." She shudders again on an inhale, but I can see her fighting madly, savagely against it. She can do this.

"You can do this," I laugh darkly as I go to her, wrap an arm around her head and bring her in to my chest. I whisper in her ear and though it is a simple statement, I mean it as a promise. "We will make a pirate out of you yet."

7

Deena

I don't have a complete grasp on reality when I wake up. All I know is that it's dark and even though I've never been afraid of the dark before, I'm afraid now. Am I back in the basement? Somehow, that thought is worse than any other. I'm distantly aware that a lot has happened since I was in the basement but right now, in the cold face of total darkness, I can't believe that I'm anywhere else.

I can't believe that I got out.

Not like *wow! I can't believe how great it is that I got out of that hell box!* More like *There's no possible way I got out of that nightmare cell because Mathilda is always and has always been one step ahead. She must have abducted me back from Rhork and the pirates somehow...*

Rhork.

I'm with Rhork.

I'm...Rhork...he...he came for me and I gave up... gave up the humans and...no...there were no humans... there were just...carpets...carpets? I shiver at the memory of carpets that I can't fully place. It's not cold — or is it? Where am I? In the basement? With Mathilda? With Rhork?

I open my mouth but I'm scared to ask for him. What if he's not here and Mathilda laughs at me? It'll crush me.

My arms are shaking. What am I lying on? It's weird and lumpy and...is it moving? Shit! What is this? Where am I! I whimper and the sound of my own voice makes me jolt. I'm just about to escalate the situation and spiral into full blown panic when a burst of light flares behind me and then dies too quickly for me to turn to face it and see where I am.

My heart is pounding. I'm not alone. There are footsteps and they sound heavy, even though they're muted by something beneath them. Not beneath me though, because I'm on this lumpy fluffy thing that feels like some sort of creature doing a dance under my shaking hands and knees every time I move.

"Mathilda?" I wheeze, paralyzed by fear and a knowing that she'll find me wherever I escape to.

The footsteps stall. A low light flares up over my head. Just a spark, like a candle embedded right in the ceiling. It's orange glow spiderwebs out from a central point and provides just enough light to douse the whole world around me in an intimacy that hits me right in the gut when I glance over my shoulder and see Rhork.

"Do I look like Mathilda to you?" His deadpan makes me laugh shakily and when I try to turn around to face him, I end up wobbling and falling onto my back. Rhork grunts when I land and his gaze sweeps my body in a way I'm completely unprepared for. It makes me heat.

"Centare," I answer, clearing my throat. "Uff." I'm turtling on my back and when I roll to one side, I recognize the issue. I'm hanging in a net. It's stretched from one wall to the other, but the holes are still big enough to stick my hands and feet through. Heck, I'd fall straight through it if it weren't for the pile of blankets underneath me. *Net, rhymes with bet, which sounds an awful lot like bed. Is this a Niahhorru bed?*

I fall back into the blanket mound again and am just about to ask him if this is, in fact, a bed, when his hands move down to the laces of his pants and my thoughts die at their points of origin. A new thought rises up: I'M NAKED AND HE'S ABOUT TO GET NAKED, TOO. HOLY SHIT!

"Shrov!" I pull a blanket around me, but it's caught under my fat ass. I yank and grunt as I do, but Rhork looks at me and speaks like he's totally calm and like this is all totally normal and like I'm not about to poop my lack-of-pants.

"I'm happy to let you inspect me more, in case you think I still might be Mathilda." My motions stall as his hands move around his hips, drawing attention to the muscles and plates disappearing beneath his pants' thick, grey material. They lace up the sides, so it takes all four hands working in coordination to free the ties. *Ties rhymes with dries*, which is exactly what my mouth and throat are doing.

In a last ditch effort, I throw my right arm over my tits and squeeze my legs together so he can't look right up the barrel of my lady bits, but he just grins in that way he does that reveals his teeth. Not just white, but radiant, they shimmer behind his grey lips like mother of pearl.

"Who do you think cleaned you, Deena?"

"C-clean?"

"Ontte. I took the gamma wand to every piece of you. Between your toes, between every coil of your hair, between your legs." His chest lifts and the plates lining it all shift as he takes large, even breaths. Meanwhile, my brain has short-circuited and I've completely stopped breathing. "Your breasts required special attention."

I pat my tits, like I'm trying to make sure they're still there. A new thought fires into my mind then and I actually manage to voice it. "The cuts."

"Quintenanrret closed them, but don't worry, he made sure not to erase the scars. You still bear them."

"Scars…"

"Yes, I told you, you'd still have them."

"What? Why?"

He looks at me like I've just asked him why there are stars in the sky. "Because if you don't keep scars from the battles you fought, how will anyone know you fought them?"

"I…" He keeps watching me expectantly, clearly waiting for an answer. I can't give him one. "I don't know."

"The correct answer is, they won't."

"Why do they need to?"

"To see your strength. On the outside…" His gaze sweeps my body salaciously, sticking every place it touches. The glue will leave a residue I know I'll never be able to wipe away, mainly because I don't want to. *He called me beautiful once. When he looks at me like this, I imagine that he was telling the truth.*

I suck in quickly through my teeth, tasting him on the air. He tastes so clean, cool in a way that doesn't make sense. Like a breeze. *Maybe one that rolls in from the ocean.* And then I blurt, "Everyone can see your strength on the outside."

My gaze follows a similarly invasive pattern over Rhork's skin and plates, his chest, his arms. Shrov, I like the way he's put together.

"Do you like the *strength* I wear on the outside?" He simpers, one brow cocked.

"Uh huh. Yeah. Ontte!" I shout — no filter at all — and then humiliation crushes me down into the blankets below. "I mean..."

He grins wildly at that and I short-circuit outright when he does. My mouth opens, my tongue lolls out, and a surge of heat fires between my legs like lightning. Instead of ignoring it like any decent, Tri-God-fearing woman would've, I make it a helluvalot worse when I reach down and cup my vag, like I'm trying to stop it from making a damn beeline for Rhork, which is *exactly* what it — and the rest of me — wants to do.

Rhork's already wide nostrils flare and the swirling patterns of his eyes start to dance even more sensationally. He seems to get bigger, taller, and then the unimaginable happens. The laces on his pants finally meet their last resistance and the entire material peels away from him, like the skin from a banana.

"Good," he says as he steps out of the material and covers the rest of the distance to me, reaching the net in four easy strides. He's just as naked as I am and he wears his nudity with a ferocious pride. I want to touch him.

"I want to touch your...strength." Shrov! Did I just say that out loud!

He freezes with his hands on the edge of the net, like he was about to climb on but now he's not.

Mortification blasts through me, but it isn't enough to douse the flames that ripple over my entire body.

"I didn't…" I start.

He cuts in. "Are you trying to torture me? You remember what I told you about Niahhorru males."

I nod, remembering…

I lay on my back, my eyes closed, trying to picture it. "I can't picture it."

His laughter echoes through the token, just a light grunt. "What part?"

"Maybe, any of it. The stars through your view pane. The ship itself. You in it." I shrug even though I'm lying down. Makes the motion feel more difficult and awkward because, in my head, I'm standing right there next to him when, in reality, I'm here in the only place I ever am.

"Interesting." He goes silent, but only for a breath. Long enough for me to try to picture him again and fail. "You have no idea what I look like, do you?"

"Uh-uh. Not a one."

"And it occurs to me only now that I don't know what you look like either."

He doesn't want to know what I look like. I tense, hoping he never knows. If Mathilda has her way, he might not. If Mathilda has her way, I'll die down here an old woman. "You've seen humans before. I'm sure you get the idea."

"Ontte, I know what humans look like, but I want to know what you look like." He says the word you with such baiting impishness, that I know he's trying to get a rise out of me. Too bad, he's conjured another demon entirely, because with that one whispered word and the thought — no, the impossible hallucination — that he might want to know what I look like — me, Deena, colony trash and colony princess all rolled into one — makes my toes curl and my belly ache.

I stifle a moan and Rhork whispers my name again with every intent of bewitching me. I'm already half-bewitched. To save myself, I break the spell by blurting, "That's not fair."

"What isn't?"

This strange hold you have over me. "I-I don't know what Niahhorru pirates look like at all."

"Centare? Being a human, perhaps it will shock you."

"Try me."

And then he proceeds to describe himself in lascivious detail, and it's strange that even the most alien things about him make me sweat. Maybe, especially them. I love that his entire body is shades of silver and that he has four arms and I love that he has these thick bits of exoskeleton, like armor, that cover parts of his chest and thighs and arms and even form two ridges that flank the giant spikes growing out of his head.

I want to ask a thousand questions, but when he gets to the bit about his cock, I forget everything I was going to say. All I want now is see it with my own eyes. This cock that, once stimulated, surges out of its protective sheath, hard and painfully sensitive until it finds its home inside of a female. In my imaginings, I even go so far as to make that female me.

"And now you. What do you look like, Deena?" He says, but I'm still recovering, already twisted leg twisting further against the sheets. I accidentally brush the scar that winds all the way up from my shin, over my knee, to my thigh and quickly wince away from it.

"Centare," I whisper.

"Centare?"

"Centare," I say again, even more quietly.

He doesn't answer. Not for a long time. Long enough to make me sweat for entirely different reasons. And then when he does speak, all he says is a word I've come to fear and anticipate. A word that I've heard before plenty of times, but when he says it, I no longer know what it means.

"Interesting."

I swallow hard and try to read his expression. Is he repulsed by me now that he has seen me? Now that he knows I've got nothing to recommend me? I swallow hard and try squinting at him, like that'll narrow my focus and help me understand what he means and what he wants from me.

"You said that the males...um...that they...you have hard bits of skin that protect your organs and that you don't have colors in your faces like Voraxians do..."

"Not what I said about faces, Deena. What I said about my cock." He lifts an eyebrow. Well, a brow bone? Whatever muscle is where an eyebrow should be, because he doesn't have hair on his face — or any other part of him — at all.

I lick my lips and zip my thighs so firmly together that they start to shake. "Um." I'm sweating again. Am I sweating? Shit. That's not very sexy. Sexy! Ha! If Mathilda heard me now, what horrible thing would she say? *Sexy? You? You're incapable of it. Defective, even Rhorkanterannu thinks so...*

"Deena."

"Um." He asked a question. Oh shit, what was it again? Males. Males and cocks. My sweat thickens and I speak as fast as I can when I blurt out, "You said that when you get aroused, you pretty much have to come or you'll be in pain."

He tilts his head forward and his gaze drops down to my tits and my arm covering them. "That's correct. And I'm dangerously close to it now, Deena. So move your hand, cover yourself, and..."

Reacting quickly, I try to pull the blanket over me, but his hand latches onto my wrist. I gasp and my other hand pulls free of my vajajay. He grabs that one too and stares between it and my tits like one or both of them has just called his honor into question.

"Shrov." He bows his head, jerks back and then it happens.

He releases me and the nest and takes a few steps back and when he stands to his full height, my gaze drops to his crotch. There's a short protrusion that looks like another rough plate, except it's slightly raised and flat on the top like a plateau. But as I stare, the center pushes up and out and from it, a cock like nothing I've ever seen before, grows.

Literally shooting up out of its shell like a flower, the thing stretches up and up and keeps growing. No, not like a damn flower, like a shroving tree trunk! The thing is massive, thick as my arm and tall and curved so that it touches his belly button. His hands flutter uncertainly around it, like he's afraid to touch his own... *thing!*...and all of a sudden, he moans.

He moans so loud and long and in anguish that it makes me jerk and stutter. I don't manage to get any words out, Human, Meero or otherwise, before he starts to, well...come. He starts to spurt semen all over the place. Thick grey gobs of it leak from the flat head of his penis, winding in ribbons down the veiny shaft.

"Holy shit." My vagina does a strange dance as a mirrored wetness starts to dampen the thick patch of curls between my legs and the blanket beneath them. I don't have the wits left to try to do anything about my current predicament with as enrapt as I am watching Rhork fight through his.

He staggers towards the curved wall to my left and presses one palm to its black, silvery surface. It peels apart, opening a small compartment. He rifles through it, throwing all kinds of gadgets over his shoulder until he comes to a long, curved tube. It's orange — one of the few things on this ship that isn't grey — and I jolt when Rhork brings it down the length of his body and fits it over his dick. He stumbles back and lands on another net, this one hanging from the ceiling, and moans even louder, even harder, his pelvis jerking up as he fucks this thing in front of me.

Ho. Ly.

Mo. Ly.

I mewl. The sound must surprise him too, because his eyes fly open and hook into mine and don't let me go. I spread my legs apart and reach between them and touch my clit. It feels so good watching him watch me like this.

His no-hair-eye-brow-brows twist up and I'm too horny to be properly ashamed that he likely finds me disgusting, touching myself to the sight of him. I'm glad I'm too horny for any modicum of self-awareness, or restraint. Because this is the most erotic thing I've ever done, and it feels shroving great.

I touch my clit, struggling to stay up on my elbow, but unwilling to lie back. I want to watch him. Want to see him through to whatever end lies in store for the both of us. The soft skin of my clit is completely soaked. Ordinarily, I'd have to wet my fingers in my mouth in order to reduce the friction of my hand on my ultra-sensitive skin, but not now. Now, all I have to do is watch him.

His hips are jerking in little pulses, making the net swing beneath him. His spikes poke through the back of it and I have no idea why, but the sight of them wrings another moan out of me.

This time, his name is mixed in the middle of it. "Rhork, baby..."

"Shrov!" He closes his eyes, blocking the sight of me out. It stings somewhere deep in my heart and mutes some of my arousal. My fingers slow. His eyes fly open and he looks at me and I stop. My face falls.

And then I jump when he jerks onto his feet. It takes two of his hands to keep the contraption around his dick in place. He grinds his teeth together and his eyelids flutter as he stumbles towards me — towards the net. Maybe he wants to lie down while he finishes...

I try to move back and out of his way, to make space for him, but it's kind of hard to maneuver on the net. It's stretched taut between three walls and the blankets beneath me act as some kind of surface. The moment I manage to get up on my knees, Rhork grabs my bad leg and wrenches it straight.

I squeal as he flips me onto my back and bites down on the inside of my thigh.

"Auhhh," I moangaspwail with my mouth open and my eyes clenched tight.

"You remember what else I said about Niahhorru males. Don't you Deena?" He rumbles, sending lightning blitzing through me.

Shrov no. I can't remember anything. Not when he wrenches me to the edge of the net with one pull, hooks my knees over his shoulders and lifts my hips to meet his mouth using two of his hands. The flash of his hot breath against my flaming, tortured clit is the only warning I get before his hard, smooth lips crash down onto it like a wave in that elusive ocean I've imagined one thousand times. I picture it again.

Heat sizzles through me, ripping a whole host of expletives out from between my teeth. I jerk and writhe as his tongue slaps down onto my most sensitive flesh, stroking it roughly, brutally, endlessly.

System. Failure.

Response. Not. Registering.

A shudder twists my already twisted leg along with all the rest of my limbs. I reach down and my fingers find smooth scalp, and then ridges and then spikes. I grab onto the uppermost hiannru tine and wrench him even closer, like I'm trying to pull him into me. He groans throatily against my clit while his mouth continues to suck and lick and nip and lave. *Stars, this is everything.*

"Ontte, it is," he answers.

I'm talking out loud again.

"Ontte, you are."

I jolt again when three fingers enter my tight opening and another probes my rear. "Holy shit!"

He enters me in both holes simultaneously and even though I've touched myself in both places, I've never been touched before in either. Not like this. My mind is completely lost, fragments scattered to the far quadrants of the known galaxy. All I've got is a Niahhorru spike in my shaking hands to anchor me as Rhork punishes me brutally for a crime I didn't know I committed.

But if I did know, I'd commit it again and again and again... I'd happily let it be the death of me.

"Rhork!"

His fingers stretch me nearly to the point of pain, but not quite reaching it, and somehow that punishing pressure is enough to make my eyes roll back while his fingers work in wretched and wonderful unison — all twenty of them. He's stroking my ass hole, using the lubricant from my wet core to ease his entry. He's got his three fingers inside of my core and they're all plated, providing a rough and delicious friction, and his tongue is still lapping up every stray bit of my arousal he can find as I leak and leak and spiral and spiral and eventually, my entire body clenches so tight there's nowhere for it to go, but everywhere.

I burst apart like a bomb's gone off inside and scattered me to the far corners of the room. My mind and its contents float out and into the yeeyar. But there is one single thing I register. One sound that's really more of a sensation that blisters through the pain of my arrival onto the shores of this beach that I've never been to before.

Rhork's cry. It's deep and thunderous and brutal and sounds oddly like my name, *"Deeeeeennnaaaa!"* It's a curse. A reprimand. I want to respond to it, beg forgiveness, run away in shame, but a tearing sound wrenches my words away from me and I yelp when I suddenly face a short, hard drop.

The net gives and I land on my back on the floor, the blankets doing more to break my fall than Rhork's hands are, which aren't so much catching as they are pulling. He's got a hold of me in all kinds of ways and I'm suddenly overwhelmed by the hands and arms situation. He's massaging my right tit and rubbing my mouth with his thumb and then he's arching over me and kissing me and he's all hard lips and soft tongue.

I can feel his other hands working at something between us and then the hard thing caught on his cock is gone and holy shit! His cock is like a firebrand! Like molten metal, it zings across my skin, making me flinch back, but I've got nowhere to run. It slaps diagonally across my stomach, before he maneuvers my hips where he wants them — between his. I'm so excited at the thought that the pirate king might fuck me that I think I have another spontaneous orgasm on the spot.

"Rhork. Fuck me," I mewl, arching up against him, mashing my oversized tits against his chest. I worry I'll scrape my nipples clean off on the rough texture of his pectorals, but you know what? So friggin be it. I'll deal with the fallout from this later and I know that there will be a fallout.

We're not using protection.

That thought excites me, too…until it doesn't.

Because Rhork is lying almost all the way on top of me now and his hands haven't stopped their ministrations and manic, near violent worship of my body, and he's still kissing me to my mind's sheer and utter delight, but…he isn't entering me.

I mean, his cock is pressed between us and I can feel it slipping and sliding between my flubbery belly and his that's made of solid stone, leaking come like someone took a hammer to a faucet and it's spraying out of control. His hips are plunging forward in micro-pulses and he's got one hand beneath my butt now and is tilting it up so the base of his cock can rub against my clit with each thrust, but I…it's…not enough.

"Rhork…" I almost beg him, in tears, to have his way with me, until it hits me like a slap in the face —

and I would know because I've been slapped before loads of times.

This is *him having his way with me. If he wanted more of me, he'd take it. But he doesn't.*

Because he doesn't want me for shekurr. Because we went onto that satellite separately, but we came off together and with a thousand tanks in our possession. He's got at least six hundred females to choose from to make his little pirate babies, and I'm not the one he wants. Of six hundred, I might very well be the one he wants least. I'm just the only one awake right now.

"Shit," I say as tears attack the backs of my eyes. I wrench away from his kiss and try to look away, even as I keep my fingers anchored around his neck, gripping one of the spikes. Because it doesn't matter that he doesn't want me.

I still want him.

"Shrov," Rhork curses and suddenly he's straining, holding everything still and I'm damn near swimming in come. It's completely saturated my tits, coming to touch my chest, all the way up to my throat. I glance quickly at his face, curious, even though I'm still a little pained, and see that his skein is pulled back and he's watching my tits like they're chanting his name.

Hell, if they could, I'm sure they would be right now. Because my dark, nearly black nipples, are wildly stiff, pointing up like two blaster rays, while my lower half is still jiggling and writhing against the smooth, silken exterior of his cock. I'm still climbing, faster and faster now, even though the pleasure only feels bittersweet at the knowing of what I really, truly want, but could never be.

His.

And when my orgasm finally comes and I feel the well of conscious thoughts drained in one rush, my tired brain finally starts to shut down. I'm lost and euphoric and exhausted from fighting and losing so many battles. Even more exhausted from the battles I've won. I feel Rhork's hand — one of them — touching my hairline and wiping at my cheeks? Am I crying? Stars, I hope not.

I drift away towards sleep and right on its cusp, I swear I imagine the roar of the ocean. And then Rhork's tender whisper, "I love you, Deena."

Wait.

What?

8

Rhork

My legs are still shaking — an uncommon sensation for me. Even more unusual is that they're shaking and I'm sitting down. But I'm smiling.

"What are you grinning about?" Tevbarannos says, plunking into the seat across from me.

We sit on the bridge, this small group of us. Tevbarannos, Herannathon, Gerannu, and Erobu. They are the pirates I trust most though, honestly, if I were backstabbed by one, it would come as no shock. Pirates are only trustworthy until they're not.

"Did you not hear the ruckus coming from his quarters?" Erobu says, sitting carefully in the seat beside mine, making sure that his tines fall straight down the opening in the center. His four arms grab the arms of the chair roughly, kneading them. He makes a brutish sound. "Damn near drove me crazy, the sounds she was making."

"You heard through the yeeyar walls?" Herannathon says, standing at the view pane and frowning at Erobu.

Erobu just grins. "They were loud."

"They?" Herannathon turns his frown to me now. "You had her?"

"Centare." I rub my face, but can't stop smiling. I'm a shroving fool for her now, fully committed. Fully stuck. Incapable of extraction. And pleased with my captivity.

"I cleaned her with the torch and it was an... *intimate* experience. When she woke, she was naked and staring at my cock like she wanted to take a bite out of it. My body reacted and I used the synthetic for as long as I could, but when she started touching herself, I had to get involved. I couldn't just stand there while she struggled to find her own orgasm."

Herannathon nods, face softening as if that's the most natural explanation in the world. Perhaps, because it is. What I don't mention, however is that there was no struggle involved. She'd have been fine all on her own, but I had no intention of sitting by idly like a failure. She had a male at her disposal to do that filthy business.

Me.

And she will always have a male at her disposal to do that filthy business.

And it will always be me.

"She enjoyed it?" Tevbarannos asks, looking genuinely interested. He is one of the youngest pirates aboard my ship and has not yet had the chance to participate in a shekurr of any kind. It may be that he has yet to even seek pleasure from one of Kor's houses.

I nod. "She did." Cursing and hollering as she was, there's no doubt in my mind that she enjoyed it. I chuckle at the thought. The memory. The itch to return to her and consummate what we started. But I won't... I won't until she understands that I am hers and she is mine and I love her and she loves me and we will continue on this path forever until one or both of us dies, likely in battle, fighting side-by-side.

"So, that's why you brought us here? To rub it in our faces?" Herannathon says. He's got a small smile on his lips, but Erobu, who agrees with him vocally, looks closer to outraged. They both start shouting, and then Gerannu tries to calm Erobu, then Tevbarannos starts asking questions about the human female orgasm and what it's like and I try to answer him over the shouting trio, and then we're all silenced when the yeeyar at the end of the space parts and Quintenanrret walks into the room.

"What's all this racket about? The human females?"

"Centare, the human *female*. The one Rhorkanterannu has taken for his own."

Eyebrows shoot up at Herannathon's statement. I feel myself get hot, a little embarrassed. Taking a female as a single male is not done. Or rather, it has never been done. Not like I plan to. My plates shift uneasily and I sit up straight, tense. I flex the fingers of my lower hands.

"Your own?" Quintenanrret has both brows raised. His skein is open, revealing his silver eyes. They glisten with curiosity and, if I'm not wrong, a hint of delight. When I don't answer, he plunks down into the only free seat in the center of the command deck where the other four of us already sit and Herannathon stands nearby. "Fascinating. You mean to mate with her like the monogamous species?"

Erobu laughs, "That's unheard of. We're pirates, not savages. And Rhorkanterannu is and has always been the model for the rest of us. He wouldn't dishonor a female like that."

All eyes turn to me and I open my mouth, but I choke both literally and figuratively. How do I explain to them — to these males who die and thrive by a code of honor that is the only truth all pirates share — that honor has nothing to do with it? That this has everything to do with the painful pressure needling my heart every time I think about my Deena with someone else?

She is *mine*. And she won't belong to anyone else.

She doesn't know it yet. She wouldn't believe it, even if I etched it into her forehead. Whatever poison Mathilda wrought in her mind has corrupted her ability to see me as a potential mate, because she does not see herself as a potential mate. Maybe she did once, when I wanted her for shekurr. But that only makes me feel worse, knowing that these human females view shekurr as punishment.

"Don't tell me Quintenanrret is right?" Erobu shouts.

Herannathon frowns at him. "There are plenty of females now, thanks to Rhorkanterannu…"

I cut him off. "Thanks to Deena."

Herannathon tilts his head forward. "Thanks to Deena. We don't need to squabble over one."

"But what does this mean? If Rhorkanterannu sets a precedent that it is acceptable for one male to claim a single female, then there *won't* be enough females for everyone. We'll have to wage war against Voraxia and claim the few that they have…"

"Don't be stupid. Even with our superior tech, we'd never win a war against Raku."

"I wouldn't underestimate our abilities, Herannathon," Gerannu chimes in. "I've been working on some very interesting modifications to the particle rearranger. I believe I might be able to bring someone *from* a planet, rather than just take us down to it…"

"What does any of this matter! We're not talking about war. We're talking about females!" Erobu shouts, stomping his foot. All of his plates lift simultaneously.

"Enough!" I grit my teeth and curl my hands more aggressively into the arms of the chair. Even my shroving toes curl into my boots painfully in the time it takes for the room to settle. "Enough."

I rub my face and plant my lower right elbow on my right knee. I drop my forehead into my hand and rake my plated palm over my face roughly. "Erobu is right. I'm setting a precedent that no pirate has ever set." Erobu opens his mouth, one arm flashing in wild distaste, but I look up and pin him with my glare and he settles back into his seat. "But no Niahhorru has ever faced extinction like we do now, either. We have never had to turn to other species, but now we do, which means that we now face customs and cultures very different from our own.

"I know you were not there, brother, but when we brought the Rakukanna and the other human on board our ship — when we stole them from Voraxia's Raku — they did not want to be had in shekurr."

Erobu grunts noncommittally, like he doesn't believe me. Likely, he doesn't. Erobu is older than even I am and has participated in countless shekurrs, two of them even successful.

But only two of dozens. And neither of those produced a litter, like the shekurrs of our sires' sires' sires. It's been three generations since more than a single kit was produced by a female. Before, females could produce a dozen kits at once.

"To take a female outside of shekurr is a great dishonor. You dishonor her, Rhorkanterannu," he spits, all petulance. But that does not stop me from wincing. *He's right.* I shake my head. *Centare. He's wrong. And either way, it doesn't matter. The needle in my chest will swing like a mallet if he even so much as suggests to rut Deena with his filthy shroving...*

"Consider what Rhorkanterannu is saying," Quintenanrret suggests, voice even and contemplative. He approaches everything like the scientist that he is. "If, to you, this may seem like an honor, consider the Lemoran species. Proud and honorable as well, they still take their mates in pairs."

"We are not the Lemoran. What the Lemoran do on their filthy rock doesn't matter."

"Have you seen the filthy rock the humans live on? Maybe you should think with your big empty skull," Herannathon blusters. I roll my eyes as Erobu's shoulders tighten and his fingers form fists.

I hiss loudly enough to avoid imminent disaster. These are my most trusted males, yet they're still a pack of animals. I grin wildly at the thought. "The humans are like the Lemoran, is the point that Herannathon's trying to make. They mate in pairs, producing one or two kits at a time. It won't get us far, but it will get us somewhere. The Rakukanna was revolted by the idea of participating in shekurr and the other human I bought from the Human Council leader was even more terrified. But, I know for a fact that the Rakukanna has given birth to a healthy Voraxian child."

"Their medical facilities aren't even as nice as ours are. We should have no problem birthing many more with the humans we have. Maybe even a litter could be produced." Quintenanrret's eyes sparkle. So do Tevbarannos's and Gerannu's.

Gerannu agrees. "We could put together something quite nice. Different from the traditional birthing houses, we could make them for...for *pairs*." He sounds the word out like he's never used it before. Maybe he hasn't, I think with a grin. I know I haven't. Not until Deena. "You and Deena could use the first house. Do you think she might be with kit already?"

My lungs inflate until they're set to burst. I exhale just as dramatically. "Centare. I haven't rutted inside of her yet."

My proclamation is met with silence and my embarrassment is renewed. My plates lift. Erobu gasps, like I've just confessed to murdering the female. "You haven't...If you're not going to share her, then what are you waiting for!"

I snarl up at him, the first sign of true irritation creeping up my spines. I fight for calm, remembering that Erobu has no experience with human females. All of the others, with the exception of Tevbarannos, were with me on the first Voraxian raid when we stole the Rakukanna from her home and brought the wrath of the Raku on our heads. It was...not a good solar for us.

"Perhaps he is following some sort of human custom," Quintenanrret suggests. Helpful, but wrong.

"Deena does not feel worthy to be taken as a mate."

Gasps. Six of them. One of them is my own. I haven't said the words out loud before and hearing them now makes them sound preposterous, even to me. Herannathon is the first to laugh. The rest fall in line. Even the stiff Erobu chuckles.

"Is this a joke? I'm not quite getting it," Tevbarannos says, sweeping his gaze around at all of us. He's smiling, but his brow is still muddled in confusion.

I don't need to tell them that Deena has been harmed in the past. Or that I love her. Or that I worry that she can't love me without first understanding that I want her and not just to use her body. Because she's been hurt in the past and because I love her and because I worry that she can't love me because she's been hurt in the past and because of that, is not capable of understanding that I love her. It's all very confusing. Wild assumptions made on my part. But to voice them now and be wrong would be to diminish her and I would never do something like that.

So I give them something small. "It seems to be something with her leg."

The laughter dies in one easy stroke.

Gerannu is first to say, "You're serious? A female like *that* thinks herself unworthy because of...what did he say?" He glances around at the others.

Erobu says, "He said something to do with her leg. Which leg? What is wrong with it?"

"Don't tell me it's a tentacle." Tevbarannos shudders. "I don't like it when they have tentacles."

"Not a fan of the Oroshi?" Herannathon laughs, making a face. "They are a, uh...unique species to couple with."

Tevbarannos's face makes the room erupt in laughter, this time mine among them. "Don't tell me you've mated with an Oroshi!" He screeches.

Herannathon laughs so hard liquid starts to pool along the lower rim of his eyes. He wipes it away with his upper hands while his lower hands smooth over his stomach. "Centare, are you mad? They don't even have females."

"That is incorrect. They have dozens of different genders, many of which would align with our definition of a compatible female. Their species is incompatible to breed with Niahhorru, though…"

"You ran tests?!" Tevbarannos clutches his throat, his chest, his jaw, his abdomen. The laughter increases as he jumps from his chair and shakes his fists at Quintenanrret. "What on Kor for?"

Quintenanrret scoffs, "To breed with, obviously. If we could produce viable kits with a species, it should be explored, even one with tentacles."

"The tentacles! Could you imagine taking one of those…those tentacles in shekurr? Oh shrov!" He starts pacing around the room while Herannathon bangs on the yeeyar exterior of the ship with two fists while the other two grab at his side. My stomach is aching with the force of my laughter now.

"It wouldn't be so bad," I chime in. "Just imagine. A pliant, supple, *wet* body on the shekurr table, entering her cold…entrance." To be honest, I don't even know how the Oroshi females are formed or how you'd even go about entering one. From the outside, they look like the Oosa, but only if the Oosa had three tentacles growing out of one side and two more growing out of the top. They have no faces, no eyes to peer into. I believe they might produce eggs? But I honestly have no idea.

Tevbarannos removes his dagger from his belt and chucks it at me. The blunt side clunks off of my pectoral and I watch him snarl around the room, clumsily engaging Herannathon in a mock battle. They wrestle on the floor while Quintenanrret continues to stodgily argue the merits of having tentacles and Erobu removes himself slightly from the fray and begins speaking to someone on the other side of the token in his ear. I try to pay attention, but I'm distracted by Gerannu, looking at me.

He's frowning.

"What?"

"Her leg," he starts, rubbing his jaw. He stretches out his own right leg and massages his thigh just above the knee. I wonder if he's aware of the action. "Is it her warrior's mark?" He asks me.

I shake my head before truly considering the possibility. Then I stop and my smile falls to form a frown even more severe than his. Deena does have a warrior's brand on her left leg. It begins just above her knee, streaks down over her leg, before wrapping around her calf and finishing somewhere near her ankle.

"I don't understand." I shake my head. "What would her warrior's mark have to do with her concern for being taken as a mate? If anything, it would only increase her desirability."

"Maybe..." I can see the wheels of his mind turning. He is old enough to be my sire and I have always counted on his wisdom and capacity to reason. And then it seems to hit him. He sits up straighter and his skein flutters and he blinks at me, silver eyes bright. "Maybe humans view scars like the princes and princesses of Quadrant One."

I lean back, aghast and horrified. "You can't mean..."

"I mean to consider the idea that humans are like the Quadrant One elite. Perhaps, they view scars as *deformities.*"

The word that comes through is an ancient one. *Deformity. Chroggh.* It's so old it's still pronounced in old Meero and comes across as little more than a grunt. I can't even remember the last time I said the word out loud.

"But her leg is not deformed," I counter. "It is still a leg." And even if there were no leg, it would not be a deformity. It would be a part of her, just as beautiful as all the rest. A sign that she survived a great ordeal and lived to sing the tales. And knowing her, she would sing them, badly and off key and every unique note would make my heart clench.

Gerannu nods again, shoulders slumping as I poke an easy hole in his initial assessment. It's Tevbarannos who speaks and it takes me until then to realize that he and Herannathon have stopped fighting. "What if she doesn't view it as a *cherr...chare...*" He shakes his head, cursing as he fails to pronounce it. "What if she views it as a khrui would? When a member of the pack loses a limb, the rest of the pack eats them?"

"We're not going to eat her," Herannathon says, frowning.

"Ontte," Gerannu says, shooting up onto his feet. "What if the humans view warriors' marks as weaknesses? Surely, if they live on a hostile planet, then the absence of one of their limbs would make them more vulnerable to attack."

"Have you *seen* that female with a blaster?" Herannathon uncrosses his arms and steps away from the wall. He takes the seat that Erobu vacated. "She fears nothing."

Pride. I haven't felt it like this before. It swirls in a thick, viscous liquid just beneath all of my plates, causing them to lift just a little. And it isn't that I haven't been proud before, it's that I feel *her* pride as if it is my own. I've never felt someone else's pride before. Huh. Funny. Charming.

The males around me all chuckle. At least, until Gerannu says, "But what if, on their planet, they have no blasters? If they are truly like the khrui then they'd have to fight with their hands." Gerannu cringes. "Could you imagine a female, even one as ferocious as Deena, against a khrui with no weapon?"

I black out for a moment. My heart stops. My entire body freezes. I fall out of my seat as if pushed. I'm on my feet, hands clutching the ridges on top of my head like my brain is attempting to flee through them. "Shrov!" If Deena fought a khrui with her bare hands, it would kill her.

Shrov, if *I* fought a khrui with my bare hands, it would be a fearsome battle, one I would not leave unscathed. There is a chance I would not survive such an encounter. But we have technology. All modern species have technology. But what if she isn't modern? From the little information there is on humans floating around the known Quadrants — most that I've gained from the lying wretch, Mathilda — humans were stuck on their satellites for hundreds of rotations and, before that, they had no access to interplanetary travel. I mean, if they had, wouldn't there be more of them?

Centare, no interplanetary travel short of the satellites and we've seen how well those went. The first crash landed on that Drakesh moon, leaving the humans to fend for themselves. The Balesilha satellite was occupied by humans who evolved cannibalistic tendencies, their technology too ancient and miserable to sustain them. Still *laying lines* to transfer power from one region of a single satellite to another. They didn't even have lights, for shrov's sake! Or they did, but their lights only functioned when not covered by the gunk growing on them. What even was that gunk? Why did their yeeyar not eat it up? Yeeyar thrives on microbial and bacteria such as that.

They have no yeeyar.

They have no blasters.

Deena has been living like an animal.

Deena thinks herself an animal.

Deena thinks her warrior's mark is a curse and not a sign of how capable she is of defeating any enemy.

I frown so hard my face aches. My whole body aches. I glance back to the door, determined to go to her and get answers about this possibility immediately, but only to disprove them. I don't want to hear her speak if she thinks any single one of these theories is true. Because she is a female who battles cannibals. She is a female who spent her whole life battling evil incarnate. She is a female who would make a worthy captain to any pirate ship. And she is still here. With me.

Mine.

The pride and love in my chest that I hold for her aches. I take a jerky step towards the yeeyar entrance to the command deck, when Gerannu's voice pulls me back. "Rhorkanterannu, where are you going?"

"To Deena," I mumble.

"What do you want us to do with the humans?"

Shrov. That's why I gathered them here. Not to talk about Deena, except to tell them that she's mine and not available for shekurr, but to talk to them about the other one-thousand-seven-hundred-and-forty-three humans we confiscated from the satellite and that are trapped in tanks held in fifty-six different chambers of this ship because there is not one large enough to house all of them.

I clear my throat into my fist as a way to clear my raging thoughts. *I will punish Deena for the way she thinks about her warrior's mark. I will shame her until she understands that she is perfect in all her glorious parts.* I shake my head harder. It's not clearing. Deena is everywhere, everything, all I can see. Her leg. That she views it as a deformity makes me sad. She is not an animal.

"The humans. Ontte." I nod around at the gathered males, but my gaze is unfocused, distracted.

"You want us to jettison the human males, right?" Herannathon says.

"Centare. I do not."

Surprise. More of it. And I know that my hoarding Deena will not be the only thing to upset my pirates today. Why I am only sharing this with a few of them first. "The object is to continue the species. If human females prove to be compatible with Niahhorru males, then it stands to reason that the human males may also be compatible with Niahhorru females."

"But...but..." Tevbarannos stutters. "But..."

Quintenanrret shushes him. "Rhorkanterannu is correct. We need to run tests before we decide whether to jettison them or not."

"We won't jettison them, even if they aren't compatible. We'll sell them."

My words are met with hesitation, consideration, then nods. "Very good," Quintenanrret says. "And the females? When should we start opening the tanks?"

Hush. They all stare. I hope only in my silence that they prepare themselves for an answer they won't like. "We need to wait."

A heavy sigh deflates their earlier enthusiasm. Even Quintenanrret frowns at me now. "You don't want to start opening tanks on the ship? You want to wait until we're back to Kor?"

"It's going to be a shroving frenzy, Quintenanrret. Imagine the terror of the human females. As far as I'm concerned, these human females won't have ever seen anything outside of their own species before. We'll need Deena to open the tanks and a controlled environment in which to do it. Some place safe, on Kor, that can't be breached and that our own pirates won't be able to infiltrate. I don't need pirates absconding with females of their liking and scaring the shrov out of them. We don't dishonor females. Nothing that even hints on non-consent. Nothing that even smells of rape."

"Rape! Seven suns, Rhorkanterannu, what are you talking about? Niahhorru don't..."

"You didn't see them, Tevbarannos. Pirates you've known for rotations. When we took the Rakukanna and Svera onto our ship, they went mad with lust. Both females were harmed, bleeding, because of us. I was glad when the Raku came for them. We didn't deserve them, then. We're going to deserve them when they wake up."

Silence.

I can see the discomfort swimming throughout the chamber and that's where I choose to leave it. Herannathon tosses a bolt in his hand up and down, curls his fingers around it, and shakes his head. "Rhorkanterannu's right. Tevbarannos, you and Erobu weren't on the ship. The rest of us barely made it off with our lives. And if the Voraxians had killed us, we'd have deserved it for what we did to those females. They weren't warriors like Deena. They were terrified. There's a chance — a strong one — that the others will be, too. Deena is special." His face clouds, lost in thought, as the others are.

My reaction isn't one I expected it to be. There's pride there, ontte, but there's also something else there. Something unexpectedly ugly. I frown. "What's that supposed to mean?"

His expression suddenly shifts as his gaze latches to mine. He stares at me for a beat until slowly, one corner of his mouth lifts. "Worried, *Rhork*?"

I start at the moniker. It sounds so wrong coming out of his stupid mouth. Worse, I didn't even realize he'd picked up on it. I frown harder. "Speak clearly, Herannathon."

He tosses his bolt, catches it again and pockets it. "You look worried that you might have some competition."

"Competition?"

Gerannu says, "Of course. There is always competition for females. It's only natural."

A meteor shower couldn't have had the same impact on the atmosphere around me. My plates all lift and I round on the room. I point at Herannathon with two of my hands. "If that's a challenge, I accept."

Herannathon steps away from the wall and tension threads the air. No one makes a move to stop us. They wouldn't. To do so would be to dishonor everyone present. But I'm still a little surprised not even Quintenanrret suggests that perhaps, I've already earned her.

That causes my mind to fire with another question — one I haven't even considered up to this moment. She doesn't think herself worthy of me. But do I think I'm worthy of her? Have I earned her? My frown is hard enough to cut glass. Meanwhile, Herannathon is laughing as he rolls out his wrists and steps between the chairs.

"How should we..." He starts, but he doesn't finish. His gaze jerks up, looking past me towards the entrance. "Do you hear that?"

I glance around, following his gaze around the command room, empty except for us. And then comes the distant voice. *Voices.* Disjointed fragments, they sound like they're being shouted from the far end of a tunnel.

"Someone activated their token to the whole ship," Gerannu says. "It doesn't sound like the act was intentional. Who's that stupid?"

"I can think of a few pirates." Herannathon rolls his eyes.

Tevbarannos stands up and shouts in panic, "I thought I heard Rhegaran. Did he say something about the humans?"

We all listen hard. Harder than hard. And so together, we all hear it. Herannathon and I exchange a look of horror, both caught in the same memory. The memory of stealing two unwilling human females onto our ship. We'd been prepared to honor them in shekurr only to realize...it's a dishonor in their culture. And with that knowledge, we were all dishonored.

"Shrov! He's at the tanks! And he isn't alone." Herannathon jerks. "Idiot!"

"Moron!"

"Oroshi-rutting madman!" Tevbrannos shouts, and we all crack at that.

We move forward towards the entrance as one single unit, but a voice that's far, far too high a pitch and not spoken in native Meero makes me stumble when I hear it. And then when that same voice fires through my token crisp and clear, spoken to me directly and me alone, I damn near stroke.

"Heyya buddy. Rhork. Rhorky bear? You there? Tekana...wait. That wasn't a thing. You can hear me."

"Ontte, I can. Deena, where are you?"

"I'm down on level twelve...I think. Whatever. I'm at the tanks. Some of these pirate punks are trying to get at the humans. Real pretty ones, too."

"Deena!" I shout, causing all five other males to turn their heads. "Deena, are you safe? Get out of there. They want you for shekurr..."

"What? Centare...I mean, no. I mean centare! I'm not...whatever. I'm just here to stop them."

"Stop them!" I choke, staggering twice more, this time bringing me up to Gerannu. I grab wildly onto his shoulder. "What are you planning?"

"Well, that depends."

"On?"

"On whether or not I have your permission to blast them. So do I? You promised me I'd get to shoot something..."

Laughter chokes my next order, making it sound like a joke. It shroving feels like it should be. Special? Is that what Herannathon called her? He has no idea. "Get down there," I shout at the pirates staring at me in a shock I feel radiating through every muscle, every bone. "I'm telling you to move."

The others exchange confused looks, but start to move. All but Herannathon, who lingers. He shouts, "Are they harming Deena?" The pirates all manage to look vexed at that.

I shake my head and answer on a half-laugh. "Centare. It's our pirates. They're the ones in danger. Deena discovered what they're trying to do and is prepared to stop them." I switch my focus back to Deena. "Centare, Deena. You do *not* have permission to shoot my pirates unless they're trying to hurt you. Deena? Deena, I repeat, you do *not* have permission to blast anybody."

Some shuffling, crackling, a wild whoop of laughter. And then cannon fire.

"Shrov!" I shout, bursting into a run as a stitch ripples up my side, bringing me to laughter, bringing me to the doorstep of pride.

She squeaks. "Opa! I didn't mean to fire! But I didn't hit anybody. I didn't hit a tank, either. Just a big pile of supplies. Looks like some cases of that awful black syrup juice. Ugh. Good riddance."

I'm laughing hard and my stomach is in my toes and I'm so shroving proud of her. I feel it in my throat, choking me like a four-armed headlock, refusing to relinquish its hold. "Deena, stand down," I bark, but my heart isn't in it. She's a pirate. We don't obey orders when we don't feel like it.

"I don't think so," she answers, but I get the sense that she isn't talking to me. Her voice is more distant. And she doesn't call me Rhork. "Back away from the tank slowly. Put your hands up. Centare, not the upper ones, all four of them. I see the blaster, you idiot."

Herannathon is running beside me as we reach the lift at the bottom of the next ramp. We squeeze in next to Gerannu, Erobu, and Quintenanrret while the yeeyar struggles to accommodate the rapid influx of people and move us down ten levels at the same time. He says, "Your female is fierce. We can hear her through Rhegaran's feed. Is she blasting them or just threatening them?"

"It's hard to say," I grin. Then I raise a brow. "My female?"

Herannathon grins impishly. "I'm not so stupid to issue that challenge, *Rhork*. Besides, I think she likes you."

"I…" I choke. I grin.

He laughs. The others laugh, too.

It's Quintenanrret who says, "She makes a fine pirate."

"She does."

"Whatever she may think, however long it takes for you to make her accept her place, we have already acknowledged her as your mate. The others will understand, even the young, impulsive ones. And together, the two of you can set a new sort of precedence that the rest of us can only hope to emulate."

And my heart lifts up out of my chest and floats away. I swallow down the lump in my throat and tilt my head forward towards the other pirates crowded in the space. All but Erobu are smiling my way. Erobu still looks uncomfortable. He shifts from foot-to-foot and offers, "Maybe some of the females will even be taught our customs, too."

I nod. "Some may be willing to participate in shekurr. We won't know that they're truly willing, though, until we find an adequate base for them where we can approach them..." The lift slides to a graceful stop, cutting me off before I can finish what I was going to say. And what I was going to say was, *as equals.*

"Come on! This way," Gerannu shouts, leading the group.

We run down the ramp towards a room guarding a cluster of tanks just as another voice fires in through our tokens. All of them at once. "Orono here. Um... Rhorkanterannu you better get to level twelve. A few pirates are trying to open some of the tanks."

"We know, Orono," I shout.

"Oh good. Do you know that Deena is trying to shoot them?"

"Ontte, we know that, too."

"Good good. What about the breach on level eighteen?"

"Level eighteen?" I give Herannathon a look as we register Orono's words and he grits his teeth, looking past the tanks as we approach a yeeyar wall leading to another room, this one where the backup cannon controls can be found. A few tanks are stored in here, too, but this isn't where Deena is holding up my pirates. We have three more rooms and another ramp to go before we arrive at the sight. *And I can't shroving wait.*

Orono shouts over the sound of chaos behind him, "Ontte. I think we've got some clingers trying to board."

"Trying to board?" Gerannu, Quintenanrret, Tevbarannos, Erobu, Herannathon and I all shout in perfect unison. The audacity.

"Ontte. I'm not sure, but it looks kind of like a Sky signature."

I throw my head back and howl out a laugh. "The audacity! Gerannu, Erobu, Tevbarannos — to level eighteen. Herannathon, you come with me and we'll join Deena in controlling the problem up ahead."

The three ordered pirates peel off with mirrored grins as they begin extracting swords from their belts and blasters from the slings hanging off of their tines. The Sky are cyber-genetically enhanced warriors of all species and make for compelling opponents. We've lost handfuls of pirates to Sky warriors. To have them here, now, when we truly have something to defend? Shrov, it's exciting.

Herannathon starts to pull his own blaster off his back, but I counsel him against it. "We'll try a more subtle approach than Deena's."

He grins. "More subtle than Deena shouldn't be hard."

"Centare. But maybe we can redirect her focus."

"Shroving comets, Rhork," Herannathon laughs, "What are you thinking? To let her lead the charge and fight the Sky?"

"That's exactly what I'm thinking." I start to laugh again as I realize that, not once, but twice in as many solars, I'll be able to experience my mate in the way every Niahhorru dreams of most — fighting a battle side-by-side.

9

Deena

"You did well." His hand is on the back of my neck and is turning my legs to soup.

Okay, not my legs. The thing at their juncture. And I'm too hopped up right now to remember that he might think I'm the most disgusting creature on this side of the galaxy. Or that he might not think that at all and might be in love with me.

Both options seem equally implausible, or plausible. Both options seem freaking crazy.

So instead, I just stare up at him with a sloppy grin while I lean back into his grip. I've got less blood on me than I did after our last battle against the rug people, but I've still got some blood on me and I like it. I think that might make me deranged or sick or something, but I don't care about that either. Mainly because none of these other people around me do either.

Wait, not people. Pirates.

But what's weird is that they are starting to feel a lot more like people to me than all the people I lived with on the colony. Or maybe, I'm just starting to feel more like a pirate. I feel like I'm home.

The thought hits me like a freaking asteroid plummeting into a too-small planet. In one clean sweep, I'm obliterated.

Oh shrov. I'm gonna start crying. I can feel it. The tears are creeping up the backs of my arms, moving slowly and sluggishly as they head toward my eyes. Up over my shoulders they climb, causing my shoulders to jolt a little and to make Rhork's face twist into a frown.

"What is it?" He says, looking down at me as we stand in the hangar.

It's a huge, vast space with small ships littering the seamless grey floor. Like most of the other pirates, we stand at one wall, watching Kor loom into view. They're all talking excitedly about beings and places and creatures I've never heard Rhork mention before. They're all talking excitedly about going home. They're all covered in the same moss-colored blood of the giants that boarded our ship.

Egama-Sky hybrids, they were the biggest things I'd ever seen, towering twice the height of the biggest Niahhorru pirate. But there were only seven of them, and there were over a hundred of us.

Us, us, us — I can hear the word echo.

We decimated them pretty quickly, battling between two yeeyar chambers and over one bridge. That had been the scary part — not falling off. And two Niahhorru pirates did. But what was weird was when they plummeted to their deaths, the others cheered. Rhork explained that it's a great honor to die as a pirate doing pirate things.

He used better words, but that's the gist of what I can remember right now, standing with one palm pressed against the yeeyar, remembering how Rhork cleared a path for me to get to the front of the fighting so I could blast one of the creatures that had a human in a tank under its arm.

My blasting didn't do much good, so Rhork pulled a sword-like thing off of his back. It had a silver blade — shocker, there — but black sparks wicked off of it whenever it connected with the Egama-creature's shield, until eventually the shield dissolved beneath it.

Rhork shouted my name and I'd fired on command, killing it just as he and two other pirates lunged for the tank, catching it as it slipped from the Egama's arms and just before it fell over the edge of the ramp.

They saved the female in it, though she'd be none the wiser. Meanwhile, a half dozen pirates came up and patted me on the back and crossed their lower arms over their chests in a sign that felt wholly reverent and accepting and made me feel like a badass warrior chick.

A badass pirate chick.

And I loved it.

And now that they're all talking and jostling me from all sides and not pawing at me because they don't want me for shekurr, but making me feel like a pirate — like one of them — I feel like I am. And I don't want it to be a lie.

"What's a lie?" Rhork looks around, his frown only getting worse.

My mouth is sticky and I sound stupid as I curl my palm against the yeeyar wall of the ship and glance towards a planet that, from this distance, only appears as a shimmery dark blue stone against a black backdrop studded with millions of stars.

"That I'm a pirate," I say bluntly, feeling weepy. Feeling whole.

Rhork looks concerned as he reaches for my chin with his bottom right hand. I wish I had four hands, so I could hold all of his simultaneously. "You are a pirate."

And then, like the sleep-deprived-adrenaline-addled-moron that I am, I burst into tears. I don't want the others to see, so I do the only thing I can. I lunge for him, wrapping my arms around his waist — careful for the tines — and bury my face in his chest. The plates are rough against my too-soft cheeks. My left and twisted leg buckles a little beneath me. His hands come around my back while my shoulders jolt.

"Thank you," I whisper sloppily against his skin, tasting blood as my lips trail spit.

Rhork chuckles and the vibrations turn me on, make me hot, make me feel something too big to hold onto. How can something that feels so good hurt so much?

"Interesting," he says and it's my turn to laugh.

"What do you mean?" I ask him, still afraid to leave the cavern of his arms.

"What do I mean? What do you mean? You're making very little sense. In fact, you've made almost no sense at all since I came upon you holding six of my pirates up at gun point. You were shouting your plant song at them. Do you remember?"

Laughing, I say, "Ontte. Of course I remember. But that made perfect sense. Every time I stopped ordering them to keep their hands up, they'd reach for their blasters. But if I talked, then they kept their hands up. So then I ran out of things to say, so I started singing."

He scoffs. "That was not singing."

"It was singing. It was a song."

"Shouting a song doesn't make it singing."

I flip my hair back, laughter chasing away the threat of tears. At least, the threat of sobs. There are still tears on my face as I plant my chin on his chest and stare straight up, up, up. I watch his expression soften into something so tender even the lightest touch might break it. It makes my lips warble all over again.

Rhork inhales deeply and exhales just as deeply. So even. So strong. So sure. "You are exhausted. You always get emotional when you're tired. Or rather, you *only* get emotional like this when you're tired." He touches the tears on my face with his fingers, but doesn't wipe them away. He just smiles down at me sweetly, like we've done this a thousand times before and like we'll do it again a thousand times more and like my brand of crazy is perfectly okay.

"You're being nice to me."

"Is that why you're crying?" He laughs and it nearly breaks the tenuous hold I have on my rapidly unraveling emotion jar. The lid's been unscrewed. The contents, spilled.

"Centare. I'm just...I don't want to go back."

"What?" He tenses.

"Can I stay?" I reach up and grab hold of the wrists of his lower arms, still trapped around my face. "Please?"

His brow furrows, flattens, then furrows again. He licks his lips, making me want to kiss them. "Deena, did you hit your head? I thought I made it abundantly clear that you aren't allowed to leave me."

"I'm not?" I gasp, heart beating hopefully.

"Centare, you're not. Did you forget what I told you when we were alone?"

I nod even though I haven't. Those little big words are tattooed across my heart.

"Deena," he sighs and shakes his head. "You were born a human, but you've proven yourself to be a pirate. Your kin, your colony, your skin, where you came from, what you think about your own warrior's marks have nothing to bear on this simple fact. You are a pirate. You belong with pirates. And now, I need you to turn around."

He moves my shoulders and head with all four of his hands, then steps up and lines my back with his front. His heat slips and slides against mine and I can't help but stick my ass out a little bit when I feel him tilt his hips a little further forward. I'm thinking about rutting and my embarrassment and worry about being rejected when Rhork taps on the yeeyar in front of us.

"Look," he says, and I look, gaze focusing on the planet looming larger before us and everything I'm thinking falls apart.

And so does the emotion jar.

I take in a gulping, gasping breath. Rhork leans down and wraps all four of his arms around me and whispers directly against my neck, "Welcome home, pirate."

Alright. Welp. That's it for me.

I fall the frick apart.

"It's beautiful," I garble unintelligibly.

"Ontte," he chuckles, holding me even tighter, nuzzling further into my neck, kissing me up and down the column of my throat, making me feel treasured and worshipped and wanted. "It is."

The glinting shimmer of its surface is revealed when we enter the atmosphere and the far curve of the planet finally slips out of sight. The planet is all towering megalithic plates of glass unlike anything I could have ever imagined. They soar almost to the tip of the atmosphere, and it's on one of those tips that we land. Like a giant ball balancing on a needle, I don't understand the mechanics of it, but I don't care. We're stopped and I can hear pirates jostling one another as they exit, but Rhork and I don't move. We just stand there on the edge of the ship, on top of Kor, looking out at its splendor.

Ships much smaller than this one zip back and forth across the sky, looking like shooting stars. Beneath them is pure chaos. Buildings of all shapes and sizes. The glass ones stand the tallest, but beneath them there are things that look black and grey and red and blue and green and yellow and brown and every other color.

"That's the Reaver Market," he says, pointing to what looks like a cluster of black tents — thousands of them — slightly to the right. "And there, Pleasure Alley." The buildings he points out are all square and look like nothing from this angle. "Apart from everywhere, gambling happens at the Cosmos Dome." A dirty, shimmery gold disc sits in the middle of so many clustered grey and black buildings not too far in front of us. "These black towers, like the one we're on now, are the Niahhorru ports. We control them all."

I wipe my fingers over the yeeyar again and again. Little pinpoints of black flare beneath my fingertips then die again as the black yeeyar moves on to some other place. "I can't believe something like this exists."

"Would you like to see your home from the ground?"

Home. *Home rhymes with dome.* The dome back on that dusty human colony is the only home I've known till now. And that sucked. This...this...this is beyond imaginings. Just like the male behind me. I turn in his arms and, before my brain has a chance to catch up with me and let my cowardice win, I pull down on his neck and lift up on my toes, climbing his damn body in order to reach his mouth.

He accommodates, pressing me against the yeeyar in a way that's terrifying because, with its clear surface, it's like there's nothing at all to keep me from falling. Nothing but a bit of technology that I don't understand and his arms. Only, right now his palms are pressed against the yeeyar as he jerks one knee up between my thighs to keep me in place. His hands are holding my neck, tilting my head back and then further back so he can plunder my mouth like the pillager that he is — the pirate.

I smile between his lips and breathily say, "Has anyone ever told you..." Insert kissing here. "...you kiss like a pirate?"

"Ontte," he answers without missing a beat. It almost sounds like he's not stopping to kiss me at all, but is speaking directly into my head. "Has anyone ever told you that you kiss like a pirate?"

"Centare."

"Allow me...to be your first." He bites my neck so hard I yelp. He laughs, laving the bite with his tongue.

"You're not my first, you know," I somehow feel the need to say.

"Not your first kiss? Ontte, I can tell. You kiss like you fight. With every piece of you."

My heart is hammering and it's not because of his kiss. It's because he's going to make me cry again. His hands are moving under my shirt now, groping my body beneath it. Well, not a shirt so much as a blanket I ripped a head-hole into and not so much my body as the rings of fat around my stomach — rings he doesn't have. I try to squirm to get him to touch some other part of me and, when he doesn't, I try to suck in.

He's insistent and I'm fidgeting uncomfortably now and for whatever reason, that makes me blurt, "You're not my first...with that either." Actually, I know the reason. I'd rather him drop me, stop kissing me and stop saying nice things to me because he now knows I'm not a virgin than because of my stomach.

He pulls back when I start to slow and looks down at me without the skein covering his eyes. In the swimming silver, I can see Kor — all of Kor and its brilliance — reflected back to me. It makes me want to cry again. He's so shroving beautiful. And I don't deserve a single piece of him. Not even one arm.

I look down and he nuzzles my cheek with his nose. Then he kisses my forehead. He pulls his hands out from under my tarp shirt and, just when I think I've gotten my wish — that he's done with me now because he knows I've had sex with other colony boys — he says, "I will slaughter any male from your past who would challenge me for you."

He sets me down bluntly and the floor is cool beneath my toes, making them crinkle. Meanwhile, I'm left feeling stupid and utterly speechless. "Wh-what?"

He grins. "Did you think a pirate would do anything less? Or have you forgotten that your people call me king? I did not come to turn Kor's head by *not* stealing what I want. I've stolen you. Now, you're mine. The males who came before will not be remembered once I take you fully. Now come. I'm hungry and I want to feast." He glances at me over his shoulder as he starts to walk away and in the look he gives me, I know he's not talking about food.

Shrov.

"Uhh… WHAT?" The word comes out too loud. I try again. "WHAT!" Well.

Rhork is standing by a pyramid in the center of the floor — a pyramid that wasn't in this room when I first entered it. He places his palm against the pyramid and its black surface wrinkles back and forms a circular opening. That's the moment I realize that the entire vast room around us is almost completely empty.

A few pirates are arguing by a smaller cruiser off to my right. A few more are walking briskly back and forth even further away than that. To my left, an opening in the yeeyar leads to a ramp. Another three pirates are laughing about something on that ramp. I can see them until the yeeyar slides shut, sealing this hangar off again.

"Deena, come home."

"Home?" I whisper dumbly.

"Ontte. The place where your soul was birthed, even if your body was born somewhere else. Come with me."

I'd go with him anywhere he wanted. All he has to do is ask. My feet propel me forward and the "gown" I wear billows around my feet. It feels like a gown, but only because he looks at me like I'm a queen.

Heat touches my cheeks when I remember that I'm limping. Holy shit. It didn't occur to me that I was limping when I was in the control room, holding up

152

pirates at blaster-point, fighting cyborg giants on floating bridges. For the better part of a solar, I forgot.

"What?" He says, closing his hand over my extended palm and reeling me in.

I crash against his chest, curling my brown fingers against his silver skin. "N-nothing. I'm just excited."

"Good." He touches my chin, combs his fingers back through my locs, tugging them just enough to ignite sensation all along my scalp. "No more crying, now. Pirates don't cry."

To that, I suck in an irate breath and stab a finger at his chest. "Centare. Pirates do whatever they want."

He swoops down and kisses me and his lips are everything. The universe and then some. The ocean. *Ocean rhymes with potion.* That's what being with him is like. Bewitching. I'm not myself. Or really, it's like the person I was is unzipped and this bold, fearless, nervous, terrified creature steps out. One who knows how to wield a blaster and kill enemies with wanton abandon, but who's so afraid of rejection it makes her bladder swell and her twisted leg burn and her heart shrivel and desiccate all at once. I want to be here. I want to belong.

"You are here. You do belong. Just let me show you, Deena," he whispers against my teeth to words I didn't realize I'd spoken. "I will show you everything. Not the things, but the ability to have them. You are a pirate now. You can have everything you want. Anything."

"Even you?"

"Centare. Because I am already had. Lost completely to you. Now come home to me and leave this thing behind."

"What thing?"

"The thing Mathilda burdened you with." He touches the center of my chest and it zaps me. I'm gutted and ripped open and I step out of me and when I look back, I see it there, a shriveled, sad, grey husk. But the longer I look, it turns to dust. I don't want to see it go, because it was me, but I don't want to be in its presence either.

This little naked timid creature carrying a blaster strapped to her heart steps forward into the triangle room with Rhork, and I leave it behind. Whatever that thing was that I saw and that Rhork saw and that Mathilda gave me. And when I look up at Rhork, it's with terror. Because I don't know who I am without it anymore.

Because without it, I'm me.

"Ontte, you are. And you are a perfect thing."

10
Deena

"This is poshkin," Rhork says, handing me a small bowl filled with something that's blue and definitely alive.

I'm having a complete out of body experience right now, taking whatever Rhork hands me and doing with it whatever he tells me. This is the first time I've hesitated in the past solar, seconds, rotations — how long have we been here? Oh, right, the triangle was the tip of one port and we rode a lift inside of it down to Kor's surface. The doors opened and sensations swarmed ceaselessly, as they continue to now. My best guess is that it's been about a half a rotation. And I'm beat.

I lift the bowl on autopilot towards my mouth before the smell — more than the microscopic squiggly blue tentacles reaching out of it — deters me. "Is this for eating?"

"What?" He asks distractedly before glancing over his shoulder at me fully and gasping. "Shroving stars! Centare." He grabs my wrist and laughs so loud that it draws stares. Who am I kidding? People have been staring at him ever since we set foot on this planet. Well, maybe a little at me, too. Mostly at me.

"Centare, this isn't for eating. It's shoes."

"Shoes?" I don't understand. "I don't understand."

"Shoes." He slips a hand into the bowl, removing half the contents. He flings the blue goop onto the filthy ground at my feet. In response, the blue tentacles start inching towards me over the ground that isn't concrete so much as its *not* concrete. I don't know what it is. It's scratchy though, almost like it's made out of the same thing Rhork's plates are.

"Shoes rhymes with bruise, which is exactly what you're gonna get if this thing touches me! Eeeaowk!" I scream and grab two of Rhork's wrists while the blue and I tap dance around one another, but it's a clever beast. When I try to kick it, the blue uses that as its opportunity to latch onto my toes, then slide over them up to my ankle. "Aaherrerhggg!" I shout in blind terror.

"Deena," Rhork snorts, but he's laughing too hard to say more. "Sh…shoes…" Is what he manages to grunt in between snorts.

"This is not shoes! Shoes don't fight back!" But, alas, I'm proven wrong when the goop grabs my foot and refuses to relinquish its hold, no matter how hard I kick. Rhork takes the bowl out of my hand and dumps the contents onto the ground near my blue-free foot and the three of us — Rhork, the goop, and I — repeat the same process.

With both feet on the ground covered in blue goop, I shudder and cringe. Then I realize that the blue has stopped fighting me and isn't, evidently, planning a takeover of my whole body and actually feels quite cool against the cuts and scrapes that have already formed on the bottoms of my feet.

"Huh." I take a few steps and the blue molds to the arches of my feet, making them feel buoyant and relieved in a way they didn't a moment ago. "Huh," I repeat.

"Shoes," Rhork says to me with a grin.

I lean forward, fighting the urge to kiss him. Luckily, he leans in and kisses me first. Someone very close to us gasps-shrieks so loudly it makes me jump. When I wrench back from Rhork, still holding his hand, I glance up into the orange face of a being that looks like it was made entirely out of fins. It's watching us, black diamond-shaped eyes pinned to me, I think.

"Ignore him. The Hypha aren't used to seeing intimacy in public."

"Um, Rhork, in case you haven't noticed, it isn't just him," I whisper.

"What did I tell you about that Human word?"

I grin, remembering him chastising me for using *um* all the way back in our very first conversation. "You're deflecting," I say.

"*You're* deflecting." Rhork pulls me along to the next batch of stalls. We're deep in the Reaver market now.

What looked like enormous black tents from above look exactly like black tents from below. Each one is the size of one of the adobe homes on the colony at the smallest, and the size of the entire colony itself at the largest. Okay, maybe not that big, but still *big*. Bigger than any standing structure on the colony, for sure.

"Everyone is staring," I rasp.

He tugs me towards the opening of the next tent where a cluster of Eshmiri stand waving colorful fabrics in the air with all of their arms. I say *all* only because I find the quantity of arms they have shocking. They have two arms. Just two. And they're also not that tall. They're shorter than I am — which is a rarity among the creatures I've seen so far — but insanely bulky in the chest.

The way they're shaped just doesn't come together because their faces are kind of...cute? They have tiny mouths lined in razorblades and they're almost constantly smiling or laughing, which sort of undercuts some of the razorbladeyness but also...at the same time...exacerbates it? I don't know! They're freaky and cute at the same time with their big bug eyes and their high-pitched laughter and the way they speak which sounds like laughter and is disorienting when it feeds through the token in Human.

"Catacat silk! Nena furs! Edena hides!" One of them giggles, practically leaping at Rhork as he approaches.

"Do you have gormar fabric?"

"Gormar. Gormar? Gormar Gormar." About thirty of them are clustered in the entrance of the tent and a flurry of activity reveals at least thirty more *in* the tent behind them. It's illuminated by large floating light orbs that the Eshmiri push out of the way when they walk. They float up into the roof of the tent like balloons, capturing my attention. They're beautiful. Like stars.

"What are?" Rhork says and I realize I'm talking out loud again.

"The lights."

"Simple torches. Kind of like the one you found in the escape pod. The Eshmiri buy them from us cheap now that we've switched to yeeyar." He turns away from me and haggles with the Eshmiri in verbose, colorful language while I turn in a circle, utterly mesmerized by the swarms of people around me.

People?

I grin. How can I possibly keep thinking of these creatures as people? They come in all shapes and sizes. Round like actual rolling balls, tall, like the stalks of mighty trees, thick in the chest with arms and legs like humans or Niahhorru, females with chests so large they cast shadows, beings with tentacles for arms and more tentacles for legs.

They also come in all colors I've seen and many more I've never imagined. Red like the colony's dust, as brown as bark but lighter and still *different* than my own shade, yellow like the sun, pale peach and an even paler, almost translucent white. Some are colors that are crosses between grey-brown and black-red and red-yellow and, above all else, grey.

There are Niahhorru everywhere, not including the ones clustered around us. I don't know if they're following with intent, but ever since we landed on the surface, we've had a small contingent of pirates I recognize following us.

A male I recognize as Tevbarannos is watching me from the tent across the…road? Walkway? Path?…from where I'm standing. He's drinking something neon green out of an enormous bottle. When I catch his gaze, he fumbles the bottle, catches it, and his plates lift in a telltale sign of embarrassment. He waves at me and I laugh as I wave back.

Suddenly, Rhork is switching in between Tevbarannos and me and is pulling something soft over my head. Meanwhile, the blanket I'm wearing as a dress is torn up the front to the neck and ripped away. It flutters to the ground at my feet while whatever Rhork's holding flutters around my ankles. Before it fully lands, there are more hands than just his four tugging and pulling the material in every direction. Eshmiri are everywhere, at least ten of them, laughing hysterically as they poke and prod and push and cut and trim… Wait a stitch… Are they fitting me into clothing?

Yes. They are.

They move back in a flourish and I'm left standing in a grey tunic and grey pants. There's a thick leather belt around the middle that somehow manages to push my stomach up into my throat *and* make me feel like I'm vomiting at the same time.

"You don't like it?" Rhork says, hiding his grin behind his hand.

Embarrassment flutters over me and I frown at him. "I…" I'm fat and I don't like that the belt brings attention to it.

Except…

I glance around. What is fat? The thought strikes so suddenly, it almost makes me laugh. Instead, I manage a snort much less attractive than the snorting laughter Rhork manages to pull off.

"What?" He says, still smiling even though his brows are pulled together and the skein still covers his eyes. It makes it harder to tell what he's thinking when the skein is down. I like it better when it's open, revealing silver eyes that are easy to be devoured by. Contrary to my feeling towards carpet people, I rather enjoy being devoured by him.

"I…" I'm *not* fat. Well, maybe I am in Human, but I'm not in the human world anymore and here, there doesn't seem to be a word for fat. Heck, I don't even know what the word for fat is in Meero. Maybe it doesn't exist.

Maybe it doesn't exist.

Maybe there's no such thing. After all, what is fat on a planet where there is no such thing as thin? Where everyone is all shapes — literally — circles, sticks, triangles and much more…fluid, amorphous things. What is fat when Rhork looks at me like that? Like I'm hilarious and maybe even *pretty*. I gulp at the terrifying thought, then quickly chuck it aside. It's too unmanageable. No, Rhork, maybe he doesn't think I'm pretty, but maybe he doesn't need to.

He looks at me like I'm someone worth standing beside.

And he's not fat. But he's not…skinny either. I frown as my gaze caresses the wholly daunting way he's built. He doesn't look like any of the colony boys, whose arms are twiggy and their bellies are either lean and wiry like Jaxal's or so concave you can see ribs. He's not skinny…

Holy cosmosy.

What if I'm *not* fat because I'm *not* fat? What if the rest of the humans are too thin?

"Deena, do I need to carry you out of here or do you anticipate answering the Eshmiri anytime in the next eon?"

"AM I FAT!" I shout.

Rhork starts. "This word you're saying is not translating properly. You're asking me if you're unhealthy?" He balks, "How should I know how you feel."

"Feel?"

He shakes his head and approaches me, pushing through the Eshmiri who are insisting that the garment is perfectly tailored and that I'm out of my mind. To the first point, they're definitely wrong because this thing is uncomfortable as all getout, but to the latter point, they're spot on.

He places his hands on my waist and frees the belt clasps, which zing with energy when he does. He throws the belt over his shoulder and caresses my belly — my *fat*. "Why do you ask and what has that got to do with these clothes?"

"No — centare — not that. I...I mean this." I slide my hands over his hands on my hips, then massage them around my front in a way I don't mean to be erotic, but decidedly is.

He's still giving me a funny look — half smile, eyebrows still both raised — only now his nostrils are slightly flared and the fingers of his free hands are reaching to join the first. He slides his hands around my lower back and pulls me to him until we're nearly flush. "Ontte, the fabric is very nice, but without the belt it won't protect you in a battle." His gaze drops to mine. He swallows. "I guess that just means you'll have to stay close."

"I...I don't mind." My voice cracks. My hands tense around his hands around my waist. I'm desperately trying to decide if I should push his hands lower to my thighs or pull them higher to my tits.

The corner of his mouth jerks. His gaze swims lower to my chest and then to my stomach where the fat is supposed to be. But he isn't looking at it like it's out of place. Heck, he doesn't even look at my *leg* like it's messed up, even though I know that it is. There must be something wrong. Something that he's hiding.

Only, that doesn't sound right either. Maybe he just...doesn't mind. But then why, on the colony, did he call me defective? *She's not even worth the ebo it would take to keep her fed.*

I pull away first.

He clears his throat. "Let's keep going. There's much to see." He turns to the Eshmiri clustered beneath him, hands them a flat silver disc. While they giggle and trill over it, he starts forward, pulling me beneath his arm. "Gerannu needs to upgrade your token. The model you have is limited. With the newest edition, you'll be able to pay for things as you need."

"Pay for things? I don't have any money."

"You will be compensated for bringing us to the human satellite. You'll be compensated well."

I cringe. "That makes me feel dirty."

Rhork stops abruptly, lifts my chin up and kisses me. His kiss is rough and unrestrained, full of a need I can feel down to my toes. It makes me whimper and makes my already feral libido rage out of control.

"There is nothing dirty about receiving bounties for a job well done. All the pirates aboard my ship receive bounties for whatever haul we bring in. The bounty this time can't be sold and is for the betterment of our species. Thus, all pirates aboard my ship will receive bounties from any male or female who wishes to interact with the humans once we figure out a safe environment for them to do so. Your cut will be largest by far."

"That still doesn't seem right. Paying to let Niahhorru meet humans. What do you even mean by that? Shekurr?"

He shrugs and starts moving forward again. Before he does, he licks his lips slowly. "If that's what they want."

"And if it isn't?"

He snarls and rounds on me again. "What are you asking, Deena? If I'd condone Niahhorru females raping human males? If I'd condone it the other way around? If *I* rape females?"

"I…well, that's what you were going to do to Svera!" My cheeks heat and I hate that the emotion I feel first isn't anger, but jealousy.

He sighs out a laugh, shakes his head, looks off towards one of the tents where Eshmiri are hawking goods that look like long spears. It's wild that even though the main thoroughfare that branches off towards so many tents is packed, there's a bubble of space around us that no one dares to breach.

"Centare, Deena. I had no designs to force Svera to do anything. She knew that and called my bluff."

"So, what would you have done with her then?"

"Nothing. Held her captive, perhaps. Forced her to drink the black fil you detest so much. Eventually, I'd have had to return her home. Why do you think I let her go and went after you instead?"

"Let her go?"

He smiles. "You think I couldn't feel the yeeyar activate in the second escape pod? It was a good plan of yours. You did force me to choose to go after one or the other. But it was always you. How could you not know that?" He tilts his head, lifts his skein, and even though he isn't touching me, I can feel his hands like the whispers of ghosts, caressing me everywhere.

And then he says, "How quickly can humans fall in love?"

My eyes bug out of my head. "Are you already in love with one of the humans in the tanks?" I say because the alternative terrifies me.

"Are you insane?" He says and I nod. Mathilda said I was my whole life and she's the smartest female I know. The worst, but also the most brilliant. "Ontte, you must be. Even if you had not heard me clearly back on my ship when I had your legs spread open beneath me, that is your first leap? The most obvious conclusion you draw is that I fell in love with one of the humans in the tanks with tubes coming out of their butts and who look dead?"

When I don't say anything, but gawk, Rhork shakes his head. He looks frustrated again, but also quite sad. Like I'm some sort of tragic project. Hopeless. Maybe irreparably. "The fact that you refuse to see the obvious is heartbreaking. But I'm a pirate, Deena. I'm too stubborn to let you break my heart. So I'm going to tell you this now, even if you aren't ready for it, because I need you to hear me.

"I am in love with you. I don't know how long I've been in love with you, but it started before I even saw you. Every move I've made since your voice illuminated my token and my whole world has been to retrieve you from your prison so I can have you.

"At first, I believed I wanted to honor you with shekurr but, when I saw you, I no longer did. Because seeing you wield a blaster like a maniac and protect yourself like a wild beast and kill like an assassin made me sure that I did not want to share you. It's not a common sensation, and one I've been struggling to grapple with but, now that I'm certain, there is no going back.

"You are my female. My mate. Mine. I won't share you and you won't share me. There are no more shekurrs in my future. There are no shekurrs in your future ever. There is only me and my cock and our kits and our ship and Kor, mother to us both even though we come from different stars.

"Now, no more doubt. I'm bored of it and there is one thing that pirates are not, and that is boring. So, I don't want to hear anymore shroving shrov about other females, shekurr, your shroving warrior's mark or whatever health issue you seem to see that I don't. If you want something, take it. Use whatever weapons you have at your disposal, including me. I am yours to wield however you want. Now come. How do you feel about gambling?"

He slides his hand behind my neck and pushes me forward. My feet are numb beneath the blue goop. I feel like the planet's gravity has suddenly given out and I'm half-floating, half-flying. I've got this goofy grin on my face now and my heart is doing this jerky little mambo in my chest, dancing to a song of my own making. *Plants! Plants! Plants rhymes with pants! Gambling shmambling! Gambling is rambling! Rumbling. Bumbling. I like tents...*

"Good," I say distantly, voice entirely divorced from my body. I look up at him and he's watching me smile like a loon, so I quickly look away. But I peek. "I like gambling," I say, even though I've never gambled before.

Only that's not true, is it? I gambled once, less than a moment ago, when I gambled on whether or not to believe him, threw the dice, and burned down the casino walling my heart without waiting to see what I rolled.

I glance up at him with more surety, grab his wrist, force him to stop and turn my face up towards his. I grab the spine behind his neck and wrench his face down to mine. I kiss him hard and with force and without caring what my stomach looks like or what the fin-faced Hydra think of us.

"I'm in, Rhorky bear," I say, voice cracking.

He growls and takes control of the kiss. Our tongues collide and he pulls me up against him and I'm pretty sure his intent is to swallow me whole.

And I'm in for all of it.

//
Rhork

It's the seventh solar that I've come back from dealings in the city to find Deena at the mok-biz roulette. It's a game involving holographic chips thrown directly at other players. It gets complicated because there are a fixed number of throws per round depending on the limb count of the thrower and the limb count of the throwee. Side bids can also be placed — meaning side chips can be thrown — to deflect throws or deflect throws and hit other players.

This solar, Deena is joined by twelve other players and twice as many spectators. The jumbled group is composed of Niahhorru, Eshmiri, two Lemoran females — distinguished by their enormous horns — an Oroshi, half a dozen Hypha, and a cluster of Egama who take up the same amount of space at the table as all of the other players combined.

I sidle up next to Herannathon, standing up on a raised arena-style seat. Most beings litter the gambling floor, but some spectators watch from this raised railed section. This one, specifically, belongs to Niahhorru. A female I've known for rotations is present and watching, too.

"Meghanora," I say, giving her a respectful nod.

She smiles and her round cheeks make her eyes slit. Niahhorru females look nothing like the males. In fact, they look quite a lot like Deena. Full hips and breasts, soft middles, their tines are a lot like Deena's hair, but much thicker, hanging like oily ropes down the backs of their heads and trailing down their spines to their full rears. Meghanora is a beautiful female, one I've had the pleasure of participating in shekurr with, but no kits came of it.

"I just came to see the human. Rumors are going around that you managed to find the lost satellite."

I smile, careful with the information I divulge. Not that it matters. I've heard the rumors flying and am aware that we have little time before the mothership is ransacked. I've been pleased that, while I attend to the matters of Kor, my pirates have been able to keep Deena *and* the humans aboard the mothership well protected.

"It has been found, ontte."

Her eyes light and her skein lowers. She turns to face me and the gormar fabric she wears shimmers, draping elegantly over her full form. "I have also heard that you kept the males."

"Hmm. Have you now?"

"Rhorkanterannu, please, don't tease me." She steps forward and places one hand on the railing, the other on my lower right forearm. "You, of all beings, should know my interest in them. Just tell me how much it will cost to make an introduction. Where are they now? Why haven't you brought them planetside?" She tenses, releases my arm, backs away. "Don't tell me — is there something wrong with them?"

I laugh and place one hand on her shoulder, giving it a light, affectionate squeeze. "There is nothing wrong with them." Except for the tubes feeding into their rear ends, the tanks that they're trapped in and their complete lack of knowledge of the events of the past several hundred rotations. "And I swear to you, Meghanora, as soon as they're ready, you'll be among the first introduced."

Her cheeks sag down her face in a way that makes my chest clench. She looks so disappointed and I am not in the business of disappointing females. "We can't do better than this, yet. I'm sorry."

She shrugs, but I can sense that her disappointment has not been eased. "You and your pirates are being awfully cagey about all of this," she bristles. "I don't know why you don't just tell us how many there are and why you're waiting. It's been solars, Rhorkanterannu, and I'm sure you've already shared with the human female."

I balk and cross my upper arms. "She is first a pirate, *then* my female. Not to mention, she is responsible for the discovery of the human satellite. Of course she knows."

That perks her interest. She turns towards me more fully then and steps closer to me in order to be heard over the renewed shouting. Diekennoranu appears on my left and shoves against my back with the force of his exclamation. "That was an illegal toss! The bid is Deena's!" No one can hear him but me and Herannathon and Meghanora and the half dozen others gathered here in this spectator's section, but it still makes my heart swell to hear him — among many Niahhorru pirates — cheering for her.

I glance down at the betting table to see Deena on her knees on top of it shaking a fist angrily at the Egama warrior on the table across from her. He's pointing angrily back at her, rising to each of her challenges in a way that makes me laugh given that she's a quarter his size, possibly smaller, and he still seems caught in her shadow.

All of the Niahhorru around the table are backing her up and I can sense a fight about to break out and I'm eager to see how this plays out.

Deena is first to draw her weapon. Aside from the gambling pits, the Niahhorru armory has been her favorite place so far. We found her a weapon she likes — several dozen of them. She has a particular affinity for blasters but, as my aim is not to start an intergalactic war, I thought it better to outfit her with a small radi-blaster, which stuns smaller adversaries and is more of a nuisance to the bigger ones, as well as a lightning stick in case she's ever battling an opponent up close.

Naturally, she withdraws the lightning stick first and starts running across the table towards the Egama, full speed. This section of the Cosmos Dome shatters into a riot and I laugh, watching Niahhorru rise up to defend their fellow pirate — even if she's wrong — and Egama rise up to defend their kinsman and the rest either choosing sides based on who they think will win, or standing back and betting on the outcome.

Herannathon and Diekennoranu jump the bannister and throw themselves headlong into the fray. Weapons remain stowed and I know that this is not a real fight by the fact that the Egama being challenged is grinning — something few of the moss-skinned Egama are known to do.

I stay where I am as a comfort to Meghanora. Niahhorru females aren't warriors. They're coddled and kept safe, considered nearly sacred in our culture. Watching Deena zap the Egama giant with her lightning stick and duck when he swats at her with his oversized hand, fills my chest with that same rush of pride that's almost become more normal for me than any other sensation. *Mine.* The thought sticks, like putty. It feels good. There are few things that feel better and all of those things involve Deena on her back in my net.

I haven't spent inside of her yet. We haven't had the chance. Between her need to "catch up on sleep," as she calls it, though I have no idea how sleep can be caught — it would seem to me that sleep is either lost or had and past or future actions have no bearing on its current status, though Deena rebuffs this line of logic — and the chaos that is Kor's management, plus new security I've had to install on the mothership and its port, I haven't had time to do more than massage and touch and lick. And I want more.

This lunar, I promised myself more.

"So, it's true," Meghanora says, voice growing dangerously wistful.

"Hm?" I have a hard time looking away from Deena, waving her stick wildly on the table. A Hypha, it looks like, got her with its finned fist, and half a dozen Niahhorru responded in kind. She's ambling up off her back, none the wearier, and is heading back to the Egama to shout at him some more. *I wish I hadn't taught her how to turn off her updated token. I wish I could hear her.*

"You plan on keeping her for yourself. I can see it in your face. You love her. Like the Voraxians love. Like Xiveri."

Xiveri. It's a concept not known to Niahhorru, but one we've heard of. One we've built up with a certain reverence. The Voraxians and the Niahhorru have always had opposing strategies for breeding. The Voraxians let fate decide for them by waiting, sometimes for a lifetime, for their gods to choose their mates and reveal them. The Niahhorru don't do fate. That's why we shekurr. Spread our odds, let as many males as it takes couple with as many females as it takes until kits are born.

I smile. "It's not Xiveri," I tell her. "It wasn't immediate. I fell in love with Deena over a thousand conversations, even ones she didn't know I was listening to. She's a fighter. She's a survivor. And she's a warrior. I could not do better than this if I hunted for such a female through the entire galaxy."

Meghanora makes a soft mewling sound. I look down at her and blink, registering the water in her gaze and feeling terrible. I bring her to my chest and give her a soft, encouraging rub up and down her soft-tined spine. In her ear, I whisper, "I do not say these things to disparage you. You know that I am honored by the time we spent in the shekurr. You are a worthy female for any male. Worthy of a thousand shekurrs to come."

She laughs. "I hope so. It's been some time and I've been...restless." She pulls back and looks up at me, wiping her cheeks. "I've been nervous to organize another for fear of the outcome. If I organized one though, would you join? I remember you from our last time. You were very worshipful."

I smile, but the smile fits all wrong. It's odd to deny a female such a request. However, there's no tingling in my groin whatsoever and, in this moment, looking down at a female who I have felt pleasure from before, I don't know if I even *could* muster the requisite amount of enthusiasm to perform shekurr with her.

And I don't want to.

Because what did I tell Deena?

There would be no other females. No sharing for either of us.

I squeeze her shoulder again fondly, then give her shoulder a soft pat. "It may not be Xiveri that binds us, but I do feel the same attachment to my mate as the Voraxian males do to theirs. I won't be participating in any shekurrs and neither will Deena. We will mate together just the two of us. I'm sorry if this is disappointing to hear."

She sulks, shoulders curling inward. "I suppose that's fine. I just worry."

"About what?"

"Our traditions. How will it work if some females want shekurr with males who want to keep them for their own and vice versa? It will be a mess."

I laugh at that and ruffle her tines. They are soft, like Deena's, but that's where the likeness ends. Female Niahhorru tines are covered in silken scales while Deena's are coarser, like furry fibers woven together into thick strands.

"Of course it will be chaos. This is Kor, or have you forgotten? You females have been spending too long in Paradise. Come to the gambling halls more often. Play a round of mok-biz. When the humans wake up, they'll do whatever they want, just like you'll do whatever you want. It will work itself out. Just never forget that we're doing this for something far more important than tradition."

"And what's that?"

Love. "Life."

She smiles a little more fully then and her gaze pans back out to the mok-biz table where Deena is waging war. "I suppose you're right. I guess I'll have to learn some patience. But — oh my." She laughs. "Your human seems to have lost the battle."

I glance down at the table, feeling light, feeling fuzzy, but when my gaze locks on Deena all that good feeling is scraped off, like skin from bone. "The shrov!"

Deena is standing on the edge of the table directly in front of the Egama she'd been fighting. Her lightning stick is stowed on the leather belt at her waist, she has her hands on the Egama male's face and, before I can pull the blaster from my back, aim and fire, she kisses him. His hand is on the small of her back — covering her entire back — pulling her close as he tastes what he has no right to.

Rage. It burns like a muted sensation of battlefield bloodlust. I have a weapon in my hand and I've already leapt over the edge of the balcony by the time Deena breaks the kiss and steps out of the Egama's hand. He catches the leg of her pant and she withdraws her lightning stick and zaps his wrist before jumping off of the opposite side of the table, leaving it in the same chaos that it was when she first started this carnage.

I am stupefied. Confused and stunned.

But also furious.

It's not a common emotion for me. Then again, few of the emotions I've felt when it comes to Deena are. I am used to sharing females. I had no problem at all entering Meghanora, spending inside of her until her quivering body orgasmed around me, then stepping back and watching eleven of my pirate brothers take my place between her thighs and spend inside of her one after the other.

But watching Deena press her mouth to this Egama male and give him the same kiss that she's given me makes my blood heat and my palms flex towards the weapons hanging from my tines.

I told her I loved her and that I refused to share and this is how she baits me? Like a true pirate. One who needs to face the reckoning that my rage will bring.

Standing at the edge of the crowd, I take a running leap, using the back of a Hypha as a springboard. I vault onto the table, remove the long dagger from my tines and throw it at Deena. It hits her pant leg right at the heel, as intended, and pins her trousers to the metal floor.

"Hey!" She shouts, turning and brandishing her weapon. It takes her a moment to locate the hilt of the dagger and then another long moment to look up at the mok-biz table and see me.

When she does, there is no contrition. There is only a glare deserving punishment. I fire on my token and push through the barrier of hers. "Don't move."

She tenses, but doesn't lower her guard. A fist finds my calf and I turn to see an Oroshi latching onto my foot, preparing to pull. I kick it away and spin towards the Egama. I pull both left fists back and let them fly into his mouth. He staggers away from the table, falling back and I might have spared the time it would take to slit him open from neck to naval had Deena not yanked her pant leg free, shredding the gormar fabric in order to escape.

I jump over heads and barrel through bodies and catch her halfway towards the entrance to the Cosmos Dome. She's blocked by a dozen bickering Walreys, flying insectoids with more credits than sense — a fact that makes them incredibly popular. I grab her arm and spin her body into mine, holding her two arms with all four of my hands.

She jerks against me, but only once. She must know that it's pointless.

Her eyes are glossy and dark and words flee my lips as I stare at her. Shrov, she's so beautiful. Unfathomably beautiful. Am I not enough? I am not used to doubt and frown. She jerks again and I lower my head and seethe in a dark voice, one that commands, "Am I not what you want, pirate? You want something larger? Something Egama-sized?"

"I could ask you the same thing, pirate." She sneers the word like an insult, but it could never be.

"I have no desire to bed an Egama."

"That's obviously not what I meant!"

"Then what do you mean?" I grip her wrists harder, snake one fist around her neck and give her a small, rage-filled shake. "I've made my feelings about you nothing but clear. If you're too psychotic to hear them, then that's on you."

"Erf!" She tries to hit me, but she can't. She tries to pull away, but she can't. "You say that you...you talk about me to my face like you like me..."

"Not like — *love.*"

"Yeah, right, but..."

"Centare. Say it. Say the word."

She opens her mouth. Her tongue flaps around in her mouth like a fish. I want to catch it and cut it out for all the anger she's causing me. I want to devour it. Trace all of its edges with my own. Lick them clean.

"Mm-hm-hm…" She grunts and it's as if all of the Meero words she knows have bunched together at the gate of her mouth, stuffing her throat full of whatever lies she's told herself. Soon, she'll explode with them. "But!" She jerkily shouts, whole face turning hot with a heat I can feel from where I stand. "BUT!" Her voice gets louder, her eyes and mouth get red. She looks like a lid that's going to pop and I can't help it. I laugh directly in her face.

"Deena, you're going to have to breathe if you want to get words out…" I chuckle.

And then she bursts. "YOU SAY YOU LIKE ME BUT YOUR HANDS ARE ALL OVER HER!"

I quiet. My laughter deflates like a worn leather ball. It rolls to a sad, floppy stop while my heart does quite the opposite. I grin down at her fully. Wildly. Her eyes widen as she takes in my expression. In the rings of her white and blue and black gaze, I can see what I look like. Like a madman prepared to conclude his greatest experiment. Like a warlord about to plunder the most sacred of temples. Like a mate staring into the eyes of his own jealous mate's.

"You were jealous to see me touching Meghanora?"

"Eragh!" She shouts, trying to twist away from me, but I'm not letting her retreat from this now.

"Answer me, Deena."

"I know who she is! She introduced herself before you got here. I know that you did shekurr with her."

Thump. Thump. The bass beats like the Egamas' great drums. Only this sound is in my chest and in my soul.

"And that makes you angry?"

"Ontte! Of course it does. You touch all over her and you did shekurr with her and you haven't done shekurr with me and I've been with you in your nest sleeping beside you — if you even come to the nest — for fourteen solars and you haven't touched me. Where have you been? Doing shekurr with her?"

"Of course not! And ontte, of course I've touched you…"

"You haven't…you don't want me! Just admit it. I'm fat and my leg is all messed up and I'm not pretty and I'm not Niahhorru and you have tanks of human women you can pick from and I'm just crazy Deena! Just let me go so I can go gamble or shoot something or play stocks with the Hypha. One of them said he'd show me where the underwater pools are on Kor…that he'd take me swimming…"

Rage grips the backs of my arms as she starts to deflate. I wrap my arms around her hips and throw her over my shoulder. I walk calmly while she writhes and curses and tries to zap me with her lightning stick. She succeeds, tagging me in the back of my left leg before I manage to wrangle it away from her.

I toss it on the ground, not caring where it falls as I exit the Cosmos Dome, make my way through the Regaragara wind market, visible only through HVB goggles unless your eyesight naturally sees that spectrum — only the Walrays do — through the Eshmiri reaver markets, down Pleasure Alley, taking a backroad to reach the Niahhorru primary dock.

My token allows me entry into the port, but I have to wait for the yeeyar built into the floor to perform a cell scan before I'm allowed entry into the lift that will take us up to the mothership.

The lift doors open into the mothership hangar and I spare little attention to my pirates there working on it — securing it, ontte, but also fixing any scrapes or damage to the yeeyar caused by the asteroid field. All throughout the mothership's hangar, I can hear the yeeyar purring contentedly. It's always happy to be treated.

"Rhorkanterannu, Deena — what are you doing two here?" Gerannu says, standing up from where he'd been working on one of the smaller cruisers.

I head to one beside it, identical to the one he's working on, and use my token to lower the bridge. "We're taking a short holiday. We'll be back in two solars, possibly three. Don't let anyone do anything stupid until then."

Gerannu nods and wipes his hands off on the rag he's carrying. "Shouldn't be a problem. The yeeyar is at maximum strength, the humans are secure in their tanks and, so far, we've been successful in fending off the Eshmiri who tried to board her. Kor will still be standing on your return."

"Oh! Hi Deena!" Tevbarannos says. He's carrying a long sack full of kintarr crystals over one shoulder, but still manages to wave one hand. "Where are you headed?"

"Help me!" She kicks her feet uselessly. "Can't you see I'm being kidnapped?"

Tevbarannos laughs. Gerannu laughs. I grin.

Tevbarannos shakes his head and waves her off like she's just the cutest, silliest thing. Mainly, because she is. "You can't kidnap a pirate. We own the skies. Have fun wherever you're off to!" He waves and keeps going, humming to himself. I notice it's the same song about plants Deena is always singing. He isn't the first pirate I've noticed who's started singing it. Garbage lyrics and all, even *I* haven't been immune.

I give Deena's full bottom a little swat and then, because anticipation is making me so anxious, I lean into her fleshy rear and bite it.

"Oy!" She yelps, kicking even harder. "You have no right to do this to me, Rhork! Put me down, now!"

"Ha! I have every right, Deena." The ship slips shut behind me and I walk her to one of the four chairs facing inward in the center of the roundish space. I lower to my knees as I set her down and remain on my knees as I spread her thighs around my shoulders. Using the token commands, I open the mothership so our cruiser can launch into the stars.

Deena yelps again as we do. Or maybe, because I've pulled her to the edge of her seat and placed my mouth over her core through the thin gormar fabric. "Mmmmhmmmmm," she wheezes and I can feel her uncertain resistance as she grabs hold of my tines. "Rhor...Rhor...Rhork! Stop it. I don't want..." She gasps as I pull back and look up at her face, the taste of her just elusive enough to drive me crazy.

I growl up at her, my skein lifting so I can read every line of insecurity and uncertainty in her expression. "I've been busy these past fifteen solars."

"Ontte, I know." She snaps her legs together — tries, but her knees meet my shoulders, which keep her legs spread. I place my upper hands on her upper thighs, massaging them in firm, gentle movements. "You've been busy having shekurr with Meghanora and all the other Niahhorru females I met. I met Trenarru, too, you know."

I smile. "Your jealousy is driving me wild."

"Stop making fun of me." She tries to block my hands, but ends up grabbing onto them.

"I'm not making fun of you. Doesn't it thrill you to know that I have every intention of returning to the Cosmos Dome when I'm finished with you here and cutting the lips off of that Egama you kissed?"

She doesn't answer. But her grip on my hands eases and her eyes momentarily unfocus. I use that opportunity to pull her further forward and nuzzle into her core, drowning my senses in her taste. "But I...I didn't fuck him. You actually had...your dick inside of both of them."

"Ontte, I did."

She punches my shoulder. I laugh against her crotch, tongue snaking out to try to reach her through the fabric. "I had them both beneath me on the ceremonial slab. I entered their heat. Spent inside of them..."

"Stop it..."

"I watched my brothers do the same. I watched twelve other pirates empty inside of them after me. And not once did I feel an ounce of the jealousy that I felt when you pressed your lips against that Egama's ugly face."

I yank her out of her seat and lower her onto the floor between the cage of my four arms and my two legs. I sink onto her so that our hips are connected and I will my erection at bay. I'm not ready. Not yet. The first time I take her, I know exactly where it will be and how it will end. I've planned for this for two hundred and twenty solars and she will not spoil my plans any more than her jealousy already has. Because her jealousy has accelerated them.

"You...didn't?" She whispers. Her voice twists up at the end, coming out as light as a feather with all the power of a scream. It causes a new pulse in my cock to beat.

I concentrate on the hard pressure of the floor beneath my knees instead of the soft warmth of her stomach against my hips. "Centare, Deena. I have never been in love before. I had no way of knowing that you'd become jealous if I touched another female. You haven't said anything of how you feel for me." I tilt my head to the side and narrow my gaze in challenge.

Deena's eyes flare with panic and I laugh, ambling off of her slowly — *painfully*. It hurts my gut just as much as it pains my soul not to rut into her immediately. Not yet, though. Soon. So very soon.

I walk to the view pane and cross my four arms. The blackness of the solar system reveals nothing. We are still a quarter solar off. "You should eat something," I say. "When we land, you'll need the energy."

"Wh...why?"

"Because I'm going to make love to you for the next two solars without stopping. I won't be able to."

"I don't understand. Why...why now? Do you even want to? You don't have to if you don't want to."

"Augh," I groan. "I thought we discussed this. Shut up and wait. Eat something. We're not too far now."

"From where?"

"Shh. You talk too much. Has anyone ever told you that?"

"Ontte. You."

"Oh, ontte. I remember. You were singing a song about a spoon."

"It's a good song."

"Centare, it isn't. None of your songs are good songs, but somehow, you've gotten all my pirates singing them."

Deena laughs. It's shaky and unsure and closer to me. I tense and shiver as I feel the warm pressure of her palm on my bare back. She traces the line of one of my plates where the sensitive skin meets thicker flesh. "Sorry for being jealous," she says after a moment.

"Pirates don't apologize. Pirates seek revenge." I turn in her arms and she lets her fingers trail over my stomach tentatively. "Just as you did by kissing that Egama in front of me. Now it's my turn for revenge. And I will take it however I please." I stroke down the side of her body until I reach her rear. I grab it hard enough her toes lift and her front collides with mine. Her full breasts mash against my chest. I squeeze them through her tunic, fondling them with the most damaging of desires.

"I will rut between these. As well as in your ass. And in your mouth. But especially here." I rub her core through her pants with the fingers of my lower right hand. I wait until her eyes close and her mouth opens. I wait until she starts to pant. She's heating up beneath my touch, getting close. And then I pull away from her and step away from her, taking a seat at the hand controls. I steeple the fingers of my upper hands beneath my chin and watch as she holds herself up against the view pane and tries to compose herself.

She turns to me with a glare and I watch her right hand twitch towards her belt, reaching for a weapon that's no longer there.

"Your lightning stick won't help you now, pirate."

"I have other weapons," she grumbles.

"Ontte." I eye her body up and down as she walks to the seat across from mine and plunks down into it. "You do. And I plan to exploit them all."

12
Rhork

My nerves are stretched taut as the small planet peeks into view. I allow Deena the luxury of looking at it while it's little more than a blue-green speck against a black universe but, before we draw close enough to distinguish its topography, I rip off a strip of her tunic and blindfold her with it.

She complains as I remove her belt and remove her shoes, leaving both behind on the ship. I remove all of my clothing and shoes, both of our tokens and, as the ship touches down onto the small planet's surface, I take her hand and lead her down the ramp, to the surface. I lead her out into the sun. It's hot here, but nothing like the underground trading stalls of Kor and far from the heat of the horrid moon colony her other humans are still trapped on.

She jolts when her feet finally touch the ground. The sand. It's soft, burnt orange, and spans the full length of the beach. The fresh water ocean spreads all the way to the horizon on my left. The trees are recessed away from the shoreline, but close enough to reach them in a few hundred paces to find shade. Waves lap and have an effect I find immediately calming, just as I did the first time I happened upon this uninhabited planet on the edge of the grey zone.

We're really too close to Quadrant Four and too close to Quadrant Five for comfort, but that's also why this planet has remained unclaimed for so long. It's too small to be of significance to either Quadrant rulers and too close to both Quadrants for either of them to want to fight over claiming it. Which means it's perfect for what I want it for.

"What...what am I hearing, Rhorky porky?" She says and her voice trembles just a little bit. I smile.

"You already know, don't you, Deena beena?"

She snorts and grips my hand firmly, fiercely. She shakes her head, centare. I chuckle and step up behind her. Bending down, I whisper in her ear, "You and I both know that's a lie."

I guide her forward, pushing her gently. It takes forever and I chide her for her lack of trust in me.

"I do trust you. I just..."

We reach the water and she jolts. It's warm, the water here. Not hot, but not quite cool. It's like taking a bath. It would be cooler if I had my choice but, as I did not create this planet from the core out, I don't.

"Do you know what trust rhymes with, Deena?" I say while, behind us, a gaggle of birds squawk loudly and take flight. Deena jolts at the sound, but I wrap my lower arms around her stomach fully. She slides her palms over my forearms with surety as the waves lap around her ankles, soaking her torn pants through to the knees.

"Must?" She tries weakly.

"Centare. The word that rhymes with trust…" I kiss the right side of her neck while my upper left hand unties the blindfold and removes it. "…is beach."

I know that I will never forget the expression that crosses her face as she looks out at the ocean for the very first time, even if there are no words in any diction to describe it. Awe, perhaps. Maybe shock. Disbelief. Gratitude, or maybe that's just what I'm projecting.

Her mouth is open and her eyes are huge. Her nostrils flare and she inhales twice before exhaling. Her fingers on my forearms first go slack before tightening when another wave rushes up her legs. She backs up into me and it must be that action that brings her awareness to my state of undress because she spins in a motion so quick it even startles me, glances down at the plate shrouding my barely restrained erection, and yells, "Ohmygosh, somebody's going to see you!"

She glances past me towards the beach, and then past that at the trees. Thin, they're only large enough for two Niahhorru to fit their arms around, but they're tall, almost gangly. They have bright red and orange leaves that complement the pale orange beach and contrast beautifully with the blue-green water that's so clear, I can see everything in it.

"Centare, they aren't, because we're the only ones here."

"We are?" She glances up at me. Her eyes are glossier than they were.

That makes me smile. Such an emotional creature, my little pirate. I stroke her cheek. "Ontte. This is a private planet. One that I bought."

"You *bought* this planet?" I nod and lift an eyebrow, willing her to understand. She does — I can see it in the sudden shock that smacks her expression — but she's resistant. She shakes her head. "Centare, centarecentarecentare. You didn't buy this planet. This is some kind of weird joke…"

"The only laughing matter is why you still have on your clothes. I'm hanging on by a thread, Deena. I need to enter you soon." Immediately.

She steps away from me and falls immediately into the water. I laugh and follow her as she backs away from me, trying to crawl, but the waves rise quickly over her head. She's inundated once and then flounders until I reach down and grab her by the arms. Immediately, I begin pulling at her garments, needing them off.

"I bought this planet a hundred solars ago. The moment I decided that I wanted to fuck you for the first time on a beach. And I didn't buy this planet for myself, Deena. This is yours, if you want it. If not, then it'll just be our sex-cation whenever we want to use it." Her shock only grows as I strip her completely naked.

She puts up no defense and shreds the last of mine. My cock starts to surge and the air is too cold against the exposed organ, but the water feels nice. *What will feel nicer is being lodged deep inside her body…* I scoop her up beneath the thighs and walk us further into the water, stopping only when it rises up to her shoulders and my chest.

I spread her legs and use her slick core to rub my cock, appeasing it for a few moments more. It's hard to stand. Hard to think.

"I will get you pregnant here," I say, voice devolving to snarls. I start to blink quickly, distorting the sight of her face.

She's got water in her eyes and a smile touching her cheeks. "You bought me a planet? Me? Deena?"

"Ontte."

"But you told Mathilda I was defective."

I shudder at the memory. My fear. Seeing her pain. "Is that what this has been all about? I called you defective and you believed I was speaking about your leg or your stomach and this thing you call *fat*?"

Deena blinks up at me quickly and nods jerkily, rather than answer.

I laugh. I laugh loud enough to fan the sensations stirring in me. They could not be hotter than they are now. "I would have told her anything to keep her from selling you to another buyer. Defective was the only word I could think of, looking at you, and it has nothing to do with your warrior's mark.

"I called you defective because you were willing to trade your life for another female's. Selflessness is considered a faulty trait among most species. It demonstrates a clear lack of a will to live. Something that, with a blaster in your hands and carpets spread before you, I know you have in abundance. But now I'm beginning to think that I was perhaps correct in such an assessment."

I drop my mouth to hers and hesitate just a breath before unraveling. "Perhaps you *are* defective, but only because you have yet to admit that you also love me. I want to hear it, Deena. Say it."

Her jaw works. My fingers curl into her rear. My upper hands palm her breasts and clutch the back of her head. My restraint is paper thin. Thinner than that. A thread. I want to break it. I want *her* to break it. I want her to know just how defective she is to me. Because she isn't at all.

"Deena…" I growl.

Her eyes unfocus and she licks her lips. "I love you, Rhorky bear."

My heart burns, my cock swells. "I know you do. You're just a pirate. Too stubborn to admit it. Now hold onto my shoulders and accept your first punishment."

She moves before I do, crushing her mouth to mine as I lift her up, up, up, high enough that my cock can expand out of its shell and stretch its sensitive head towards her entrance. The flat head makes entering her more difficult, so I reach between us with one hand and finger her folds, spreading them wide with three fingers.

She moans against my tongue, tasting sweet, like the ocean water calmly ebbing around us in the magic we create. "Fuck me, Rhork."

I wince as I grab the head of my cock and bring it quickly to her heat. I have to use two fingers to keep her open and another hand to guide me. The head of my erection meets resistance and I momentarily panic that I won't fit.

"You'll fit. Keep going," she says, reading my mind.

Removing my hands and centering them on her hips, I push her down and piston my hips. The pleasure that blasts through me makes my knees buckle. Water was, in retrospect, a poor choice. I'm going to drown us both.

I stagger towards the beach, collapsing onto it with Deena beneath me, but Deena's moving, pushing on my shoulder. "Roll over. Your tines…they'll go in the sand."

Confused, but exhilarated and far too delirious to think beyond her request, I roll onto my side and, from there, onto my back. She's right. My tines sink into the soft orange and I'm left staring up at Deena, framed by the sun as she squats over my hips and works my shaft into her body, little bit by little bit. Her full breasts are a canvas to paint. I want them in my mouth and sit up. From there, I begin licking and biting.

"Oh shrov!" She shouts, hands finally finding my shoulders, knees finding the soft sand on either side of my hips.

I look down and suffer a small fit at the sight of my cock stuffed into her body almost, but not quite all the way, down to the plates. And then she starts to move. The slightest rotation of her hips makes my mind blank and semen begin to fire.

"Fuck! I forgot about...the come!" She laughs wildly, throws her head back. Her long coils — a style she calls *locs* — spray sweet water across my cheeks. It looks like diamonds and feels like rain. She is everything.

No Niahhorru male has ever been rutted on his back and I don't know what to make of it. I brought her here to punish her, but instead, I believe I might be the blissfully unaware recipient of Deena's complete and utter thanks.

"You like the beach, then, do you, pirate?" I growl, holding onto her hips and thrusting mine up every time she slams down. The slapping sound fills me with pleasure and fear and a shattering sort of surreality. This cannot be real. For all her talks of defects, this female is perfect for me. The most perfect female in all the Quadrants.

I massage her stomach in a way she likes because her panting picks up, elevating and escalating. She starts to fondle her left breast, but I bat her hand out of the way and quickly reclaim it. "This is mine, pirate, and if you try to steal from me again, you will be punished." But there is no such thing when even her voice is the most acute torment to my discipline. I'd do anything for this female.

"Punish me, Rhork," she moans. "Touch my…"

She doesn't need to finish as my lower hand moves from her hip to her clit. I wet my fingers in my come and smear it over her curls, using it to massage her sensitive skin. I rub and pinch and massage her thoroughly. It takes her instances — less than breaths — before she starts to shake and shiver, losing the rhythm she'd been following, and collapsing forward onto my chest.

When she screams my name, she makes me feel like I own the cosmos. Or perhaps, like we are the only ones in it. Without my token in my head, I feel uncommonly clear. With her in my arms, I feel wholly focused. There is only this thing between us and it will never end, because it is shaped like forever.

I groan, coming more forcefully in response to her pleasure. Thick grey gobs of semen soak her curls, soak my plates and the stones they protect, soak the sands beneath us. I want it deeper inside of her and growl, flipping our positions so that I'm on top and she's beneath me and I start to pound into her hard. I want it to imprint on her memory, the weight of my thrusts. I want her to think about them when she closes her eyes in the dark. I want her to think about them every time she sees me interact with another female because I want her to know that they are all for her. Only for her.

I want her to know that, in exchange for her love and her body and each one of her terrible songs, I'll buy her however many planets she wants, breed her in all the galaxies oceans.

"You're mine, Deena. My pirate. My warrior."

"And you're mine, Rhork. And if I ever see you... with your hands on another female again..." She grabs onto my throat, not hard enough to hurt but hard enough to grab my attention. "I will cut them off. All four of them."

I bark out a laugh and dive into the shape of her mouth, then feast.

13

Deena

Rhork is insatiable. He fucks me on the beach and then in the water and then on the beach again and then on the ramp of the ship and then standing up against the side of the ship and then he pushes me onto my knees and commands me to lick the come on his cock until it's clean and I do and then he pushes me onto my back and ruts between my breasts and then we leave the beach and head for the trees and he takes me again up against a tree trunk, but when it starts to shake too badly, he lowers me back to the ground and I ride him until he begs me for mercy and then I roll over and he tries to enter my ass, but can't fit, so he sates his desire to have my ass by humping me between the ass cheeks while fingering my clit until I come and he explodes and then we start the whole process all over on the beach until the sky turns dark and then starts to lighten.

"Rhork, I need to catch up on sleep..." I moan, boneless lying on the sand. Sand covers all of me. Rhork covers all of me.

He pulls my body under his and slaps my knees apart, settling between my hips. His cock is still rock hard and still coming and his face twists in pain whenever he comes out of me to change position. "Pirates don't sleep and they certainly don't try uselessly to catch it."

"This pirate might."

"I'm your captain. You'll sleep when I tell you to sleep." He slams my hips down to meet his, breaching the barrier of my swollen, sore lips in one move.

My eyes roll back into my skull as I grow deliriously hot all over again. The sand is soft between his skin and mine, but still grates when our bodies press together. I wince at the sensitivity on my clit and, like the mind reader he is, Rhork staggers onto his feet with me wrapped in his arms and takes us back to the water.

He's clearly not operating at full speed, because he staggers and splashes wildly into the waves, which are picking up. I smile, too tired to laugh, as he collapses to his knees with the water at chest height, and smooths the sand away from my clit, then starts to lift me up and down and use my body like he used that strange come machine on his ship.

My hands are loose around his neck and I'm not doing any of the work, but he doesn't seem to mind and I definitely don't. "I'm just like that come receptacle you had on your ship…"

"What?"

"The orange one."

"Ah…ontte," he snarls against my cheek, biting it savagely before licking the bite clean. "The machine for relief. A place for me to put my cock and my come whenever I'd like. Will you ever deny me, Deena? Even when you are tired?"

"Centare," I gasp as another orgasm builds in me. I shake my head, damp locs whipping around my shoulders and sticking to my neck. "I won't."

"When I want you, you'll spread your legs, isn't that right?"

"Ontte." My chest constricts. My gut contracts. His words are disgraceful as all get out, but I can't find myself anything but aroused by them.

"And when I want your mouth on me, you'll lick me clean, won't you, Deena?"

"Ontte."

"On your knees."

"However you want."

"Ontte. However I want. And when I want to drink your nectar, you'll pull down your pants and let me bury my face in you, won't you?"

"Ontte."

"You'll ride me on the net, drinking my come with your body. You'll relieve me whenever I need, letting me empty into you again and again."

Oh fuck yes. "Shrov!" I clench.

But his hips lose their speed and momentum. He stills for one painful second. "That wasn't an answer. Will you let me use your body to drain my cock however I want? Whenever I want?"

"Ontte!"

"Then ontte," he says, resuming his pace while my body climbs back to the dangerous ledge it'd been balancing on. "You're like this come relief machine. But that is only one of the many things you are to me."

"What are the rest?" I squeeze out through clenched teeth, inner thighs quivering, whole body shaking with a need to fall off that precipice and hit however many waves on my way down.

"Family," he says with no great ceremony and my whole chest rips apart, giving him all the space he needs to reach in with all four of his great, gobbling hands, and resuscitate my long dead heart.

An orgasm rips through me and Rhork's mouth somehow manages to find mine as he guides me through the rapids. I'm taken away, dragged in the undercurrent, skin pulled from flesh and rearranged on the other side. In this new shape and form I am a pirate, even though nothing about me is any different than it was.

It's just the inside parts. They're all Niahhorru now.

Because Rhork has given me something I didn't know was real. Love *without* pain.

My eyes roll back into my skull and I shout out a whole host of expletives before finally, the thing I meant to say pops out, "I LOVE YOU, RHORK, TO THE MOON AND BACK."

He laughs against the column of my throat, against which I feel the unmistakable scrape of his teeth. "Which one?" He whispers.

I slap his shoulder, but hold him tight as I feel his body tensing and his chest bucking and his hips jolting as he finally releases on top of my release. He groans my name and I feel like a goddess, one who rules the stars, one who can't be caged. *Never again.*

Rhork groans and it's the strangest feeling — his cock shrinking and eventually, pulling out of my body, splashing grey come everywhere. Some of it is swept away by the water, but not all. We drag ourselves as one single, connected unit until the water only laps at our feet. Sand rolls up and down my back, attacking my hair and the back of my neck. I'm gonna need a thousand passes of the cleaning radiator gun that the Niahhorru use in order to get rid of all this gunk. *I love it.*

He rolls onto his side but stops me when I try to roll onto mine. Instead he holds down one of my shoulders, keeping me on my back. He takes both of my ankles in one of his hands and pushes my knees to my chest, rolling me back, back and further back until I'm balancing on my shoulders and my butt is way up in the air.

"Uhh...Rhork?" I giggle at the compressed way my voice sounds.

Rhork doesn't laugh though. He just smiles, cheeks sunken, eyes sunken, looking completely and utterly spent. He arches over my body and kisses my forehead. "To make sure."

"Make sure?"

"That my seed takes. I want to see a dozen kits from this. And in case there is any chance we've not done a thorough enough job, I'll make love to you again on the coming solar." He groans and falls onto his side, releasing my feet. He smiles up at the lightening sky and that expression alone is like a thousand armies attacking my heart all together, all under his command. I don't stand a chance. I never did. I lost the moment I heard his voice through the power of that magical token.

I lost the first time I heard him say, "Interesting."

Because this is. He is. All of it. Everything. The ocean. This world. I want it all. I want everything. I want it with him.

I edge towards him over the sand and he wraps his two left arms around my body and holds me close. I can't stop touching him. I run my fingers over his plates, his neck, his jaw. I kiss him, wanting him to know, "I love you. I really do."

"I know, but you are dangerously close to being rutted again. Just give me a moment, Deena." He inhales, then exhales, clasping my hand in one of his. He pulls me down onto his chest and I lay my head on the plate covering his pectoral. It's scratchy but I don't mind.

"This all feels so surreal," I whisper as I look up at the purple sky. "Sometimes I think I'll wake up and find that I'm still stuck in that box in Mathilda's basement."

"Not a chance of that. I would come for you wherever you are." He inhales, then exhales, and I ride his chest like a wave. "Do you miss your people? Your colony?"

I scoff, "Centare. Those people are the worst." Rhork laughs as I rub my hand over his stomach and he plays gently with my hair. "I mean it. They're so busy trying to figure out how to stay alive and take from each other that they don't even realize that they don't need to take, because there's enough for everyone. They don't even know how big the galaxy even is. How much of it there is still to explore. It's pure abundance. And even though they have the ability to travel off-planet now with the help of the Voraxians, they don't. They stay put and keep fighting over stones and sand. They're nothing like us pirates."

I can feel Rhork's smile leak through his voice as he says, "Centare. They are nothing like us pirates." He lifts just enough to be able to kiss the top of my head. I close my eyes, just enjoying it.

Then I say, "And you know what rhymes with pirates?"

"What?"

"Nothing at all. Because we're special."

"We are."

And then something clicks. "Hey, what were you planning to do with this planet anyways? Besides have sex on it?"

"My imagination only got us to this point. I have nothing planned for after."

It's my turn to laugh at that.

"Besides, this planet isn't mine. I bought it for you. So you could see the ocean. Was it everything you imagined it would be?"

"Centare. I had no way of imagining this. It's... incredible."

"I agree." He pats my bottom and I fight the urge to want to mount him again by distracting myself.

"But you know what I was thinking? It'd be a pretty big waste of a pretty rad planet to just use it for the off-chance we feel like leaving Kor or the ship for a sexcapade. And we've been looking at building secure housing facilities for the humans on Kor. But what if we built them here instead? I mean, it would be such a cool place to wake up after however long they've been sleeping. It'd be isolated, a planet they could call theirs, if they want. Otherwise, the cool ones that want to be pirates can join us or go to Kor and do whatever.

"It's way better than the colony. And hey, we could even build trading ports out here, if we wanted. That would give Niahhorru a chance to meet humans in casual commerce type settings, instead of whatever forced introductions you had in mind and then when the humans are more established, maybe they have something to offer besides just their ability to breed.

They could, I don't know, bake something or build something. Harvest something. Whatever."

Rhork doesn't say anything for some time after I've finished prattling. I stay on my back, staring up at the purple sky, watch it lighten around the edges, getting yellower and yellower.

Finally, when the silence has gone on for too long, I elbow him in the ribs. "Rhork? What do you think?"

"Interesting."

Ninety-eight solars later…

14

Deena

I was less nervous when I went out with Herannathon street racing at the Gogo tracks. Of course, I'd still been a little nervous. Rhork hadn't exactly been thrilled to find out where I was given how pregnant I was — and still am. My belly precedes me like a damned trumpeter announcing my entry everywhere I go.

The extra weight is a little annoying. My leg hurts more often and Quintenanrret tried to encourage me to stay seated more often and be less active. But really, let's face it. He was as crazy as I am to think that I wouldn't be out every solar exploring and I think he knew it, too, because along with the recommendation to stay on the mothership, he also gave me a pale purple powder to rub onto my leg whenever it starts to smart. He said it's made out of the excrement of some giant purple bird — as if that would deter me.

There's nothing better than exploring Kor and, as pregnant as I am, I can't say that I hate the attention. I mean, when I asked Herannathon to take me street racing in the first place he'd had an impossible time saying no. No one ever tells me no anymore and it's freaking fantastic.

So, bird poop it is.

The Eshmiri at the next stall over draw my attention with their colorful fabrics. These are lighter, silkier, and much more beach planet appropriate. I'll need to stock up, seeing as we'll be opening tanks as soon as the coming solar.

So far, we've unloaded all one-thousand-seven-hundred-some-odd tanks onto the beach planet and stowed them in a newly constructed and ultra secure facility. Eighty homes have been built along with stalls for the first marketplace and a birthing center. A little optimistic, I thought, but I later found out that Rhork had that commissioned first and exclusively for me.

Such a softie.

He'll make a great dad.

A dad! Holy shit, I'm pregnant!

Pregnant rhymes with eggplant. I wonder if our little grey and brown kits will look like eggplants when they pop out. According to Quintenanrret, it's looking like I'm going to give birth to six babies all at once and in the next fourteen to twenty solars. I don't think I've wrapped my head fully around that, but Rhork seems to think this is all totally above board and normal and is freaking excited about it.

It's cute to see him excited. Heck, they're all excited. Every few moments, a new voice fires into my token asking me about some random thing the baby might need or that I might like. No matter my reply, the pirates always get me the thing. Even the things that crawl and have stingers and that Rhork will undoubtedly punch them in the face for, and that we have to return or rehome.

As such, I can focus on buying things for the new humans we're about to wake from their long sleeps, instead of the new hybrid Niahhorru-humans I'm hopefully going to bring into the world calmly and peacefully.

I slow, twisting the beautiful silver bangle Rhork gifted me so many solars ago, after I told him about the human concept of husband and wife. I'd told him that there was an exchange of rings and he'd shown up a few solars later with this bracelet. I hadn't had the heart to tell him that the rings were worn on fingers and, instead, bought him a bracelet at the reaver markets the next solar just like it. I grin at the memory.

Meanwhile, all of the Eshmiri reavers descend on me all at once. It's like the damned creatures have a sixth sense for this stuff. They know where I'm going to stop and have their disc readers out even before I know that they're carrying the items I need.

Scratch that. Do I ever really *need* what they're offering me? Centare. But want? Ontte. And I've got Rhork's magic silver disc to make it happen.

Negotiating with other species while pregnant has its advantages, too. Seems like *everybody* in the whole dang cosmos is nicer to pregnant ladies. The Egama, in particular, get real flustered every time I get close. And I do get close. But only when Rhork's bad and I feel like making him jealous, or when I feel like instigating a fight. I like fighting, but Rhork says I'm not allowed to fist fight anyone in these final days. He says if I want to fight, I've got to blast them.

I frown at the thought, realizing it's been way too many solars since I blasted anybody. "Humph."

"Which color do you like?"

"We have pink and green and blue."

"Or white!" Another one shouts, thrusting a swatch of fabric into my face and stroking my cheek with it.

"Wow," I answer, "it is soft." I slide my hand over my belly as a baby does a little dance. Nerves mount. I'm only fourteen days away from delivery and I'm oscillating between nervous wreck about to poop myself and the proudest mama in the known cosmos. I...I never thought I'd ever be pregnant. It isn't that I always wanted to be...it's that I thought I never would be.

I was trapped in a box, in love with an alien I never thought I'd meet and I was sure, if I did ever meet him, wouldn't look twice at me.

And now he calls me his *wife* and tells me he loves me and I'm pregnant by him.

With six babies.

HOLY SHROVING SHIT!

"I...um..." There's that um again. I shrug my shoulders down my back and use both hands to hold my belly up. "I'll take this one," I tell them and they immediately all start giggling and packaging up three times the quantity I asked for.

I reach into my pocket to retrieve my chip, but a hand slides over mine, holding my palm against the curve of my stomach. My butt cheeks clench. My toes flex in their rubbery covering. My ears perk back. My mind goes blank, thoughts scattering wide.

Because the hand that gently cups mine is familiar. It's the same dark brown shade as mine.

"You chose incorrectly, Deena. You should have gone with blue. It matches your eyes."

Mathilda's voice catches me off guard and for a moment, I imagine that every solar I've spent out from underneath her thumb was one I dreamt up. Cold sweat comes to cover me. I feel like a child watching her raise her palm and then bring it down against my cheek. All I did was ask her about my mother, where she was. Then she hit me. I guess that was the better option for her. What was the alternative? Admitting that she killed her own daughter in order to be able to sell hybrid babies to the monster that enslaved us? Admitting that she's a monster just like him? That even though she's human, she's formed from the same carbon that Pogar is, and is just as rotten as Balesilha, too?

I inhale with a start. My toes wiggle in my shoes. My hand flexes for the lightning stick hanging off of the belt around my hips. My ears perk forward and capture the high trill of the Eshmiri giggling. It sounds like giggling, but I can hear them through my translator shouting curses and insults at the woman standing behind me.

My grandmother.

My captor.

My nemesis.

She thinks she can intimidate me. Scratch that. *She* thinks she can intimidate *me?* I'm a motherfucking pirate. Hear me roar.

"Rhork," I say it out loud, but there's a sudden pressure against my back just above my ass, right at belly-level, that makes me hold my tongue.

"Not another word or the mutants growing in your belly will meet the same end as your mother, by the same hand, too."

I inhale, then exhale. I meet the Eshmiri's gaze and he's watching me with an expression I find quite strange. He's frowning. I've never seen an Eshmiri frown before. I try to communicate with him through gaze alone, but he's easily distracted by another customer. Shroving Eshmiri.

He waddles off, the crowd in front of me disperses, and I'm left staring into the darkness of the Eshmiri tent behind him. There, two eyes watch me. Even though I can't make out the shadow-covered face they belong to, I can see that those white eyes have neither pupil nor iris. Creepy. Creepier still, a surge of black smoke crosses them, followed by blots of what looks like red, before the face retreats back into the shadows without ever allowing me to fully glimpse the Eshmiri it belongs to. At least, it must be an Eshmiri, though I've never seen a reaver with eyes quite like that.

"Hi there, grandma," I say, tension threading my tone, but no fear. It surprises me.

It must surprise her too, because she doesn't answer right away and she doesn't laugh in that creepy villainous cackle, like she ordinarily would. "You sound pleased to see me."

"Of course. This is the family reunion I always hoped for." My voice trembles just a little bit in the middle and I can feel her lean her weight further into my back, barrel of whatever blaster-tip more aggressively digging into my flesh. I will my token on, but Mathilda says, "Don't even think about it. I have a mobile disabler active. It has a wide radius. Not even your shadows will be able to reach out through their tokens."

Her hand curls around my shoulder like a claw and she starts to rotate my body away from the Eshmiri tent and back onto the main road. She pushes me forward. "As you can see, your pirate friends are a little incapacitated at the moment."

Shrov.

Herannathon stands at the stall opposite this one with all four of his hands raised. Behind him are two Drakesh warriors, characterized by their long white hair and dusky red skin. They have blasters trained on him. Of course, given that this is Kor, no one seems to care. I have half a mind to laugh until I realize that Tevbarannos, Rhegaran, and Ewanrennaron are in identical positions.

Shrov!

Shrov rhymes with stove. I feel like cooking Mathilda on a stove right about now. She deserves worse. How is she here? How did she find me! And who in the shrov are these Drakesh? Are they working for her? My thoughts jump the tracks that they were on and I suddenly arrive at a few conclusions based on the things that I know now. Because not just my belly has gotten bigger these past however many solars, but my brain has practically exploded with all the new gunk Rhork and my pirates have been feeding it.

This gunk enables me to postulate a few theories. Heh. Postule. Sounds like pustule.

Focus!

How is she here? *Exile.* It has to be. Kor is where the Voraxians exile all their unwanted creatures. Svera or Miari or somebody back on the colony must have figured out her game and shipped her off to the grey zone where they hoped she'd die even though they didn't have the tits or the stones to off her themselves. Cowards.

How did she find me? *I stand out.* Belly aside, I'm damned conspicuous. Even on a planet as diverse as this one, a single human still garners attention. A single human mated to Kor's overlord? I might as well carry a blinking sign with an arrow pointing down at my head.

Who the shrov are these Drakesh? *Hmm....* Here, I'm not so sure. They could be more exiles? But what's strange is that they seem to be following her orders. Are they *working* for her? That seems unlikely. Drakesh are known for their hatred of other species. It seems like a stretch that they'd ever work for a non-Drakesh, no matter the payment.

The thoughts turn over and over in my head as she leads me down the main road past the last of the Eshmiri tents. We turn right and head down Pleasure Alley, away from the Cosmos Dome and the Gogo Racetrack, which is good for her. Everyone knows me there.

We don't go deep into Pleasure Alley, but stop at the third building in. The structure is wedged between two huge pleasure houses — one run by the Oroshi, the other by the Oosa, which means the streets outside are littered with every kind of species and all the genders they contain between them. Tentacles slither and cocks hang so long they nearly touch the ground. Breasts hover like inflatable balloons, some species with six or seven of them. Skin tones glitter in all gemstone shades. It's a good spot for a hideout. No one would stand out here. Maybe, not even a human.

The Oosa building is bright yellow, covered in lights. The Oroshi building looks like it's made out of the same material their tentacles are, blue-green and kind of squishy. The building wedged between them is black and brown and green — Breen? Glaown? — and completely run down. Mathilda presses me up against the front door and for a moment, I wonder if she's going to try to push me through it without opening it at all...

And then she does.

The facade of the building shimmers and makes a popping sound as I'm shoved into it, or rather, into the building behind it. The interior is nothing like the outside. It isn't glaown at all, but a lavish and decadent green. It was always Mathilda's favorite color. She'd send her human minions to the far side of the planet to harvest green leaves from the tallest trees just so she could dye her fabrics. At least three warriors died in their attempts. Did she shed a tear? That's a hard *no*.

The pale green carpet fibers are long and swish around my ankles, feeling like strands of silk caught in suspended animation. There's a divan against the far wall, stacks of pillows spread around it. To the right is a dining table built for ten and there's a staircase leading up to the right of that. Paintings that look like something with tentacles painted them hang lavishly over the divan. Sprawled across it is someone I did not expect.

My hands flinch towards my lightning stick but the male just clicks his tongue against the backs of his teeth. They're pearly white and match his hair. It's white. His eyes are black. His skin is red. I haven't seen this male before in the flesh but make no mistake in thinking that I don't know who he is.

Pogar. Drakesh. Exile. Rapist. Murderer. Bo'Raku, once, but he hasn't been that for rotations. Now, all he is is a whispered menace, a haunting shadow...

His reputation has carried even though I wish it hadn't. When he was exiled from Voraxia, it should have been the last we ever heard of the male whose crimes include mutiny, thievery, rape, kidnapping and murder. He bought the hybrid babies Mathilda sold him. He bought the kit that would have been my hybrid brother or sister. I wonder where she or he is now…Clearly, he didn't keep them. He probably sold them off and I know better than anyone what kind of fate awaits a human in this grim and greedy galaxy when they don't have a pirate family to back them up.

Family. And I don't mean the blood-relation standing just behind me with a blaster pressed to my stomach. And I don't mean the kind of family Pogar had given that his son, Peixal, was just as foul as he is. What he did to Kiki? There's a special place in the afterlife for that level of scum. For the lot of them.

No, I mean the kind of family who will buy my future kits a poisonous animal to cuddle and who will fight a giant with me because I say he cheated at a game of mok-biz and who will trick me into eating a living insect by claiming that it's really a sweet and who will show me how to reload a blaster bigger than I am and who will stand shoulder-to-shoulder with me and sing songs I made up about plants and planets and spoons — maybe even not sing them, but shout them — up at Kor's many moons when the sweet wine is at its sweetest and the lunar is at its deepest.

The kind of family that, some day, I hope to pillage a Voraxian ship with. The kind of family who will help raise all six of my coming kits because they already think of those kits as their family, too.

It's hard not to feel calm and strangely protected even as I stand between two of the sickest most sinister beings in the galaxy. My voice belies such a calm when I say, "So. You've been making friends, gramma."

She shoves me forward. I stumble, then brush down my dress. I got too big for my gormar pants, so now I just wear this giant grey gormar tarp. Rhork calls it a dress, but I'm too big for dresses. It's a tarp. But no matter what it is, I feel beautiful in it because Rhork still looks at me like I'm a perfectly formed star.

"I have. It looks like you get that skill from me, Deena." She eyes my stomach as she comes to stand in front of me. I see the blaster now, for the first time. It's an old model compared to the one that I use and I almost tease her for it — I would have, had Herannathon been using it — but then I remember that even the old models plug holes into things just fine.

"Actually, I didn't make friends. I found a family, but I don't suspect that family is what you brought me all the way to Pleasure Alley to talk about. It hasn't ever really been your strong suit, now has it, *grandmother*?"

She gives me a funny look and I struggle looking into her eyes. Every time I do, it makes me think about what she cost me. What she cost the entire colony. So many lives, wasted. So much suffering. So much pain. So much of it mine. But that's all over now.

The colony is firmly in the control of the Voraxians — the good kind — and Miari and Svera. And I'm a pirate and my man controls the most important trading port in the entire galaxy. And I'm a protective mama bear who won't let anything hurt the strange multiple-armed hybrids growing in my belly. They're *mine* and she no longer owns me.

"You seem different," she finally says.

"I am different. You, on the other hand, don't seem to have changed at all." I glance around theatrically. "I see you've still got great taste."

"Thank you."

"I'm bored," the former Drakesh king says. "Let's get on with this. Our allies are waiting."

Noooooow, this is getting interesting. "What's the plan, Mathilda? Hold me captive for another fourteen solars, wait for me to give birth, sell the hybrids, slit my throat? I mean, you should be familiar with all that. It's what you did to your daughter. Do you remember killing your own kid?"

Mathilda's hands tighten around her weapon. Her eyes blaze. She doesn't like when I talk about this. Somewhere deep down, I think she has an entire Hell full of demons tearing her apart for what she's done, over and over again. My words just bring them up. At least, that's the idea.

I smile, because talking about my mom reminds me then of what I need to do. What pirates are best at. *Revenge.*

"Did she cry out for her mom when you killed her? Did she beg? Mama, mama no please! Aaaarg!" I make a clutching motion and grab my chest, pretending to fall. Mathilda's front teeth clench. She opens her mouth and starts to talk, but I speak over her. "Or did she tell you what she thought about you? That you are the worst mother in the history of all mothers and the worst human in the history of all humans? Did she call you a fuckwad? A bastard? A bitch? Did she call you an ugly old hag? You are, by the way. Did she tell you that her daughter, Deena, would one day become a pirate seeking revenge and tear you down to the nothing that you are?"

"You are…" Mathilda lifts her blaster and takes a half step towards me.

Pogar rises to stand and steps up beside her. He grabs the barrel of her blaster and tips it up. "You are allowing your frivolous human emotions to take control. If you intend to live, then…"

"You *dare* threaten me? This plan is mine."

"The plan is yours. Everything else belongs to me, including the contacts, the allies and the battleship. So come. Grab the female and join me or stay here and allow her mate to tear you to pieces. I could not care less what fate befalls you, female."

"She can't communicate with him and your Drakesh soldiers subdued her guards."

In a fluid motion, the red-skinned alien reaches out and grabs Mathilda by the throat. He arches down towards her and speaks directly into her forehead. "You think that those are the only eyes Rhorkanterannu has on Kor? You are misguided. Now let's move. I have no desire to linger here. The attack is prepared, the plan already set into motion. Bring the girl. Come, human."

Mathilda looks furious as he releases her neck and heads for the stairs. Muscles in her cheek and neck both twitch. Her long grey locs swish around her shoulders when she tracks him with her gaze. My hand flinches towards my lightning stick in a way that's visible, hoping to distract her while my other hand reaches through the hole in my pocket for the battle kilt tied around my waist underneath the dress I'm wearing. The tarp.

"Don't move. Come here."

"You just said not to move."

"Don't be smart with me. We both know you never were."

I shrug. "Seems like you've lost a bit of those smarts, too. What's your plan here? You think that guy's not gonna betray you? That's literally why he's been stuck here the past half dozen rotations."

"Luckily, our interests happen to align. When I take back the colony, he'll take his revenge on Va'Raku, who stole his planet from him."

I roll my eyes even though I've got no clue what she's talking about. I don't know anything about Voraxian history, but I don't let it show. I just keep reaching slowly for the micro-blaster hanging off of my belt, refusing to move forward. Refusing to go with her. If I go with her, then the battle will get a thousand times more difficult.

"*Riiiiiiiight*. Because the colony is just gonna open up its arms and welcome you back after they exiled you for slaughtering human females and for teaming up with that ugly dude. Makes sense."

"They won't have a choice. Why do you think you're here, Deena? It's certainly not for the pleasure of your company. I mean look at you. Pregnant, rounder than a moon, and cripple. Rhorkanterannu was right. You truly are defective."

The words are intended to slay, and some part of me feels that they're true until I remember looking straight ahead into a mirror as I put my dress on early this solar. The distant sun had just begun to rise. Rhorkanterannu was still in bed — a first, since I almost always sleep longer than he does — and I looked at myself naked and I looked at him naked, sprawled out on our net behind me and I thought to myself, *damn if we don't make a sexy, sexy family*.

"There's nothing wrong with my leg." I straighten.

Mathilda stiffens. Her pupils contract.

I shrug with one shoulder while my hand finds the blaster and fixes around it. I carefully unclip it from its holster, speaking as I do. "The only thing wrong with it, is that you're the one who broke it. You said it was to protect me, so I wouldn't have to go into the Hunt. I think it was to protect *you*, so you wouldn't have to look into the mirror and see a woman who killed both her daughter and her granddaughter."

"Stop talking, Deena, and move."

"Why would I?" I balk. "I don't get why you need me anyway."

"The pirates won't fire at our ship when we leave the port with our mercenary army if you're on board, and the humans, as stupid as they are, won't let the Voraxians fire if you're on board either. All of these creatures you call *family* that you've surrounded yourself with are too sentimental for these Quadrants. You're what ensures that we make it door-to-door without any fight. They're too stupid to know any better than not to die for you."

"You're probably right. Svera always was too self-sacrificing for her own good. But, I'm not like Svera. I'm all about staying alive and keeping my kits alive, too. So, I hate to break it to you, grandmother dearest, but the only one who's gonna die this solar is you." Underneath my dress, I aim through the tarp at my grandma and I pull the trigger.

The little blaster heats underneath my touch and my arm momentarily flinches. Killing someone who raised you — even if they also tortured and contained you — is harder than I thought it would be. And even though my will is sure, my fingers are unsteady. The tiny little ray gun is the newest of the new models and has no recoil at all, so my feet remain rooted as the blast tears through my tarp and knocks into Mathilda. The shot nails her in the hip, spinning her around. She manages to catch herself on one of the dining room chairs, but I fire again, this time hitting her in the leg.

The irony that she's limping now on the same leg I limp on makes me smile, but only briefly before I realize that she's somehow still got ahold of her blaster and is pointing it solidly at me.

The critical difference between me and my grandma? When she aims a gun at her kin, she doesn't hesitate to pull the trigger.

The room explodes in bright white light, I cover my belly with both hands and I open my mouth on a silent scream.

15
Rhork

"Yo, Rhorkanterannu." The voice slips into my token. I allow it to do so because I'm surprised to hear from her. Eshmiri reavers don't make a habit of befriending Niahhorru and this particular reaver doesn't contact me. Ever.

"Ashmara," I answer, leaning back against the yeeyar view pane, so far above Kor's surface the world beneath it looks like it belongs to the galaxies tiniest of creatures. We're prepping the mothership for departure to the beach planet that Deena's made a habit of calling Reqama, the Meero word for *gift*. Erobu and Gerannu are arguing about the command settings we'll need to land effectively on sand in a craft of this size. I'm a little bored watching them fist fight, but have made no move to intervene, so Ashmara's distraction has come at a good time.

"To what do I owe the pleasure?"

She doesn't answer right away and I can hear the high-pitched trill of many Eshmiri in the background. I wonder where in the cosmos she is. And then she surprises me. "I'm on Kor."

"Interesting." I pause, allowing myself to think through the possibilities of why she's here and, more importantly, why she's sharing this information with me. I come up with very little of substance, so I press, "You don't normally share your whereabouts with Niahhorru."

"Yeah, well don't make me regret it. I just...I saw..." She clears her throat. I stand a little straighter.

I lift my right hand and the thirty or so pirates on the command deck turn as I capture their attention. Something is wrong. I've never heard her like this and immediately, I feel unease. Despite the fact that she is Eshmiri, I've always had a bit of a soft spot for her. She's a reaver and reavers and pirates share a mutual dependence. They steal from us, we steal from them, and then we come together on Kor, drink ourselves stupid, and trade all of our stolen parts. They don't have kings or queens like the Voraxians who are bound to their planets by nothing but history. They are free. She is free. And freedom means confidence in everything, something I don't hear now in her tone.

"What is it? Are you safe?"

"Ugh. Don't ask. You're so annoying when you ask. I'm a reaver. I'm perfectly capable of handling things on my own. I just saw something weird and I wanted to tell you."

"What?"

"I saw your woman. Your human. You knocked her up real good, didn't you?"

"I did. She is beautiful, isn't she?"

"Yeah. She is. But uhh yeah. I saw her and she was haggling with Tintin at the market, but she didn't finish negotiating. Another human came up to her and led her away and it didn't look like a friendly sort of meeting. Just thought you should know."

I grimace and make my way to the exit, rounding up pirates as I walk. "Gerannu, stay here," I order before turning my attention back to Ashmara. I'm surprised that she's left her communications open.

"You see which way they went?"

"I didn't, but I asked around. Some Eshmiri said they saw the grey-haired human leading your female towards Pleasure Alley. They weren't alone, either, Rhorkanterannu. There were Drakesh soldiers with them. Looks like they had your guys subdued."

I growl, feeling hot, feeling restless, feeling shroving exhilarated. It's been too long since I murdered somebody — since I've been faced with a real opponent. "I've been waiting for this. I'm surprised it took her so long."

"You knew your lady was gonna get got?"

"She isn't getting anything. You think I'd let my human wife carrying a litter of my kits in her belly walk unprotected through the streets of Kor?" I laugh. The thought is rather hilarious. "I am a Niahhorru pirate. And I run Kor."

Ashmara exhales a little easier on the other end of the line. "Sorry. Forgot who I was talking to. Your guys looked worried though."

"Herannathon and them? Where are they now?" I'm more worried for them than I am for Deena.

"Not sure. I'll ask around though. See if I can lend a hand."

"Don't let me pull you from the markets. This problem will be quickly eviscerated."

"Were you using your mate as bait?"

My chest rumbles in satisfaction as I enter the lift, pirates smushing themselves in to fill its entire space. The excitement brewing between us now is infectious. "Of course."

Ashmara's sharp laughter crackles through the line. "You're something else, you know that?"

"Ontte."

"Still, I'd like to stick around. Traitors aren't anything to brush off. You might need some support."

"Traitors litter my streets and I've been prepared for this one. I got word eighty solars ago that this human traitor was spotted in the markets. I've been trying to root her out, without success. You've just made my job much easier so, as far as I'm concerned, your work here is done."

She pauses, doesn't hang up, doesn't say more. Then she curses as she undoubtedly runs into someone. I can hear their irate rebuttal through the token. "I'm going to stick around. I mean, if I can get your permission, Rhorkanterannu."

"Is that deference I hear in your tone?" I balk, feet hitting Kor's streets as I burn a path towards Pleasure Alley, a dozen pirates in line behind me. More join us as we walk. They don't know where we're going, but they know it has to do with Deena. And they're starved for a fight.

"Ontte," she says in Meero. She still carries the high, giggly Eshmiri accent when she speaks in our tongue. It suits her perfectly. For as savage as this reaver is, the high pitch to her tone only succeeds in making her sound more frightening. "I'd like to stay. I met Svera. You were right. I did find her in the pits."

"Good. I'm glad."

"She gave me a little history lesson. I know about this female, Mathilda," she spits the name with the disdain it deserves. I believe her.

"So you know about your own history, then? You may be linked to my female."

She answers stormily, "I know. But I don't want to be involved with them. Svera wanted me to come meet all her precious little people, but that's not my world. I'm not a human, Rhorkanterannu. I'm an Eshmiri reaver. So don't tell Deena about me. I'd like to see this through and make sure that foul woman who sold me is dead, but I don't want to open old wounds. Mine or your female's."

My fists tighten, hatred building in my bloodstream towards this human traitor. How I've longed for this moment. The moment I'll finally get to hold that wretched woman's heart in my hands. Then tear it into four pieces and swallow all the parts. Centare...maybe I'll feed her to the Doredore sharks. They eat slowly. Or maybe, I'll just let Deena decide. So long as the end result is painful, I don't really care how the traitor dies.

"I understand."

"Good. Just let me know when you find her or if you need my help. I'm heading that way now."

"Centare, don't come here. If you want to help, go after my missing pirates. There were four of them guarding Deena. Herannathon, Tevbarannos, Rhegaran, and Ewanrennaron. Locate them, then head to Pleasure Alley. We're coming around the far side of the Cosmos Dome, so we'll meet you in the middle. Look for smoke."

"Smoke?"

"Smoke. If I know Deena's kinswoman, she'll have already tried to kill her and the shield she's wearing will incinerate anything on the block if that happens."

Ashmara laughs, "You really are a hell of a pirate."

Pride swells in my breast — this time, my own. "She is one hell of a wife. One worth protecting."

"Ugh. Don't make me choke."

Chuckling, I click out of our conversation as Pleasure Alley rises up before me. We round a glowing orange building, built for Walrays and all thirty-seven of their genders, but it doesn't look like they're conducting very good business now. No one is. The street is full of creatures of all species running in every direction. We're slowed considerably, until I break out a Niahhorru shield that's built out of sound waves. It repels anything it comes into contact with and sends people in front of us scattering.

My pirates form a V behind me, me at the tip, and we spear forward through the throngs until we reach the most successful pleasure houses on the row belonging to the Oroshi and the Oosa and the small, derelict building between them. The flat roof has caved in on the upper level. The left side of the lower level has a hole in it and from that hole steps my woman. My wife.

I stow my shield and extend all four of my arms out to her. "Deena, did you let Mathilda escape?"

Her chin snaps up, then her mouth falls open. She has soot on her cheek but not another spot on her. Her hands cup the underside of her belly. It looks heavy and I am momentarily annoyed that she doesn't have a carrier buzzing her around the city. She insists on walking, even though she's carrying so much extra weight now. I feel my mouth opening to chastise her for this but, instead, am rewarded for my concern by a fist to the gut.

She punches me hard. "I just got shot! Are you seriously asking me if Mathilda's okay?"

"I didn't ask you if she's okay," I say, massaging the space on my stomach as I quickly issue orders to the pirates behind me to canvas the house. Most are too busy being concerned that Deena let Mathilda escape, just as I am. And I suppose a few are also wanting to make sure that their pirate comrade is alright. Just as I do now.

My hands stroke her body, loving the feel of it. It's hard not to be distracted by the softness of her skin or the fullness of her stomach, reminding me that I impregnated this female and filling me with the proud urge to lay her on her back and rut into her again, just for good measure. Just because I can and just because she loves it.

Deena stabs my chest with her finger. Her full lips flatten and twist as she shouts, "Aren't you at least a *little* concerned that I just got shot?"

"You didn't get shot. You're wearing your wedding ring." I cuff her wrist, fingering the atomic metal.

She glances at it, then grins, then quickly tries to squash her expression as she turns her angry face back up to me. "This is a force field?"

I drop my mouth to hers and take her quickly before rasping against her lips, "You really think I'd let my *wife* wander the streets of Kor without a force field? I'm a pirate and, have you not heard what they call us?" I kiss her again, much more softly. "They call us lord and lady of Kor."

Her head falls back and she laughs. "You're crazy."

"It's why I'm perfect for you."

She fingers her cuff with renewed interest and, when her eyes turn up to mine, they're glossier than they were. "You could have told me that if someone tried to shoot at me, my bracelet would shoot back."

"I didn't want to worry you."

"Well, it was pretty scary when she fired. I thought that was it for us."

She rubs her stomach. I place two of my hands over her one and hold our kits between us. "Never. We have access to the most advanced technology the Quadrants have to offer. I traded a small fortune to the princesses of Quadrant One for this one. They make these there in order to protect the royal family. I had to modify it of course. It also includes an anchor. If anyone tries to take you on board a non-Niahhorru ship off planet, the ship won't rise."

She chuckles at that and shakes her head. "Shoot. I should have let them take me then, I guess. They'd have been stuck planet-side."

"They would have been. And Mathilda's just lucky she only tried to fire on you with a blaster. If it had been anything with more power, the response would have leveled the entirety of Pleasure Alley. The Oosa wouldn't be happy."

"Let me guess — Nikkowerranorru modified this, not Gerannu."

I grin at the image of Nikkowerranorru, Gerannu's psychotic apprentice, as he explained the details of the modifications he made to this ring. I nod. "Which is why I had to test it."

"You tested it?" She yelps. "On yourself?"

I nod again.

"Augh." She rubs her face roughly and turns from me, shaking her head. "I don't think I want any more gifts from you, Rhorkanterannu."

I make a face. She only calls me my full name when she's angry with me. "Don't be angry."

"I *am* angry. I thought I was gonna die and meanwhile, you *planned* for me to be attacked and you knew Mathilda was here, didn't you?" There is genuine hurt in her eyes now. They are glossier than they are ordinarily.

Panicked, my lower arms reach for her, but she evades my grasp. "Deena…"

"Don't!" She shakes her head and gnaws on her bottom lip. "Don't say anything else until she and Bo'Raku are dead."

"Bo'Raku? Bo'Raku was never exiled to Kor."

Her narrowed gaze returns to my face while my blood sings through my veins. "Don't lie to me, you knew he was here."

Ah. She does not mean the recent Bo'Raku, Peixal. She means his sire. I nod. "Ontte, I knew Pogar was here, on-planet, but the last I heard, he defaulted on gambling debts and was in an Egama prison. He was there? With Mathilda? You saw him?"

Deena's anger cracks. She crosses her arms over her full breasts and raises one of her furry eyebrows. "Ontte. He was there. He spoke with Mathilda about a plan. They wanted to kidnap me, not kill me, and to use me to get off planet. You guys control the ports and they won't be able to leave without your approval, right?"

"That's right." And Deena was the key to their entire operation. And now she's here, safe, with me.

"So, they won't be able to leave now without a bartering chip?"

That doesn't sit right with me, either. The two of them working together...they are the most devious of all beings I've ever come across. It doesn't seem likely that their plan would rely on something so easily disrupted. But perhaps, they were boxed into a corner. Perhaps the Egama have something to do with this. Perhaps, the rapist Pogar and the murdering Mathilda had no other allies...no other chips...no other options.

"What are you doing that for? I don't like it." She reaches up and grabs my hand massaging my jaw and pulls it away from my face. "Is there another way they might get off planet? Because if they do, we're stardust."

I frown. "Why?"

"Because they were talking about going after the humans. They wanted to use me as a chip to get off Kor, but also as a way to get onto the colony. They think that Svera and Miari won't let the Voraxians fire on their ship if I'm on it."

"They want revenge."

"Maybe. Sounds like my darling nana also thinks she might be able to take the colony back."

I guffaw. "Preposterous."

"Ontte, well, she's crazy. We all know that. But she's definitely not going to be able to do any of that, because we're going to catch her. Right, Rhork?"

"Of course. No one leaves Kor without our knowing..."

"Rhorkanterannu! Deena!" I hear Tevbarannos's voice — not through the token, but in person. He's panting, rushing down the street, past the mob that's mostly Niahhorru at this point. He has black blood smeared across his chest and one of his lower arms looks broken or dislocated. He cradles it against his chest, teeth clamped together as he struggles to breathe through them.

"Tevbarannos!" Deena shouts, turning to face the Niahhorru with her arms outstretched. He was always one of her favorite pirates. "Shrov! What happened to you?"

"The Drakesh that took us," he heaves, skidding to a stop while the Niahhorru gathered make space around him.

Deena reaches forward and takes one of his less-injured-looking arms. "Shrov. You're hurt. Did the Drakesh do this to you?"

"Ontte," he heaves, then shakes his head as he uses her shoulder to right himself. I call for Quintenanrret in the meantime. "Centare." He nods, contradicting himself. "Not the Drakesh. Well, the Drakesh at first, but then the Egama..."

"What?" Deena and I say in the same breath. I exchange a glance with my wife and see two things that make me smile. Her worry. Her exhilaration. She has not forgotten how much fun it was fighting Egama-Sky mercenaries that very first time.

Stars, my female is perfect.

I reach out and touch her neck, pulling her away from Tevbarannos as Quintenanrret appears at his side. He has a scanner in hand and passes it quickly over Tevbarannos's limp arm, finding the break and then repairing it just as quickly.

"Thank you," Tevbarannos says, sucking in his next breaths a little more easily.

"The Egama," Deena presses at the same time I say, "The Drakesh." The smile we exchange this time is pure fire.

Stars, my female is a perfect pirate.

"So. The Drakesh took us. I didn't understand where they were taking us at first, because they didn't seem to be ready to kill us, even though they could have, right away. Instead, they took us to one of the Niahhorru ports."

"Which one?" I ask.

"South Star."

South Star? "Interesting," I muse. The North Star port is where the mothership is housed. If the Drakesh were trying to overtake a ship, I would have assumed it would be that one. Of course, they'd have gotten nowhere in it, because that ship is anchored to me and can only leave planetside when I'm at the manual controls in the command center.

"Right. So they took us to the South Star port and then they tested all of us against the yeeyar reader until they got to Herannathon."

"I see. Herannathon's ship is docked there?"

"Ontte." He winces and clutches his side while Quintenanrret mutters curses and insults and tells him to be quiet and let him seal his wounds without complaint. The rebuke ends in a small shoving match between them.

Deena groans, "Oh for shrov's sake! Pirates, focus!"

Tevbarannos's mouth twitches and several of the pirates standing around listening on chuckle. She shouts again. "Would you just finish the shroving story? Where are they now? Why did they want Herannathon to open the key to his ship?"

"Because Herannathon, the filthy pirate," he says it as an insult, though in Meero, such a term is only ever an endearment, "*stole* one of the females in the tanks. The human females, I mean. I mean he stole the shroving tank! He had it on his ship and the Drakesh knew about it. They tried to unload it with the help of two Egama mercenaries and they might have succeeded if your Eshmiri friend, Ashmara, and her crazy horde hadn't shown up. They blasted the shrov out of the Egama, wounding one of them.

"The Drakesh killed the injured Egama — I guess, so he wouldn't talk — but instead of unloading the tank, they were cornered and just all piled onto Herannathon's ship and took off."

"Shrov!" I bark. "They took Herannathon with them?"

"Ontte."

I'm less furious with the fact that they stole one of my pirates then I am with the fact that stealing my pirate means that they have what they need to be able to take his ship off planet. That tank is as good as lost to us now.

"How did this happen? Shroving Herannathon!"

"I've never seen him like that before," Tevbarannos says. "He was losing his mind. Said that the tank belonged to him. He was talking about the sleeping female inside like you talk about Deena."

"Huh," Deena says, eyes wide. "You think he's in love with her already? He doesn't even know her?"

"It doesn't matter," I mutter, trying to refocus these pirates, though Deena's assessment is correct and Herannathon's behavior, odd. "What matters is whether or not we can find that ship again. The cloaking device on Herannathon's ship is strong."

"Ontte. That's why I had to come to tell you in person. The Drakesh took our tokens. But Ashmara and her reavers took Rhegaran and Ewanrennaron to track the ship. They're on its trail."

I exhale, slightly more relieved than I was, "Good. We'll go after them while you clean up this mess and find me Pogar and…"

"Hey! They're not here!" The voice of one of my pirates shouts up from the open hole carved out of the building Deena emerged from. I squint and see Nikkowerranorru standing in the opening holding a blow torch in one hand and, in another, a radium knife. He shrugs. "Your traitors are gone."

"What?" Deena shouts, starting forward. "I saw them both go up the stairs. And I shot Mathilda twice. She can't have gone far."

"Ontte. There's red blood on the stairs. You musta tagged her good. But there's no body. There's an opening though in the wall where it looks like they might have tunneled out, except it just leads to the alley behind this one. Big alley though."

"Big enough for a ship?" I ask.

"Ontte." He nods, gesturing back towards the house with his blowtorch. "And there's scorch marks on the ground."

"Interesting." I frown and quickly fire on my token. "Gerannu? Gerannu, what's the status of the mothership? Any communication requests come through to you to allow a ship to travel off planet?"

There's static. *Static.* "What the shrov is going on? Did you build faulty tokens using out of date yamar?" I tap the token in my ear, as if that might encourage

Gerannu to speak through it. "Nikkowerranorru. Why can't I get through to Gerannu?"

The male steps through the opening and approaches us with one hand raised. The other is fiddling with a circular device built directly into the skin of his lower left wrist. I've never seen this device type before and ask him about it.

"Experimental tokens. We meshed some yeeyar bits with something we bought off the Lemoran."

"They're a primitive species."

He nods. "They are. But their crystals aren't."

Suddenly an image flares to life, bright as a flame, above the disc on his wrist. In it, I can see a face. Gerannu's. And it's covered in black blood. All that's visible are his teeth, because he's grinning. "It took you long enough to think to use this channel to get through to me Nikkowerranorru," Gerannu hisses.

I step forward and grab Nikkowerranorru's wrist. I speak directly into the token. "What the shrov is happening up there?"

"Mutiny. Erobu let twenty Egama mercenaries on board and then gave permission to a series of ships to take off from Kor. The warriors they sent were Egama *females*. Their cries disabled us. Their jammer took out our tokens but I managed to tap into the yeeyar of the ship and rig up a scrambler. After that we managed to take back the command center, but we couldn't stop them from opening the hangar and stealing a dozen of our battle cruisers. We're tracking them here and they're making good progress towards your planet, Deena."

"Shrov." My curse is complemented by the curse of a dozen or more pirates who can hear this.

"We need to alert the humans," Deena says.

I balk. "Against Niahhorru battle cruisers your Voraxian allies don't stand a chance."

"Then we need to give them one."

"It's risky, Rhorkanterannu," Gerannu says. "We don't want war with the Voraxians."

"There won't be a war," Deena says and she starts off at a run — a waddle. "Because I'm leading the charge."

Quintenanrret starts after her first, even before I do. "Deena! You should be resting. You're in the final stages of your pregnancy."

She pulls her nano blaster from underneath her dress, points it at Quintenanrret's feet and shoots between them. He jumps into the air and I grin so hard it feels like my cheeks are composed of stone and are cracking right up the middle. "If you *dare* suggest that I don't join you on what is sure to be the most exciting battle of my lifetime, then you are even crazier than Nikkowerranorru."

"What did I do?" Nikkowerranorru shouts behind me.

"Quintenanrret, step aside or issue a challenge," Deena says, rising up onto her tip toes. "I will fight you."

Quintenanrret beams and my heart swells with pride. I step up behind my mate and place two hands on the center of her back. "You will monitor her every step of the way," I say, maintaining Quintenanrret's gaze, "But this is the pirate who will lead us this solar. Follow her."

We hurry down the streets, Deena opting to allow me to carry her, for once, so that we make better time. As we board the mothership and I issue orders to pirates to clean up the mess made by the mercenaries and Erobu, and for Quintenanrret and his apprentice healers to assist Gerannu and the others who've fallen, Deena heads directly to the control room, takes the primary seat and begins tapping into the controls. I kneel before her as the ship rises up into the sky, away from Kor's surface.

She wears a grim expression that unsettles me. "What is it? This is sure to be a shroving good time. You should be pleased."

Deena meets my gaze. Her eyes dazzle in their intensity and their verve. I place one hand on her knee, another on her belly, and then skim her jaw with a third. She takes my fourth free hand in between both of her palms and says to me quietly so that no one can hear, "Rhork."

"Deena, my mate."

"Why didn't I kill her before?"

"What are you talking about?"

"I had a chance. One single chance just now when she took me captive. I didn't know about the shield you gave me and I thought she was going to kill me and our kits, but I still hesitated. I had my finger on the trigger, but I hesitated. And then when I shot her, I missed."

I bring her hands to my mouth and kiss all the knuckles. The ten of them that there are. "You are a pirate, Deena, not a killer. Pirates are still able to feel. Still able to love. That is something that killers can't do — killers like your kinswoman."

She sucks in a breath, looks deep into my eyes, nods once and then again with more conviction. "So, it isn't wrong that I want to blow her out of the sky?"

I grin rakishly and squeeze her every place that we touch. "Centare. She is a female who has long outlived her welcome in this lifetime."

Deena releases a shaky laugh, then nods resolutely. "Pogar, too."

"Him perhaps even more than her."

Deena turns to the controls and begins drawing up coordinates that will take us to the human's moon. Not her human moon, to be sure, because her place is always, has always been and will always be with us. "Let's blow them both to dust."

"I follow your lead, pirate."

"Good." She swivels in her seat, releasing me everywhere and rising to stand, one hand on her belly and the other on her lower back. "Nikkowerranorru!" She shouts across the command center. From the chaos, the pirate appears at her side.

"What is it?"

"I need you to show me to the controls for the cannons. The biggest ones you've got. And can you break through the life drives and access the communication tokens of the Voraxians?"

He makes a face. "Cannons, I can do. Communications, I can't from here. They're better protected than that."

"Can you send a signal of any kind?"

"I can get you through, but only when we're in range."

"Good. Then get me through."

"Whose communication token should I try for?"

"The queen's."

16
Deena

"Shrov! There are so many of them!" Banging hits the outside hull of our ship for the bagajillionth time. Quintenanrret has strapped me into the command seat, refusing to allow me to get up and storm around the command center like the other pirates are doing, but limiting me to the controls built into the armrest of my command chair.

Rhork streaks past one way, shouting, "It's the most frustrating feeling in the world, being fired on with my own shroving ships!"

Gerannu shakes his fist at him from the seat across from me. "Those are *my* ships! I built them!"

"This is *my* ship, I built this one! Don't you know of any way to override them from here?"

"Centare," Nikkowerranorru tosses into the mix. "They're built autonomously."

Gerannu says, "But there is a failsafe. We could tap into their yeeyar communications and broadcast through their ships."

"And what? Appeal to their reason?" I shout as another crash bangs the yeeyar and a splinter stabs my

238

mind as the yeeyar token in my ear reacts to what's happening to its larger counterpart surrounding us.

"We just need to distract them for a few seconds. If we had a break from the cannon fire for even a moment, then we could use the destabilizer! It would stall twenty of their ships at once."

Even though our ship is larger than all of theirs combined, the dear sweet bitch that is my grandmother and her red-skinned rapist ally somehow managed to get together a mercenary army of forty freaking ships. Meanwhile, we've got the mothership and a dozen more ships on our side, but the combined firepower of their ships — *our* ships that they stole — is pretty formidable. I'm starting to wonder if going to the humans' rescue was such a good idea for me and mine.

Then I glance around.

Just like Rhork promised, everybody here is having a shroving good time.

And so am I.

"What about a song?" Tevbarannos shouts.

I brace as I'm jostled around again, then shout back, "You want us to sing to them?"

"Worth a shot. Everybody ready? Good. Now sing!" Nikkowerranorru's words fire to life just as the token line opens between all of us. I can't make out whose voice it is that starts up first, but sure enough they're wailing at the top of their lungs the miserable song I made up.

"If you lift your green leaves up to the sun, then you'll grow big and strong." Overlapping voices make this song an immediate mess. "Plants sway in the breeze created by the wind and even when there's no wind...

they find a way to rise again…" I start to laugh. Really laugh. And soon I'm not the only one.

Our ship shakes again and I can't decide if it's just me, the combined laughter of everyone, or an actual explosion. "Stop…" I howl. "It's so bad…"

"It's terrible!"

"Worst song I ever heard."

"I kinda like it…"

"Plants rhymes with *this isn't working at all*!" I shout over the sound of the other pirates talking about my deplorable songwriting skills and the sound of the next cannon exploding against the ship, this one hitting the view pane in a beautiful pink explosion.

The shield shimmers through the viewer, beyond which, I can see a brown speck coming closer and closer against the Voraxian galaxy behind it. Between us and it is a swarming fleet of little ships that look like insects, at the smallest, like boulders at the largest. Or maybe that's just what it feels like they're flinging.

"We need backup!" I shout.

"On it," Rhork says, lifting a hand to his token and shouting at the mysterious reaver called Ashmara. "Ashmara, where are you?" I can't hear what she says, only Rhork's answer. "Redirect. We need support out here… It's alright. Herannathon will rescue the female in the tank…If his feelings towards that female are even half so bright as mine are to Deena, then centare, I don't question his strength in this…Ontte, I am a sentimental shrov…now, get the shrov back here! We need a diversion…"

He continues explaining the particulars to her while Nikkowerranorru rushes to my side. "Got it."

"Got it?"

"A line through to the queen." He extends the flat disc on his wrist towards me and I'm shocked when I see Miari's face floating above it.

"Holy xok!" She shouts. "Deena, is that you?"

"Yes, it's me!" I say, switching to Human, surprised by how out of use and out of date my mother tongue feels. I clear my throat. "Are you on the colony now?"

"No, I'm in Illyria, but Svera is. But Deena, are you safe? Can we rescue you…"

"Shut up, Miari! Sorry, but no. I'm not in trouble. I'm a pirate. I'm pregnant. I'm mated to Rhorkanterannu and right now we're trying to save everybody on the colony's freaking life!"

"What?" Her expression shifts, her red face going from worried to terrified. "What's going on…"

"You idiots exiled Mathilda instead of killing her and now she's formed an alliance with the old fucker, Bo'Raku!"

"Bo'Raku? But he's…"

"No, no, no. Not him. His dear old dad, Pogar. And now Pogar and my dear old gramma have amassed a mercenary army and are coming to try to take the colony back! We're fighting them now…still in the grey zone, but we're incoming too fast and we aren't going to be able to stop them before they reach the colony surface unless y'all send backup…"

I can hear a male's voice in the background rumbling something about a trap.

Feeling manic and hysterical, I shriek, "This isn't a trap! I'm serious! You need to put me through to Svera! Or you need to warn her! We can't hold on much longer and I'm mondo preggo. I'm not going to let my little kiddos die for you guys, so if y'all want to live, then you need to trust us pirates."

Miari pauses, but only long enough for me to see a range of emotions flash behind her eyes and then crystalize into a single decision. One she voices when she says, "We're coming now. Hold the line. I'm opening my life drive and patching you directly through to Svera."

A moment passes. Another boulder hits our view pane and shatters to brilliant purple on impact.

"Hold on!" Corvenarennu shouts, and I can feel as he and the other navigators pull deep in the token world and redirect the ship into a dizzying dance, one that makes my stomach lurch up into my mouth and makes me feel like I'm about to pee myself. I think I do pee myself a little bit at that and I laugh wild and recklessly.

"What?" Rhork says, appearing at my side. "Are you alright?"

Another spray of cannon fire is followed by a chorus of cheers from the pirates in the control room. "Never better. What's going on?"

"What's going on?" Svera says at the same time.

Rhork answers us both. "Hello Svera, pleasure to see you."

"Rhorkanterannu! If you've done anything to Deena…"

"Deena here. And no, he didn't do anything to me except knock me up and make me a pirate."

"You were already a pirate," he says, bending forward to kiss the tip of my nose.

"There's no time for this!" Miari shouts, severing the moment. *Sigh… Lucky for me, I plan to make sure that there are many, many more.* "Svera, Deena appears to be mated to Rhorkanterannu and right now they're only a few clicks away from the Heimo colony. Apparently, Mathilda and the exile, Pogar, are fast approaching with a mercenary army. I'm sending the scans to Krisxox now. Is he there with you?"

"Of course." And then in the viewer, I see a red-faced male appear with bright white hair holding two little tiny infants in each of his arms.

"Oh em geeee!" I shriek. "You had a baby?"

"Twins," she answers. "Miari gave birth as well."

"Congratulations!" I shout while Krisxox, looking into the life drive and, seeing Rhork, snarls, "I'm going to skin you alive."

Svera places her hand on his chest, absently giving him a couple distracted pats. "There won't be any of that now."

"Do you have any idea what he cost us? What he could have done to you?"

"He's right to want my skin, but unfortunately, I have no desire to give it," Rhork chimes.

"He's trying to help us," Svera says.

"This is obviously a lie. He's manipulated Deena…"

"Hey!" I roar, slamming down my fist, which only makes me squirm as I feel like I'm peeing even more. "I'm not manipulated. I'm running shit here! So shut up and help us!"

Krisxox snarls — at me this time — and Rhork grabs Nikkowerranorru's wrist like he'll break it. Nikkowerranorru punches him in the chest with another hand and Rhork lets go and I shush him up in time for Miari to say, "She's telling the truth. Look at the scans! You need to get Xhen'Raku's ships in place and bring up the shields."

"Shields!" This time it's Nikkowerranorru shouting incredulously at the queen, "We need cannons! Big shroving cannons!"

"If we fire, how will we know which ships are yours and which aren't?" Miari asks.

And then a male appears in view behind her. With blue skin and black hair, I recognize him as Raku, king of Voraxia. He's glaring at everything caustically, and even though my male is unsettled and unseated by nothing, I can still feel him tense slightly at my side.

"Rhorkanterannu," Raku says in a deep grumble.

"*King*," Rhork sneers out an insult — an insult to any Niahhorru pirate, anyway.

I punch him lightly in the stomach. "Play nice," I mumble.

Raku says, "It would appear that we're locked in a temporary truce."

"Very temporary," Rhork answers at the same time that I say, "Not that temporary." And Svera says, "It could be more." And Miari says, "A truce between us would be productive. And if Deena's running things that side, then I say we've got a good chance of making it happen. It's called moving on, something we humans know quite a lot about. Because even though Rhorkanterannu has done terrible, terrible things, can you not say the same of your own kind's behavior towards us? If anything, the Voraxians have done much greater harm and much more damage to the humans than the Niahhorru have. And humans, we can see now through Mathilda's actions, have done equal damage to what you Voraxians have done.

"So if these Niahhorru pirates can save our colony now and if Deena vouches for them *truly*, then it's something we should consider. Old wounds are better left as scars. Don't you agree? Or should we rehash the past now and leave the colony we've spent a rotation building back up to ruin?"

Miari's tone is stone, her gaze even and level as she stares at her mate. Her Xiveri Mate. And even though he might be king and totally, just a little terrifying, I understand exactly why she's queen and capable of withstanding or perhaps, taming, his might.

She has might of her own to rival it.

And as she stares at him, colors wash over his face in an expression of emotion only shared by Voraxians — bright lights that appear above his eyes where eyebrows should be, turning his face first neon yellow now before the color is disrupted by a smidge of grey. From the little I know of Voraxians and their colors, that combination of colors means something like shame.

He flicks his gaze back to us through the viewer just as another explosion rocks our mothership.

"The Rakukanna has spoken. We will proceed for now, with trust. Arm the battleships, Krisxox. Take to the skies. Don't let anything touch the colony soil."

"I won't," Krisxox grumbles. "I'd still like to skin him, though…"

As Svera issues some kind of response, I'm distracted by shouting behind me. More cheers go up. "Did we take out another ship?"

"Looks like we didn't. Your Eshmiri friend did, Rhorkanterannu," Tevbarannos shouts over to us from controls built into the wall.

"Ashmara," Rhork says to what looks like no one. He grins with one side of his mouth. "Give me a moment. Let me patch you in…"

"What? Centare!" She's still talking as her face appears in the viewer.

"Holy shrov!" I shout out loud. "Is that..." But my words are drowned out by Krisxox's snarl, "Ashmara, you filthy pirate!"

"Why, thank you," she answers. "You're looking better than you were the last time I saw you."

"Forget about shroving Rhorkanterannu, *you* are the one I'm coming for. I'm going to rip out your lying tongue!"

"You'll have to catch her, first," Rhork says. "Not an easy task considering the Sky bounty hunter who holds her contract has been trying for rotations. Is he close?"

Ashmara shakes her head, white curls fluttering around her face as she glances over her shoulder at something — someone. "Nah. Not even a little. And while I'm enjoying this family reunion here, my ship's not made out of yeeyar, so if y'all have a shroving plan, please get on with it! We can't take another hit!" Her whole body sails out of the frame of the viewer for a moment, before cutting back in. This time it's an Eshmiri's face in the viewer and he's shouting angrily at all of us in Eshmiri. Well, giggling.

Their line cuts off and Rhork issues orders to deploy the destabilizer. "Wait!" I shout, shoving up and out of my chair as I head to the view pane while Quintenanrret shouts at me to sit back down. "Won't we hit Herannathon and the human?"

"Shrov! Ashmara, is Herannathon's cruiser anywhere in the vicinity?"

"Centare," she grumbles and her face appears over Nikkowerranorru's wrist again. This time, she's got her chin tipped up and a bottle trapped between her fist. She upends clear liquid into her mouth, letting some of it drip down the long column of her throat. It's a smooth, flawless dark brown, just like the rest of her skin. She's stunning.

And she's also *definitely* not Eshmiri.

This chick is half-human.

With white hair like the Drakesh and white eyes that lack a pupil, she looks like she got to pick the most random pieces of alien and human anatomy and shove them altogether. I'm momentarily annoyed Rhork didn't tell me.

She finishes draining the bottle then releases a satisfied sigh before chucking the glass over her shoulder. "They looked like they were heading into Quadrant Five. At least, towards it. Can't get more specific than that. But what about us? When are you deploying that machine?"

I glance over my shoulder at Nikkowerranorru who looks at Gerannu who looks at Corvenarennu at the controls who gives us all an apologetic shrug. "Was I not supposed to deploy it already?"

"Shrov! Tintin, get us the shrov out of here," Ashmara shrieks over her shoulder before turning back and shaking her fist at us through the communicator. "You assholes! I'll send your pirates back to Kor in shooters or in body bags if we make it out of this..."

Her voice cuts off and I stand with both palms pressed against the viewer as I watch one little nut-sized ship zig zag wildly away from all the others. It comes closer to us as it moves and I get a better look at the ship being flown by the Eshmiri reaver who is somehow, also partially human. It's a piece of crap. I make a face and Rhork, at my side, laughs.

"It is a piece of crap. The Eshmiri aren't known for anything other than their cloaking technology. Ashmara's ship is all metal."

"Why didn't you tell me she was half-human?" She could be my sister. The thought makes my heart hurt.

"She asked me not to."

"Why?"

Rhork shrugs and turns his gaze towards the view pane and the destabilizer activating beyond it. It looks like a huge shimmery net stretched across the expanse of the cosmos. From here, it appears to be moving so, so slowly, but the ships that are trying to move away from it, can't. Like a net, they seem to be caught by it, their cannon fire quickly absorbed into the blue and sending shimmers sparking every place an explosion should be. The net passes over the first ship, sweeping straight through it, but what it leaves behind is a shell that's completely dark. There are no lights, no energy, no power.

As I watch this, mesmerized, Rhork says simply, "She is an Eshmiri reaver. Just like you are a Niahhorru pirate. It doesn't matter the body she was born into."

I nod, understanding, and feeling more sure than ever that that female might just be a sister Mathilda and Pogar stole from me. "She'd make a great sister."

Rhork sucks in a breath and glances down at me. "You think she is?"

"Ontte. I can feel it."

Rhork's expression falls and this marks one of a limited number of times I've ever seen him unsmiling. "Does it pain you?"

I nod, returning my gaze back to the ships as Rhork gently combs his fingers through my locs. He's been helping me tighten them, says he finds it therapeutic. I think he just does it to hear the pleasure sounds I make when he's gently pulling on my hair and massaging my scalp.

"A little. Makes me think of my mom. From what I remember, she was a fearsome woman. A loving, wonderful woman. I'm just sad that my sister never got to meet her."

"Then perhaps you can give her new life now by ending the life of her killer."

My chest tenses. Rhork drags his fingers over the yeeyar view pane and a handful of controls flower beneath his fingertips. He expands the scanner and I can see clearly as he zooms in on one of the ships. He taps it twice and suddenly — shockingly — I can both see and hear *into* the ship.

"We only have a few more moments before the ships are released from the destabilizer and can reactivate their controls. If you plan to end her, you'll have to do it now, Deena."

My thoughts blank, my heart squeezes and sputters, my stomach turns, and I feel all the babies in my stomach kick at once, or maybe it's just my intestines turning. "I...how?"

Rhork drags another control closer to me, this one a dark square large enough for me to flatten my palm against it. "Just lay your hand there and will the command through the yeeyar. I will confirm your request..."

"So will I." I jump and see Tebvarannos behind me. Behind him is Gerannu, Nikkowerranorru, Corvenarennu, Walleenonnu, Reffarannu, Berreto, Tarrowrennan, Terronathon, Tennora, Quintenanrret. A dozen others. They're all murmuring and smiling at me and rubbing their hands together. It's Tevbarannos who puts his hand on my shoulder first. Then Quintenanrret places his hand on my back. Nikkowerranorru puts his hand directly on top of my head and when the others look for places to reassure me without Rhork punching them, I start to cry. I start to laugh.

Rhork has hold of my right hand. He gives it a squeeze and leans down and says against my cheek. "Family is not bound by blood. Family is bound by love. You are and have always been a pirate. You are and always will be loved by each and every one of us."

I look at Mathilda through the screen. She and Pogar are shouting at each other. She's holding onto her side, bleeding. He's holding a knife out towards her, but he's looking worse than she is, covered in coppery blood from his right shoulder to his right ankle. Whatever she shot him with must have hurt because he's staggering with every third step as they circle each other, debating whether or not to try to land on the colony, even if their army doesn't make it past the Voraxian defenses.

Pogar wants to land. This is clearly a mission with a solitary purpose — wreak as much havoc as possible, even if he dies in the process. Meanwhile, Mathilda wants to evacuate, escape, regroup and try again another time. *I can't let her live. Every other life in the good and glorious galaxy is in danger if she does.*

I lift my hand and try to remember what it was like to have her for a grandmother. Were there any good times? When she broke my leg? When I discovered that she killed my mom? When I cried myself to sleep when I was small and she stood in my bedroom doorway and did nothing but watch me and tell me how disgusting I was?

I had a nightmare three lunars ago and woke up to Rhork, Quintenanrret and Herannathon all standing over me singing me my own song about plants. I rolled with laughter, almost falling right off the net, then we all got up and, even though it was the middle of the lunar, they took me to an underground river party where we drank and danced the lunar away. Well, they drank. I ate.

Family is love. Mathilda is not love. Mathilda is only evil.

"Hate to rush you, pirate, but you've got to the count of fourteen before the destabilizer loses its effect," Corvenarennu says.

I exhale and place my palm to the square. I will my command through the yeeyar in my token and can feel as that command is confirmed by the pirates standing around me and by the pirates all across the ship. I glance up and Rhork's stare is fixed on the image of Pogar and Mathilda stabbing at one another with their hate and vitriol, but my stare is fixed on him. I feel the rumble of the ship as the cannon prepares to fire and as it fires, I whisper, "I love you."

He doesn't respond right away. Instead, I'm left to watch a bright purple explosion flare in the reflection of his gorgeous silver eyes. He blinks and it's gone when he looks at me.

"Is it over?" I squeak.

He touches my cheek. "She will never hurt you again."

I exhale shakily, not sure how I feel. Nodding and swallowing down the knots in my throat, I turn, only to find myself immediately surrounded. "We are sorry, Deena."

"If it makes you feel any better, we're going to have fun shooting Erobu's ship out of the sky."

"Oh ontte. Have you located it yet?"

"Ontte, it's here. Who wants to shoot?"

"Me!"

"Centare, me."

"Rhork should do it," Tevbarannos says. "Or Deena."

"Deena already got to have her fun. Let me."

"It wasn't fun for her, it was her kin," Rhork snarls around at whoever last spoke. More hands come around me, dozens of them, fighting for place as they murmur weak apologizes. I start to laugh with how hard they squeeze until Rhork forcefully bats them all away. "Stop handling my mate like that." He grabs my shoulders and steers me towards the chairs in the center of the command center while issuing orders to the other navigators to hunt down the scheming Erobu and the fleeing Egama mercenaries. No reason to stop the fun now, I think with a small, sad chuckle.

"Are you alright?" Rhork says to me as he steadies me against the rapid movement of the ship chasing clusters of Egama mercenaries away.

I open my mouth to respond when Gerannu shouts, "Would you all stop firing the incinerators! For shrov's sakes those are expensive battleships! Destabilize them, then we can use the reverse transporter Nikkowerranorru and I rejigged to pull the ships back onto the mothership. Then we can battle the Egama hand-to-hand!"

Murmured assent crops up all around us, but one voice is slightly louder than the others. Sprinting past my seat, Tevbarannos shouts, "I'm heading to the hangar! I'll be the first one to bag an Egama." His knees lock. He looks at me and gets all bashful as he extends his blaster my direction. "Unless, you think bagging the first Egama would make you feel better, Deena?"

I laugh and snort simultaneously, which makes Rhork laugh and Tevbarannos smile. "Centare, I think I'm okay. You go ahead."

He shrugs and starts towards the doorway while several others grab blasters and brush past him in their effort to get there first. "Alright then, I'll bring you an Egama head when I come back…"

"You don't have to do that either!" I roll my eyes, but he doesn't hear me because he's still speaking.

"…and a new tunic. Though I don't have any of the gormar fabric you like."

"A new tunic? What for?"

"Ontte. For your wet spot. Did you sit on something or did you…" He pauses, then makes a face. "Did you get scared and pee your pants?"

"What?"

"What!" Rhork turns me around in the most embarrassing display ever and lifts up my dress so that the base trails around the backs of my calves. Then he *sniffs* it. "It has no color, so it isn't blood and it has no scent so it isn't piss. What is this? What did you sit in?" He strides over to my chair and curses. "It's here, too. Gerannu, what sort of malconstruction is this?"

Gerannu balks, "That isn't mine…" And the two males start arguing about this and other constructions that, in the past have gone wrong — or haven't.

Meanwhile, I palm the space over my ass in concern as I also realize that the liquid coating my butt is drying on the insides of my thighs. And that's when my brain and belly start to churn.

I gasp. "Shrov the saints!" I grab my stomach and my toes curl and I hallucinate that moment with Mathilda in that house with Pogar all over again. "I'm shot!"

Time stands still, and then throttles forward all at once, with pirates tripping over themselves to arrive at my side. Everyone lifting their weapons in search of the enemy. Pointing their blasters around at each other and everyone accusing everyone of treachery. Rhork arrives at my side and palms my chest and my stomach in a way I'd ordinarily find quite pleasurable, but don't.

"What is it? Where is it? I don't see any marks..."

And then Quintenanrret, bless his bawdy, pirate heart, sends a screeching tone blasting through all of our tokens simultaneously. Everybody buckles, including me, and in the brief silence that follows — punctuated only by curses and groans of pain — he shouts, "Let me through!" He starts shoving pirates left and right until he arrives in front of me where he drops to one knee. He presses two hands against the bottom of my stomach and then grins up at me from this strange position of genuflection.

"Deena, you've gone into labor." And then his smile falls and his eyes widen in what can only be described as pure panic. Which isn't exactly great since *he's* the healer. "Deena's gone into labor!"

"Deena's gone into labor!"
"She's what?"
"Labor!"

"What's that?"

"Babies are coming!"

"Kits?"

"Kits are coming!"

Rhork, at my side, starts to stagger to the side and might have fallen had Nikkowerranorru not been at his side and caught him. Rhork blinks many, many times. So many times I start to laugh. Panic-laugh, but laugh all the same. Kits rhymes with wits. Because mine seem to be scattered. Lost to the chaos of Kor that exists wherever pirates are, no matter the planet.

"I'm going to be a father?" He asks Quintenanrret, but the healer just grimaces.

"Not if we can't get Deena to a medical facility — and fast. We don't know what birthing looks like for a human female and I don't have any of my equipment here."

As he starts speaking, a pain — well, more like a discomfort — squeezes my stomach where my ovaries usually live. Or maybe lower. I can't really tell. But I start to feel immediately dizzy. "Is dizziness part of it?"

"Shrov! Centare, it isn't. Rhork, she's early. I don't know if this is normal for a human giving birth to Niahhorru babies or not. We need a facility…"

"I need to sit down."

"We're far from Deena's beach planet," Corvenarennu says.

Rhork shouts back as several hands lower me gently into a seat. Hands keep trying to offer me things and someone has the audacity to offer me black fil. I grab it and launch it across the room as hard as I can. "No fil! I will smash your face if you try to give me any of this again, then I'll give birth to these aliens inside of me and they'll smash your face, too!"

"Idiot," somebody says and laughter crops up somewhere in the crowd, arguing too, of course.

The discomfort subsides, but the dizziness doesn't. I hold my head in my two meager hands and close my eyes. "Nikkowerranorru?"

"Ontte, Deena, I'm here."

"Is Svera still there?"

"Centare, but I can get her back quickly."

I nod. "Maybe do that. Rhork?"

"You want to land," he says, dropping to his knees at my feet and placing his palms on my calves and belly.

"Ontte. I think there's a birthing facility on the human colony."

Silence. Then a moment later, Svera's voice cuts in. "Oh! You're back. We thought we lost you forever. Oh. Stars! Deena, are you alright?"

"I'm dizzy…"

"She's gone into labor," Quintenanrret answers on my behalf. "We need to make use of your medical facilities to help her deliver…"

"This feels like a trap…" Krisxox says again while Rhork damn near loses his mind at my side.

Svera, luckily, has the force of presence to say, "Krisxox, shush. Grant them permission to land. You'll need an escort. Our fighters are still trying to round up the last of the Egama."

"Round them up?" I wheeze as another dizzy spell washes over me. "Why aren't you just shooting them out of the sky?"

"Because we'll give them trials."

"And then send them to Kor?"

Her jaw works at that and she has decency enough to blush. "Alright, we'll figure out what to do with them when you land. An escort is on its way. Can you wait another quarter solar for us to get to you..."

Rhork cuts her off with a condescending scoff, "We don't need an escort to reach your planet. We'll use our machine and be there in less than a blink. Just make sure the space directly south of your medical facility is clear because we're incoming in the next five...four...three... two..."

17
Rhork

We exit the mothership — all eighty of us — and storm towards the medical facility with blundering force. The Voraxian and human soldiers awaiting our arrival are quickly overwhelmed, which is fine. We aren't here to fight. We're here to celebrate and bring little hybrid kits into the world. Deena leads the charge — in my arms — and Svera rushes out to meet us even though her mate attempts to block her at every turn.

He fails.

I start to wonder if *all* of these human females don't have a little space pirate in them, though certainly none are more pirate than mine is. Deena is shouting orders even as I bring her from the surface of the hot dusty rock these humans occupy into a silver lift and take her down a long hallway decorated in vibrant colors and into a room that is...passable.

I frown around at the facility. It's perfectly pretty but I don't see any yeeyar anywhere. Are they using ancient technology here? A female Voraxian escorts Deena and I into a separate room divided from the first by a panel of glass that my pirates quickly remove so as to create a single room large enough to accommodate about twenty of them, but not more.

The Voraxian healers make sure of that. "It needs to be sterile!" The one with the strange title like Fi-lemoree or Fileee, snaps. These titles are unnecessary and confusing so, in my mind, I deem her Fifi.

"Sterile conditions are not created by allowing a horde of blood-covered pirates in...augfff!" Fifi throws her hands in the air and returns to my female lying in a plush furry nest just as another bout of pain washes over her. "I'm familiar with Niahhorru birthing, but only through study, never in practice. Are any of you bloody pirates familiar..."

Quintenanrret steps forward, taking the space beside her. Even though she is a tall female, he still towers over her. He removes the gamma wand from his belt and quickly sterilizes his hands with it. He does the same to hers when she lifts her palm towards him as if to shake his hand like the humans do or offer him some kind of Voraxian greeting.

"No time," he answers and her mouth quirks.

"You're right. Her vitals are elevated and I can feel that the kits have begun to turn. But she hasn't yet had many contractions..."

"You mean this pain sensation?" He says, then shakes his head when she confirms. "Niahhorru females release their water, have three of these pain sensations, then they must push."

She nods, then checks a screen on the wall — a physical holo screen — *dear stars, what sort of technology are they using here!* "You need serious upgrades," Gerannu says, as if reading my mind. He stands at the front of the crowd, doing his best to hold others back while also glowering around at everything. "Is that an ion laser? Ion! That technology has been out of date for six rotations!"

Krisxox, who is standing close to him and also helping keep Niahhorru back and out of the way, snorts, "You pirates wouldn't know structure or organization if it stabbed you in the gut..." I meet his gaze and am surprised when his brow illuminates in shades of brown and grey, Voraxian colors that, when coupled, can mean *uncertainty*. Not bad considering a little while ago he wanted to tear out my heart.

A dozen pirate voices speak all at once and Deena laughs. "Oh stars," she says as her third pain wave comes.

Svera leaves her mate's side, much to his terror and chagrin, and starts to make her way towards me. Standing close enough to Deena to touch. I feel... uncomfortable...and clear my throat as Svera approaches, her warm shoulder coming close to brushing my outer arm. She smiles up at me and my mouth opens. Then she reaches towards my female and places her hand over our joined hands.

"All is forgiven. Thank you for taking such good care of Deena in our absence. You did a much better job than we humans ever did." And then her gaze turns to Deena and a crease appears between her eyebrows. "I'm sorry we failed you."

Deena's face twists while the Voraxian healers begin pushing Deena's dress up to reveal the slit between her legs. I feel oddly uncomfortable with pirates looking at her in such a way, but I don't dare ask them to leave. I would not deprive them of the magnitude of this moment — should everything go well, and it will. It has to. The alternative is too painful to imagine. I just squeeze Deena's hand tighter and watch as she tells her kinswoman, "I got her, Svera."

Water wells along her lower eyelid as she drops her head back and spreads her legs. Quintenanrret pushes aside the too-tall stool built to Voraxian proportions and drops to his knees. He shoulders his way between Deena's legs and asks for tools which Fifi already holds at the ready. She slaps a scanner into his palm and he brings it to Deena's stomach while his fingers probe my female's insides in a way that makes me want to snap those fingers clean off.

But Deena doesn't seem to mind. She's uncomfortable, that I gather, but she trusts him. Trust. A pirate? I sneer at the thought. There's only one pirate I trust, and it's this one holding my lower right hand. The same one who holds my heart.

Svera nods. "I saw. I'm so sorry I exiled her. I just… sorry! Alright. Just concentrate."

"Centare…it's…a helpful…distraction." Deena exhales a little more shakily. Sweat appears on her brow. Fifi mentions giving her something for the dizziness.

"Fifi, will that hurt Deena or the kits?" I ask.

She opens her mouth, then snaps it shut and smiles as she says, "Of course not. I'm here to save human lives, not harm them."

"This is no human," I answer her. "This is a pirate."

Her expression softens and she tips her head forward slightly as she brings a diffuser below Deena's nose and asks her to inhale. She does several times and when she leans back, she seems to breathe a little easier and her gaze is no longer so unfocused.

"Thanks, Fifi," Deena answers, making Svera giggle and Fifi's forehead brighten in surprise. Then Deena says to Svera, "Whatever you're feeling guilty about, don't."

"I should have killed her."

She shakes her head. "*I* needed to. I needed to see her ship blown apart in the sky and know that this solar, when I bring mine and Rhorkanterannu's kits into the world, that woman can't hurt them. I just wanted to thank you for letting us help after everything Rhork did to get us here."

Svera's cheeks redden again and she pulls back her hand. I flex my fingers, not liking the feel of her skin against mine. It tastes too much like failure, like an alternate path that could have been and would have deprived me of the female in my arms. "All is forgiven."

"The xok it is," Krisxox shouts across the room, clearly paying attention to his female's every word, even though they are speaking in Human. I'm surprised further when his next words are in Human and not in Voraxian. I can only understand them through my token. "You still need punishment!" He stabs his finger through the air at me.

I suck in a breath, prepared to defend myself and my female if it comes to blows, but it's my female who says, "I think we have something else we can offer..." Her forehead creases. She exhales in big heaving breaths. "Have you considered...ever moving off...of this rock?"

Svera makes a face. "We have, of course, but there are few safe places for us humans in the cosmos, and we can't survive the climates of the uninhabited places in Voraxia..."

Deena nods and I notice that her hand has begun to clutch mine tighter and tighter. "How…do you feel… about the beach?"

I grin, elated, shocked, pleased. "You'd give them your beach, Deena?" I say.

"It's not mine. It's for the humans, and you know as well as I do that I have no desire to babysit all those people. Let Svera do it. It can be a port controlled by humans. They can let whoever come onto it that they want so long as those beings include Niahhorru." She gives Svera a questioning look then, but Svera just frowns.

"I haven't said we'll move, of course, we have a good setup here."

"Just wait til you see it. You'll be sold on sight."

Svera smiles, then frowns, then strokes Deena's leg. "You should be concentrating on this…"

"Centare, keep talking…" She squeezes everything together. I pull her hair back from her shoulders, hoping to keep her cool, even though it is already cool in here. Surprisingly so, given this moon's awful climate. "We found the human satellite, Svera."

"You did?" She gasps. "How was it? Are they advanced? Did they treat you well?"

"Centare," Deena hacks out on a laugh. "They're carpets." Her voice twists up in a mirror of her expression. I drop to my knees and press my face closer to hers, wishing I could take her pain, or offer her anything in this moment.

"Pirate, what do you need from me?" I whisper.

"Tell me…tell Svera…about the beach…"

I smile and I tell my pirate about the beach as she brings the first hybrid Niahhorru-human kits into the known galaxy, one after the next after the next. Quintenanrret passes them off to my pirates, much to Svera's shock.

"Is that safe?" She asks me at a point, some half-solar later.

"There is nothing safer than a Niahhorru kit in the galaxy. Every pirate is its father or its mother."

Svera's mouth slams shut and she smiles at that.

It takes all lunar, but Deena manages to persevere and bring all six kits into the universe healthy and safe and on her own. I think at some point, as I look down into the little brown face of one of my own little girls, I start to sob. In fact, I think we might all be crying. Except for Deena. She's laughing like the madwoman that she is.

Svera is looking confused as she coddles one kit close to her chest — a boy. There are two girls and four boys and already the competition to name them is fierce. Lines in the sand have been drawn. Tevbarannos states that he will blast all of us if we don't name one of the kits after him. The healers have an impossible time trying to wrangle kits away from them and check them over. They appear healthy, but much, much too small for Niahhorru kits. Their tines are so soft. Like feathers. I touch the little brown cheek of the little girl in my hands and place her on Deena's chest with reluctance. I don't want to put her down.

"Shrov!" I curse as I lean away from Deena, holding my little girl. "Gerannu! Where are the atomic rings I ordered?"

"Shrov! They're on the ship! Nikkowerranorru, go get them."

"*You* go get them. I wasn't the one who forgot them…"

"Someone go get them!"

"Centare! You shroving idiot, don't take the kit with you!"

"I want to keep holding him. I barely got a turn…"

"Stars!" Svera shouts, bursting out laughing as she takes one of my babies towards her mate. I snarl and point a finger towards him threateningly, but Svera just shakes her head at me sternly, then says to her friend, still spread open on the nest trying to recover her breath as she gives birth to whatever alien thing comes after. "Are you pirates always like this?"

Deena smiles sleepily, sluggishly and caresses the soft hairs growing out of one of the kit's tiny heads. Both females got human hair and appear to have no tines, while all four boys got tines that I expect to harden to be stronger than even mine. My pride, in this moment, is limitless.

"On special occasions…they're much worse."

Svera laughs and has tears in her eyes as she returns my kit to my arms after having shown it to her mate. He nods at me and I see his hands flexing, as if he's wishing he had his own kits with him in this moment. "We'll leave you to celebrate as a family. My mate and I will return to ours and contemplate what you've told us about this arrangement. A common Niahhorru-Voraxian-Human trading ground and a new potential base for all of us Humans to live on together?"

Her gaze falls to the far wall where Fifi and Quintenanrret stand speaking about the smallest of my kits — one of the little girls. But I know that even though she may be small, she'll grow up to be like her mother —

the toughest pirate Kor has seen yet. As I watch the pair of healers, however, I notice something odd happening in Fifi's face.

Her gaze is trained on Quintenanrret with focus and her forehead...well, it's alight in a whole host of colors that I know only one way to interpret. Svera is covering her mouth with her hand, evidently already having noticed.

"Oh my," Fifi says, taking hold of Quintenanrret's arm. He stares at her agape.

"Does this mean..."

"I'm your..."

"Your my Xiveri Mate?"

The two start to grin at each other like lunatics while I stare on, stunned. This has never happened before. Has something changed for us?

Us. Voraxians *and* Niahhorru.

Or perhaps, we've never given it a chance. Perhaps, the humans have given us more than one way to reproduce — not just through their genetic compatibility, but through their ability to bring us together.

I continue to stare, agape as I reel at the possibilities that now lie before us while Svera speaks on, "It would appear that this type of arrangement will work out quite well. And you've already sold me on the concept of this beach. But, Deena, with your skills in negotiation and leadership, I think you should consider joining me and Miari in leading this effort."

"Thank you, Svera, but centare. I'm a pirate to the bone. We'll definitely have a house there to visit, but our family belongs in the stars and on Kor."

The room quiets sometime later, once the kits have been nursed and once all of my pirates find a space to sleep on the floor around this much too-small nest. I lie on my back, stabbing through it without care with my tines and I tuck our pirate babies between us, all six of them.

And as Deena finally falls to sleep in my arms and the first kit begins to cry and I prepare for the first of many entirely sleepless lunars, I take the kit outside and stand on the lift, without lowering it.

This scorching world is only warm now, made bearable by the grace of darkness. Wind slips over me, over us, offering reprieve. I keep my little kit against my chest, her head leaning against my shoulder. She is quiet now that she's outside and I know that she's a little girl after her father. She doesn't want to be contained. She wants to be set free.

I look up at the dark sky and at the brightness of so many distant planets looming against it. My ship gleams like a smooth shell against the horizon and I trace its shape with two of my arms as I speak into the shell of my smallest kit's tiny ear, "This is your ship, little Melianora. One day, you will grow to command it. You will be the most savage of all pirates. I know this because I know that you are much more than you seem.

"You are your mother's daughter. You will lay waste to armies, battle giants, discover new galaxies, build new ships, and more. Much more. And no matter where you go, and no matter how distant the galaxies are that you travel, just know that you are and will always be loved."

Twenty-eight solars later...

18

Deena

Oh shrov. Shroving golly gee wiz. Shroving gosh. Gosh rhymes with slosh, which is exactly what my belly's doing now as I stand with my palms upturned and the blaster close on my belt.

Miari hadn't wanted me to wear it seeing as we're supposed to be introducing new humans to this beach world in a non-threatening way, but I saw what those people became on the Balesilha satellite. I didn't die then and I don't shroving plan to die now.

Miari shoots me a glare as my hand twitches towards my blaster.

"I'm not going to shoot anybody," I grumble, but it might be a lie because if anybody tries to eat me, I am definitely blasting the poop out of them. I've got a lot more to lose now.

I glance towards the trees where the Niahhorru pirates are waiting. Some had wanted to hover in using Eshmiri cloaking technology, but then the Voraxians got jealous because they don't use Eshmiri cloaking shields and they wanted to see the first humans, too, and then they got into a big fight and Rhork punched Raku and then Krisxox attacked Rhork and then Gerannu and

Diekennoranu, Corvenarennu and Quintenanrret attacked Krisxox and then I attacked Raku. At this point, the Voraxians got confused since they aren't, evidently, used to fighting females. Raku let me punch him a few times. It was insulting that he refused to fight back.

But then Miari screamed at all of us to calm down and now here we are, just us three humans on the beach. Well, three *almost* humans given that Miari is a hybrid.

"Svera," she says, glancing to the trees, same as me.

Her mate is in there somewhere next to mine. The arrangements for this whole affair are tenuous at best, but what's clear is that this beach planet is a gift from the Niahhorru, protected by the Voraxians, and governed by the humans. The Niahhorru and the Voraxians will be allowed onto the planet in reasonable numbers — no more than five percent of the planet's population will be Niahhorru, and another five percent Voraxian. As the humans population grows, so will that percentage, but for now the goal is not to overwhelm them.

Them, not *us*.

I giggle out loud at the thought and Miari shoots me a funny look. She looks so odd standing here on the orange sands. Her skin is as red as the leaves on the trees and, against the orange beach, she almost blends in.

I smile at her and wave even though we're only standing a few feet apart. She just rolls her eyes and shakes her head. Tucking her brown-blonde curls behind her ear, she glances up at Svera and says, "Go ahead, Svera. Open the tank."

Blarg. That's the sound that it makes when Svera flips the switch that Gerannu prepped for us. With one touch of her human palm to the yeeyar-modified sensor, the glass front panel swings open. After that, we have to move fast. I move up to meet Svera and reach my hands into the nasty blue goop. Granted, I thought my blue shoe goop was gross at first, too, but this is much worse.

"It's sticky, Svera," I mewl.

She just gapes at me over the top of the tank. Her hazel eyes crinkle when she smiles. "You gave birth to six kits one right after the other and you're complaining about this liquid being sticky?" She laughs at my expression as I stick my other arm in, too, and shakes her head. "Tri-God help me, you truly are a strange pirate."

She smiles and pride fills up my entire bawdy pirate heart.

I find an arm in the liquid and yelp, totally freaked. Then I remember what I'm here for and I latch on. I'm stronger than Svera is so, when I pull, the female's body rises up to my side of the tank first. I use my other hand to tentatively lift the back of her skull out of the water. As soon as her face hits air, she starts sputtering and coughing, twitching and jerking.

It's freaky stuff.

Blech. Gross. Learn how to breathe, why don't chya? I'm muttering in my head. Wait, was that out loud again? Svera is giving me a disparaging look, so I assume that it was.

"Up and out," she coaches me, and I lift when she lifts and together, we pull the dripping wet body out of the goop.

The first human to be awakened in two hundred rotations is a female with medium brown skin and big, round lashless eyes. She's pretty. Even bald. And she's freaking her shit out!

With the coughs wracking her body, she can't move except for where we put her and where we put her is right at the edge of the water so that the gentle waves lap at her toes without dragging her under. The powdery sand displaces under her bottom and the hard horizon stares us down.

It's sunny today. The light is bright yellow, almost golden, and touches everything with a lovely orange tint. It contrasts wildly with the green-blue sea, which is so clear I can see small fish swimming near the ocean floor. Newly introduced by the Voraxians, the species seems to be thriving.

We both back away from her, giving her space. I'm on my feet in a crouch with my hand directly on my lightning stick now while Svera kneels beside the female totally empty-handed. Idiot. *Okay, she's not an idiot, she just hasn't met any flesh-eating carpets yet.*

As the female continues to choke, Svera eventually grows bold enough to grab the female by the shoulder. Surprising me, Svera shakes her. So, maybe I was wrong. Svera's got a little pluck.

"Hey!" Svera shouts. "Breathe. You can do it. Follow my breath."

The female turns her attention towards Svera and, while she's staring Svera down, I creep up to her… edging closer and closer and closer…and then wham! I smack my hand over her ear and shove a Niahhorru token into it. She screams. She screams a lot. Scrambling to her feet, she backs away from us, then immediately falls into the ocean, forcing Svera to go after her.

I'm not that kind.

Instead, I draw my blaster. From the beach, Miari shouts, "Comets, Deena, how many times do I have to tell you? Don't xoking shoot!"

"I'm just being cautious!"

"You're worse than the boys!" And I know she doesn't mean my sons or Svera's, but that she means the boys that I brought onto her planet. All eighty of them.

Meanwhile, Svera's managed to rise up into a crouch. The warm ocean water soaks her dress through up to the knees. She's wearing sandals, which I find funny since the sand is so soft and I took off my blue goop shoes the moment we landed. Then I'm distracted from the shoes and the boys and the babies they're carrying when the female in the water rises up onto her feet and manages to stay there.

"What's going on?" She says, or at least, that's what the token translates. "Where am I? Who are you? And what is that!" She points at Miari and releases a shriek, which makes me immediately despise her.

I actually manage to wrap my hand around the blaster and pull the trigger this time. "Deena!" Svera shrieks.

"What? I blasted above her head! She's fine! But she does *not* get to talk about Miari like that! What does she know, anyway? She's barely more than a carpet!"

Svera gives me a look that might have made me whither before, but doesn't now. Not even a little bit. "What are you talking about?"

The female is screaming full-out now, shaking and panicking. It's honestly quite boring. The only thing that riles me at all is the fact that Miari's backing away from her towards the trees, looking uncomfortable.

"FTS," I tell her, racing forward and grabbing her wrist, then towing her towards the shore. "You don't get to be made small by a would-be carpet." I shove her forward and push her so that she's standing directly in front of the human.

The human female falls back at the sight of her, but I don't let that stop me from striding forward, grabbing the woman by the upper arm and dragging her towards us. "Listen up here, toots. This lady is the queen of an entire quadrant. She's half-human, half-Voraxian. That's a species you're going to need to learn about. I'm a human and I just gave birth to some babies that are half-Niahhorru — them's be the pirates. And you, my dear, were asleep for almost two or maybe even three hundred rotations — that's almost a thousand years in your early human time — so you've got a lot of catching up to do. Not to mention, we saved your ass from being eaten by cannibals, so I'd say some appreciation and thanks are in order. Whadda ya say?"

She stares at me like a frog — *heh, just kidding* — she stares at me totally *agog*. She doesn't react. "Okay then," I say and place two fingers in between my lips and whistle through them. I whistle loud. That's just for the effect, though, because all the Niahhorru on this planet right now can hear me through my token and, one-by-one, my boys come forward. All of them.

Rhegaran, Ewanrennaron, Tevbarannos, Quintenanrret, Corvenarennu and of course, Rhork. They step out of the trees and, in each of their arms, is a squirming little cutie. My heart sings — and not a song about plants this time, but a song about my kids. My perfect little kids.

I grab the female by the hand and drag her, despite her resistance, towards Rhork. He comes forward holding our daughter, Melianora. Of all the babies born, she's the smallest and I can tell already that, even though she's only twenty-eight solars old, she's already got daddy wrapped around her little fingers. All twenty of them.

When we step up close enough, I take Melianora from Rhork, even though he looks like he's going to stroke when I do. I hold the baby against my chest and then I pass her, without warning, to the human. *Take that.*

"Oh…oh my god," she says and I roll my eyes. Yet another worshipper of the Tri-God. Svera will be thrilled. "This is a…a baby."

"That's right. And she's only half-human. She's half-alien — well, alien to *you*. And these others," I say, pointing back behind me at Rhork and the other pirates as well as Krisxox — Svera's mate — and Raku — Miari's king — and the hybrid-Voraxian babies draped over their arms. "They're also half-human."

The woman meets my gaze and I can tell she's overwhelmed because her right leg starts shaking. Looking at her, I almost feel sorry for her. She has no warriors' marks on her whatsoever. She must not have fought any battles at all before they strapped her into that tank.

I take my kit from the female and coddle Melianora close to my chest. Rhork steps up behind us and the human female looks at us…and keeps looking at us. As her stare finally focuses, I can see the thoughts in her mind turning and then solidifying into a single realization.

We are not the same species.

We look nothing alike.

We are a family.

The best, most kick ass family.

"I'm Anushka," she finally says and the corner of her mouth jerks, surprising me completely. Hope…

crushed. Because then she shakes her head and blinks rapidly. "I must be dreaming."

I groan, "Svera! Miari! I did my best."

They laugh and corral around the female called Anushka while I turn back to face my mate. The Niahhorru pirates gather around us, holding my other kits. I kiss each baby on the forehead and then Tevbarannos, too, but only because he asks for it.

We make our way further back towards the trees while Svera and Miari do more talking with the human and she does more gawking at the aliens and their kits.

"How is it going?" Rhork asks, sparing a glance at the human females some time later as they prepare to open a second tank.

I shake my head and sigh, "Who knows. I don't think that first chick is a born pirate, though. Way too easily overwhelmed."

Rhork laughs against the top of my head just as Ferannu, in his arms, starts to squeal. I swap babies with him and then Tevbarannos comes and takes Melianora and then babies are swapped all around until I'm not sure who's got a hold of who. But I don't care. I know that each of these males would die for one of my kits if they had to. Because that's what family does for each other.

"Have you heard from Herannathon?" I ask Rhork.

He shakes his head as he strokes my hair while I breastfeed the little one right there on the beach. Gently, he guides me underneath the shade of one of the trees where it's cool. Pirates come by and hand me babies periodically and periodically, I hear a scream as another tank is opened on the sandy shore. By the time the sun sets, there are a dozen new human females awake and three male tanks open, too. One of the human males is even conversing what appears to be amicably with Meghanora and the two other Niahhorru females who joined this merry expedition.

I try not to be irritated by the sight of her. It's easy though, holding Rhork's kits and when I look up into his face and see him staring at me, as if we're the only two fools on this beach.

Bonfires spring up right there on the sands and soon Niahhorru laughter and jibes are being punctuated by the unnatural sound of languages being translated from Human and Voraxian. Dang. Even the pirates and the prim and proper Voraxians seem to be getting along. That's not to say no fights break out. Of course, there are a couple. I'm pretty sure my boys start them all.

I lean my head on Rhork's shoulder and sigh as he kisses my forehead. Then my cheek, then my nose. I tilt my lips up to his and let him kiss me once more. I close my eyes and in the background, I hear the roar of the ocean.

"I'm ready," I whisper.

"Ready for what?"

"To be a pirate again."

He laughs against my lips and I shudder with desire. Knowing that my body needs to heal for another thirty solars is pure torture. Rhork pulls away first and kisses my temple, then takes the baby in my lap from me and gently cradles Gigimorannu in his lap while she softly coos herself to sleep. My babies sleep hard. Makes sense, since they're so exhausting.

"You're ready to leave already?" He asks.

I nod. "I'm a pirate. I belong in the skies, pillaging and marauding. Besides, I remember you promising me that I'd get to shoot something as soon as I was feeling better. I'm feeling better, Rhorky bear."

"Good. Because I had a few ideas to pay back the Egama who joined Pogar in his mutiny. I believe it will need to be a family affair."

I stare up into his silver eyes as he stares down into mine. Gigimorannu, who'd been softly sleeping a moment before, starts screaming like a banshee between us. Over that sound, I manage to be heard as I shout a single word up at my mate, the male I love most in all the cosmos.

And all I say is, "Interesting."

Thanks so much for joining Rhork and Deena on Kor! I hope you enjoyed their story! Reviews, even the one-liners, are very much appreciated on Amazon or Goodreads.

To get access to future books filled with hot, possessive alphas and the resilient, warrior women they worship _first_, not to mention freebies, exclusive previews and more, sign up to my mailing list at www.booksbyelizabeth.com/contact.

Until next time,
Stay interesting ¤°´´`°¤,,,ø*

Elizabeth

Continue the journey and be…

Taken to Lemora

Pagh! Raingar hates flesh peddlers more than most other things. But the female with them may be a problem because when he looks at her, his horns start to itch and his grumpy stone heart starts to beat.

Taken to Lemora: A Grumpy Alien Romance
Xiveri Mates Book 6 (Essmira and Raingar)

Available in paperback anywhere online books are sold or on Amazon in ebook or hardback

1

Raingar

"I hate these things."

"Yeffa. We know," Merquin says without looking at me over the back of her seat. Tana and Reyna are focused on the controls ahead. Bebette, on my right, scrunches her nose at me and, in an act of horror, takes a step closer and gives my shoulder a light pat and a tight squeeze.

I shove her angrily off. "Stop that!"

She just smiles back.

Tana is too busy staring out of the view pane — I know she stopped listening to me rant half a rotation ago — so I redirect my ire onto Reyna instead. "Why I was chosen as representative of our people is utterly beyond me."

"You're a clan leader," she says dryly.

"There are other clan leaders."

Reyna huffs out of the corner of her mouth, "Yeffa, good point, Raingar. That's why we're *all* here."

My face heats. I shift, my rough skin feeling uncomfortable under the Lemoran customary tunic I'm wearing. Doesn't matter that it's spun of rough catacat silk. It feels like barbed wire. I yank angrily on the collar, stretching it out so that it gapes. A small rebellion. *There.*

"Nob!" I stomp my right foot and shake my right fist around at all of them and at the translucent kintarr crystal exterior of our ship and at the stars beyond it and mostly at the monstrously gold planet looming closer and closer — *that's* the cause of the sickening sensation in my stomach.

"You all *chose* to be here. You could have sent someone else from my clan. You could have sent Gorman! He would do just fine to represent my clan. I don't speak for all of them."

"Funny," Bebette chirps in her spry, bubbly brogue, "because last I checked, you were the one who got on the ship."

I open my mouth to rebut Bebette, but I can't think of anything to thwart her insouciant, giddy logic. *I do speak for all of them. I was elected. And that's why I'm here on this blasted ship and Gorman isn't.* "Pagh!"

We near the dock and I start to pace, squirming in my skin. It doesn't fit right. Everything is tight and hot and irritated. The skin around the base of my horns itches and I reach up and rub it thoughtfully. Merquin must notice the action because when I look away from the hideous gold planet, I find her watching me thoughtfully for the first time since we left Lemora and my ranting started.

"Are your horns bothering you?" Her brows are drawn together over her wide nostrils.

Like all Lemoran, her appearance is made notable by horns, which begin above her ears and swoop down towards her cheeks, following their path before curving dramatically up and ending a good Lemoran foot's length above her head in hazardously sharp peaks. She has big hands and blocky fingers. Hair? What hair? She's got horns and rough textured skin all over. Blocky shoulders that stick up in hard ridges like she's made of rocks.

With skin that ranges from light brown to darker brown, she actually looks like a rock. We all do. And her size? Well, that doesn't help negate the rock-appearance any. She's built like a mountain. I'm a male — the only male clan chief — so I look just like her, only bigger and rockier and without the breasts. And with a larger curl to my horns. And with...uh...extra between my legs. I stand out! And because I'm male, all the other wretched species that have females that they keep tucked away want to speak to me! And I hate it!

"Nevermind about my horns. I'm not getting off the ship. You know all those stupid species with only males for rulers will come and talk to me. They don't care that I'm the youngest clan chief. I'm not going. I don't want to talk to them. I've already concluded most of the business I needed to from the holoscreens anyway. That's why they're there, after all. So that when the dire occasion calls for it, we can broker agreements with off-world idiots."

"*Most* agreements," Tana says, voice rich with impish emphasis that I don't like. I don't like it at all.

"*Practically* all. If I thought I'd have to come to these gatherings, I'd never have let you monsters install those holoscreens in my keep in the first place. You know how much I hate those things. I hate the way the dignitaries' faces press in on me from the safety of my own ohring keep. Why couldn't we just keep the old boxes? The ones you could only speak through?"

"It's more effective not to negotiate with creatures that can see us," Tana says.

"We do make quite intimidating negotiators." Bebette's gaze flicks up to my horns and she sticks her tongue out at me like something about this situation is funny, the blasted wench.

"I don't negotiate!" I jab, but Reyna talks over me.

"And think about it. If you hadn't gotten those holoscreens from the Voraxians, you'd have to do *all* your negotiating from here."

I gasp in horror. Merquin snorts. Bebette laughs. I shake my head and sputter gruffly, "I still don't like it. I don't like *any* of it!"

Reyna and Tana sigh in unison but Merquin is staring at my horns again as Reyna guides the ship into the enormous golden hangar alongside hundreds of other ships built out of so many different materials I can name and even more that I can't.

There are ships barely bigger than insect pods and some as big as mountains. A sleek ship catches my eye across the hangar. It's black exterior is *shifting*, moving around like it's got a mind of its own. It creeps me out and I know that it belongs to pirates, which surprises me. They don't usually attend these things.

"What do you think..." I start, but Merquin's stare is so intense it rips the thoughts right out of my grasp. "What?" I bark out at her as the ship banks between a monstrosity of a ship that's all pink and gold and another ship that's small and bright blue. Both most likely belong to one of the Quadrant One princes or princesses whose planet we've just arrived on. They have *sooo. many. princes and princesses*. And I hate all of them.

She squints at me while, behind her, Tana drops the bridge and the slightly more oxygenated atmosphere on our ship whooshes out into the gold-and-prince-filled world we've landed on. I hate gold. I hate princes! I hate whooshing! Pagh!

"You sure you're feeling alright?" She's got one eye slightly squintier than the other even though both eyes are locked to my horns.

I realize I'm fingering the base of my right horn, completely unaware. *I never touch my horns. What's wrong with me?* I drop my hand and cross my arms over my chest. The depth of my chest makes it difficult, but I struggle against the strain in my shoulders and bark, "My horns are fine! I'm not getting off of the ship."

The other clan chiefs roll their eyes at me and descend the bridge into the gold hangar in this gold world. Alone, I glance around at the hated clans exiting their ships in smiles and giggles and walking around the circular platforms to reach the various entrances to the golden castle that link directly from this open air dome to the many hallways that lead into the king's palace. Ironic, considering that the last king died rotations ago. Now, there are only princesses and princes. Loads of them.

My blocky hands twitch against my ribs, where I've got them tucked under my arms, as if I'm purposefully restraining them from reaching for the controls. I debate what level of pain and suffering I'd be in if I were to commandeer the ship and fly back to Lemora without the other clan chiefs. *A world of pain,* I decide, then reconsider, *Nob, not a world of pain. World*sss.

I huff after them down the ramp, shaking my fist as I shout, "Fine. But I'm not going into the castle!"

In the castle, standing at the edge of the ballroom, looking in on the horrifyingly bright colors and the hundreds of kings, queens and chiefs gathered, I growl, "Pagh! I'm not going into the ballroom!"

In the ballroom, I edge backwards, toe-heeling my way farther and farther from the crowd that's gathered until I bump into horns — Reyna's. She nudges me forward. "We all know why we're here," I hiss under my breath, "and these beings still feel like pressing their ugly faces in on one another and pretending that they care about the answers to the questions that they ask. Pagh! *'Oh, how are crops farming in Quadrant Eight?'*" I say in mock imitation of a Quadrant One prince. *"'Oh, very well? That's so lovely.'* Nob! It isn't. Don't they know that Quadrant Eight farming is impossible! The Oosa only eat synthetic foods!"

As I'm speaking, a contingent of Walreys from Quadrant Five fly close enough to be heard — close enough that I can see myself reflected in the enormous purple orbs they have for eyes. "Kintarr for sale?" Is what we hear through the translators *they* wear. We wear no translators, but we speak Meero, the universal trading language, and that's what we hear through their two-way translator boxes now.

"Nob!" I shout back in Lemoran, before shouting the word in Meero for good measure, "Centare!"

Bebette chokes back a laugh. Reyna shoves me in the back. Tana drops her face into her hand. Merquin pushes me aside and approaches the Walrey contingent with the diplomacy that I lack. "We have kintarr for sale. We sell at thirty-thousand credits per pouch, three million credits per tun, or resources and wares of equivalent value. We're interested in Walrey silk threads…"

"And Walrey honey," I blurt. It has healing properties that my clan uses both for medicinal purposes and recreational enjoyment. Its popularity is only increasing at the markets.

They reply, "Raw or treated? Treated will cost more."

"Untreated. We treat it ourselves with our own dyes, but we would like to buy some of yours, specifically the amber and yellow shades. We can't manufacture shades that light."

"And the Walrey honey," I whisper again, irritated that I'm here. Irritated that I'm negotiating. Irritated that no one is ohring listening to me!

The Walrey out front makes a buzzing sound, the transparent wings on his back flapping too quickly for me to see them at all. His thin forelegs rub together in front of his fanged maw and he nods his head. "We'll only be able to give you amber and gold. The yellow is out of season."

"Fine. But we expect at least one tun of silk and two tuns of dye for every kintarr pouch."

The Walrey's need time to confer. As their leaders turn away to face the others, I hiss, "Walrey honey." Merquin flaps her hand at me behind her back so the Walrey's can't see. I growl in a voice that's deeper, but louder, "Wal. rey. hon. ey."

"How much?" Tana leans over to whisper in my ear.

"Six pouches. I'll trade pouch-per-pouch for kintarr." She lifts both of her hairless, protruding brows, clearly surprised. Kintarr is one of the most valuable commodities in the known quadrants. To trade one-to-one for it is unheard of. But I don't negotiate. The others might, but I don't. So I pay what I can afford for what I think is the value of an item's worth.

I nod, then say, "We value it highly in my clan."

"Apparently." Her surprise releases and she nods at me once. I am satisfied my request will be taken and the order will be placed with Tana, so I use the opportunity to back out of the ring of Lemoran clan chiefs and head for the closest exit. I need air. I have no idea how I'm going to survive another half-lunar of this. That's how long it will take me to get off this planet with no shrubbery and no trees and another solar's journey after that, I'll be back on the moss-covered rock that I call home.

The ballroom entrance is guarded by a curtain. I slip behind it into a foyer that's almost entirely made of helos — a brilliant white and black stone — with chandeliers dripping from the ceilings in the shape of stalactites. Wait a second...did they make those out of... Pagh!

"The damn lights are made out of kintarr! Probably from my own ohring mine! Those are a rare energy source. Not meant for decoration!"

I'm still shouting up at the ceiling when a cheery voice booms across the room. "Raingar!"

I wince. I've been spotted. Pagh!

I growl and look sideways over the edge of my horn at the Niahhorru pirate sprinting towards me. Seeing my own horn in my peripheral vision, I realize I'm touching the base again. What the...

It's *tight*. The skin has been tight ever since we entered orbit. I wonder if it's the stress of this horrible place. Yeffa, that must be it... All I know is that I just don't like it.

"Raingar, how are you?" I notice that he's wearing the traditional grey tantu leather pants Niahhorru pirates always wear — a clear sign he's breaking with the formalities of this nonsensical affair — and I remember that he's one of the few beings here I like.

Tolerate.

Can endure.

Meanwhile, I'm trapped in this ohring tunic made out of a silk that came from a bug that lives deep in the earth of Quadrant Four and has three butts through which it excretes said silk and no eyes. "You're looking as pleased as ever," he says, spreading all four of his silver arms and beaming at me with his shiny teeth.

I grunt, upper lip lifting in a snarl.

When his smile holds, my shoulders slump forward, defeated. "What do you want?"

He doesn't answer right away, but the massive silver orbs of his eyes shift left then right. His lips stutter as he spots an Oroshi captain walking by with its guard — a *female*. The Oroshi spots Tevbarannos, too, and gives him a subtle wave of one tentacle when it passes by — a look I would never win, not even from a creature that is all green-grey tentacles and nothing else. Herannathon, another pirate I admire, once told me it's because I don't smile and look around at everyone like I'm one wrong word away from committing a brutal, bloody murder, but I know what I look like.

Like a rock.

But ohr what I look like. We Lemoran are the best species in these eight quadrants. Decent, hardworking beings with honor woven into our rocky outer skin, and threaded through the pink blood we bleed. Not like these honorless pirates with their four arms and their bright smiles, and even less like these gaudy quadrant one morons with their one thousand princes and one billion princesses, and even less like the spineless Oroshi who are, well, quite literally spineless.

"What are you doing here? Last time I saw Rhorkanterannu, he told me that he'd rather be caught in an Oosa orgy than ever come back to Quadrant One."

"Better an Oosa orgy than an Oroshi one." Tevbarannos shudders and continues watching the Oroshi until it disappears up the stairs and out of view.

I try to picture what coupling with an Oroshi would be like and immediately retreat from the image. "I suppose you're right," I huff.

Tevbarannos laughs easily. All the ohring pirates laugh easily… "I'm actually looking for someone."

When he doesn't say more, I roll my eyes. "Good luck with that." I stomp off, but he shouts after me, "You haven't seen any Egama here have you?"

"Of course I have! They're giants — bigger than I am. They're hard to miss." I wave him off and stomp towards the stairs, but he rushes after me and shocks the ohr out of me when he grips my bicep and tries to lead me somewhere to the left. "What are you doing?" I remain rooted and glare at him with a frown.

He cocks his head and gives me a pleading look, but when I still don't budge, his look turns frustrated. He crosses his lower arms over his chest, and then his upper ones on top of those. "You are a stubborn brute. Herannathon warned me about that."

I'm curious as to where Herannathon is, but the words damn themselves behind my teeth. My horns are aching again, more noticeably now. I growl and start to walk away, up the stairs where I can see Oosa rolling back and forth over the floor — they're gelatinous-looking blue beings and I hate conversing with them. They always want to have sex with each other mid-interaction! Realizing they're blocking almost the entire landing above me, my shoulders sink even more.

Suddenly, Tevbarannos is there, politely asking the Oosa to move out of his way. He catches my gaze when he has a path cleared and ushers me forward — not towards the divan with Quadrant Five warriors spread across it engaged in a gambling round of mok-biz with some Hypha delegates — bright orange creatures that walk on two feet, have two hands, and are made remarkable by the set of fins that shoot out of their heads in every direction, *and* that are the second most populous species of Lemora — but toward a less crowded hallway.

Here, he catches my elbow with his lower left hand and drops his voice to a whisper, "I just wanted to tell you that if you stick around, you'll run into Igmora and Tyto." He makes a face that I can't interpret, but when his eyes shift nervously, I frown.

"What do I care? They're flesh peddlers. We don't have any occasion to trade with them. Goodbye."

"Wait." His grip tightens on my arm. "Have you seen her?"

"Her who?"

"Their newest…acquisition." He has the decency to look embarrassed and drop his gaze as he says that.

Meanwhile, my face is burning for entirely different reasons and all of them come down to rage. "You mean the sex female they're looking to sell? Nob! I told you already, I don't deal in females. On Lemora we males believe in coming by our females the old fashioned way. Through hard-earned courtship!"

I start away again, until he says so quietly I almost miss it, "I heard that the female they have for sale is a *human*." Human...I haven't heard of that species before and I thought I'd heard of everything.

And though I don't give an ohring ohr, a tight pressure fills my horns, all the way through to the tip before rattling back down and settling in with a dull, aching throb. It's an ache which only gets worse as I turn away. It makes me wonder something ridiculous! Incredulous! Outlandish. Ha-ha-worthy...

If maybe, just this once, I should give this bawdy pirate my attention and actually *listen* to him.

"Human? What's human?" I say despite my best effort.

Tevbarannos closes the space between us and speaks like he's divulging sacred rites. "A new species class, they're under Voraxian and Niahhorru protection. They are...um...very...I mean the females...they're um...soft?"

I wait. He doesn't say more. "Are you asking me?" I shout at him. The nerve! Pagh!

"Centare," he says, shaking his head. "I mean." The hard plates that cover portions of his chest lift — a Niahhorru sign of embarrassment. I throw my hands in the air, remembering that even though I am the youngest clan chief, I'm still several rotations older than Tevbarannos. He's the youngest pirate I've met that counts among Rhorkanterannu's inner circle. Rhorkanterannu is the pirate king of Kor, though I'd never dare say that to his face. Pirates look down on kings. Absently, I wonder what they think of clan chiefs and less-than-quietly harrumph.

"Out with it, Tevbarannos!" I roar.

"I mean they're um…the females!" He jumps, like someone has just come up behind him and tapped him on the shoulder. He even turns around, but there's no one there. His upper shoulders shrug and he exhales, looking exhausted. He rubs his forehead and runs his upper right hand over the top of his head, where his tines shoot up like thick tusks.

He has a whole row of them studding his spine and though his are not as thick as some of the pirates' I've seen, they're certainly thick enough to impale someone if they were to run into his back on accident. I sigh whimsically… *I wish I had tusks. I wish I had tusks covering every inch of me!*

"Look. I'm only here alone because there aren't that many pirates Rhorkanterannu trusts to go looking for humans. They're delicate and very, um…easy to want to keep? Especially the females. Though some of our Niahhorru females are going mad for the human males, too. They're a very *alluring* species. I'm here searching for a human female. Herannathon is looking for her, actually, but we haven't seen Herannathon in two dozen solars."

"He's missing?" That *is* something of significance. I almost feel…sorry. I liked running into him at these stupid ohring functions, though I'd never tell him as much.

"He isn't *missing,* so much as he's *searching.* We've gotten reports from an Eshmiri friend that he's tailing an Egama battle pod."

"An Eshmiri friend?" I balk, jowls quivering with the force of my surprise. "What do you mean an Eshmiri friend? Do you mean fiend? Is that what you meant to say?"

Tevbarannos laughs though it doesn't look like he meant to. He shakes his head and smiles at me with all of his pearly teeth. "Centare, Raingar. A friend. Her name is Ashmara and she's a friend of the Niahhorru and the humans. She caught his signal some time back and, according to her, he's been waiting for the Egama to dock somewhere to gather supplies, but they haven't. They should be running out of food soon, so he's hopeful, but he hasn't been able to latch on mid-flight. They seem to know he's on their trail at all times and are consistently evading him."

"Well, good for all of them, including your Ashmara friend, whoever he is," I say, trying to get him to correct his previous insinuation that this Ashmara character is female. All Eshmiri are male. Everyone knows that.

I start to stomp off again, but Tevbarannos holds me back, the ungrateful whelp. "Rhorkanterannu sent me to try to help, just in case the Egama thought to stop here to trade. But then we heard that Igmora and Tyto had a female of their own and we wondered if maybe Herannathon made a mistake and the trade was conducted already."

"Well, why don't you just ask them! I don't understand what you're telling me all this for. I don't deal with flesh peddlers, pirates, hoomains, or any of the lot! I am Lemoran!"

The male groans at me, like *I'm* the insufferable one. He rubs one hand down his face and blocks me with two when I try to shove past him. "I'm coming to you because I want to know if they've extended you an invitation to see the female. They are asking for a pouch of kintarr just to view her and since you hold the most kintarr here, I was hoping you could tell me if she matched Herannathon's human's description."

My jaw opens, then shuts. I can nearly hear it creaking like a rusted hinge. On the one hand, I'm appalled by the idea of flesh peddlers — even ones so renown as Igmora and Tyto who spend *rotations* grooming their acquisitions to become the most exotic and skilled pleasurers in the galaxy — but I'm almost, just a little, *offended* that Igmora hasn't come to me.

She knows that if she wants kintarr, there is no one here to match our supply. Does she think even less of us Lemoran chiefs than she does Rhorkanterannu's youngest pirates?

I frown and narrow my eyes. "You were approached?"

Tevbarannos nods so guilelessly it makes me immediately annoyed because it's impossible to be annoyed with him. "By Igmora herself?"

He nods again.

I frown harder. "And you made an offer," I say. It is not a question, but an assumption.

"Centare, I told you. We're not looking for *any* human. We're looking for a human. A female. She has light brown skin...almost like helos? But not quite so bright. I'm not sure. It's white but not white and pink but not pink. Do you know what I mean?"

"Nob!" I growl, huffing between my lips, "How *should* I know? I haven't been approached!"

Tevbarannos's eyes widen. "Truly? But...but...but," he stammers.

"Out with it!"

"You hold the most kintarr!"

And I feel myself heat slightly. My horns...they're feeling even more tender than they did. They haven't felt tender like this since...ever. Since never. Even when I was a youngling and my horns were growing in, my head hurt, but my horns didn't hurt at all. Now it's the ohring horn part that hurts. That rough exterior could penetrate the flesh of any living creature, Oosa included — we're their greatest adversaries in the gladiator's arena of Evernor. But pained as they are like this, I couldn't attack a Walrey! I hate it. Just like I hate this whole ohring conversation. Hate it! *And I hate that Igmora didn't approach me most of all.*

"I..."

Tevbarannos cuts me off. "Word is that the current bid for the female is already up to four."

"Four pouches of kintarr for the female?" I huff, somewhat assuaged. "That doesn't seem like so much for a female cultivated by those degenerate..."

"Centare, centare." He shakes all four of his hands at me before slowly repeating, as if speaking to a youngling, "Four *tuns*, Raingar. Tuns, not pouches."

I choke on my own saliva. Tevbarannos is clapping on my back with two of his hands, which doesn't help matters much. The only thing that *would* help me regain my breath — and my sanity — is knowing that he made some kind of horrible joke and that he didn't just offer the two most despicable creatures on this side of the quadrants enough kintarr crystals to power a small city for a rotation. An amount that would take my entire clan half a rotation to mine.

"Shrov," he curses in Meero.

"Ohr," I curse in Lemoran, still choking. "Who offered them four tuns? Who offered them that much?

Don't tell me it was a pirate. I know you don't have that much kintarr or access to it and I swear to the stars, if you or Rhorkanterannu try to rob me, I'll rip off two of your arms. The bottom two."

He chuckles. "If Rhorkanterannu wanted to rob you, you'd never know he was there."

"I don't doubt it." I straighten up, clutching his shoulder as a support so hard he winces before prying my fingers off his skin. "That still doesn't explain who has access to that quantity and from where they acquired it."

"I saw her approach the Egama and the Oosa as well."

"I thought that the Egama sold the female?"

"We aren't sure."

"But if they did, why would they bid on her?"

He shakes his head. "Egama mercenaries might have sold her. These Egama here are of the federation."

"Hm," I scowl, then rub my chin thoughtfully — *though what I really want, is to rub my horns.* "They wouldn't have anything to do with one another."

"Precisely."

I stare down the hall, thinking back to the Egama giants I saw in the ballroom lurking over the other guests. One-eyed giants with moss-colored skin, they stand twice as tall as I do.

"I pity the female," I grumble, then I remember that I don't deal in flesh and I don't negotiate and I'd *never* pay that price for anything, *unless, maybe, it comes in a honey jar.* I start away from him again. As I do, the base of my horns don't just heat now, they itch. It's like the shell encasing them is contracting bit by bit, trying to smash them to pieces.

Tevbarannos blinks at me with his enormous silver eyes, looking young and innocent and confused, more than anything else. "You aren't even curious to see what she looks like?"

"Nob."

"Herannathon was right. You're a real bore, you know that?" He says with a grin.

It irks me, making me want to grin, too. "Pagh!" I shout, shrugging his grip off of my arm. "I don't have time for this..."

But as I turn to walk out of the tunnel, I'm arrested by the sight of the last being I'd have wanted to see among all the beings in these great and miserable cosmos. *Why oh why did they have to elect me to be clan chief? Gorman would have done a fine job!*

"Raingar." The sound of my name in that voice I've heard before makes me cringe. I turn down the hall, only to be halted by Tevbarannos blocking the way.

"Move," I shout at him.

He just stares past me in frustration. "Igmora," he says and for a few moments — the most painful of my life and that has nothing to do with my horns' sudden itchiness — we dance around one another, neither moving the respective direction we'd hoped.

My shoulders slump forward before electricity radiates up my spine at the gentle press of treacherously soft fingers against my bare arm just below the arm hole of my sleeveless tunic. My shoulders roll back, double time. My rough skin sizzles under her touch. She knows how to touch a male. How to manipulate. It's what they do, Igmora and her scaled mate.

"Igmora," I say stonily, turning to see the female with bright orange skin. Some say she's part-Hypha part-Voraxian, but I don't know. I don't care. All I know is that she's orange and about as gentle as a whip. She stands slightly shorter than I do, but is waif-thin and covered in a slick fabric that catches light and turns it all manner of color depending on the way she moves. It attracts the eye, but I don't dare look anywhere but into hers. She sees everything. She knows what males like. But I don't like anything that can't be found on Lemora.

I hate everything.

But I like my rock. My rock is nice and the people on it, solid.

She rolls her eyes, the color of pitch, so oily and black. Her gaze flashes to Tevbarannos. She slinks past me, slides her other hand over his shoulder and pulls away from me in the same fluid motion. "Don't worry, I'm not here for you. I come with some news, Tevbarannos. For a small price, I'd be willing to give you a viewing. It won't be as…*intimate* as the viewings some of the bidders will receive, but I'd be willing to let you have a look to confirm your…" She casts a dismissive glance in my direction before pulling Tevbarannos past me and dropping her tone so that I can no longer hear it. She has his attention — *all of it* — and then she…they both…she…*she…*

She turns her back on me.

I…I am not a particularly proud male, but I don't like that. I hate it. And I do something unexpected. Instead of keeping silent and continuing my hunt for the exit, I shout, "A decent male prefers his female strong and salt of the earth! Not a fragile pet that he had to pay an obscene amount of kintarr for!"

"Alright, Raingar," she says without looking over her shoulder at me. "I am aware of your feelings on the matter. You don't need to worry about receiving an invitation from myself or my mate. I wouldn't dare dishonor your Lemoran sensibilities."

"You...I...pagh!"

"The exit is down the main hall to the right. I know that's what you're looking for, anyway. Goodbye, Raingar. Good luck with your...negotiations." She glances at me over her shoulder and offers a smile that's either menacing or filled with humor. With her, it's hard to tell the difference.

Then she and Tevbarannos disappear around the corner. I follow. I follow them out into the main hall but where they go left, I go...well, I don't go anywhere at first. I just stare in the direction they've disappeared wondering what's unnerving me more — my curiosity, my pride...or my horns. *I'm touching them again.* The itch has settled into that stultifying pressure that I despise more than Igmora and the sum of her unsavory parts.

Air! Wind! Fresh air. Not this perfumed princess piss. I stomp towards the exit, past the mok-biz table, past the Oosa coupling openly on some atrociously bright green benches. I shudder and it has nothing to do with how I feel seeing them and everything to do with the strange taste of the perfume in the air, which seems to be giving me an even more severe headache. The scent makes me frown.

I think about what Tevbarannos said about this newly discovered *hoomain* species. *Soft*, he'd called them. I wonder if he means they're like the Oosa or the Oroshi. I doubt that, though. He also called them *alluring* and very few would qualify the Oosa or the Oroshi as alluring, outside of their own species. I can't picture her, but I pity her. Based on what Tevbarannos said, she'll go to either an Egama warrior who's likely to break her on their first coupling or an Oosa clan who's equally likely to suffocate her with their blubber.

I'm still thinking about this sad female coupling with a blob or a beast when I reach the tunnel that leads to the exit and stomp down it. There are a few doors in this hall. Which did Igmora say to take? The one on the right? I can't remember. There aren't any beings here to ask — not that I would have asked even if there had been — so I pick the farthest door down the hall on the right and push the door open...

My jaw unhinges, easily this time. A hinge so well oiled that air flutters in and out of my gaping maw breezily. For a moment, I forget where I am. Not where. Who. I forget *who* I am.

All I know is that this is not the exit and that my horns have discovered the very definition of pain and yet, I could not care any less.

The scent suffocates me and I inhale once, and then again for good measure and a ghastly thought occurs to me...

I don't...hate this.

2
Essmira

My fingers are shaky and my heart is slamming against my chest. I'm sweating uncontrollably and a female never sweats.

Females don't sweat, or shake or slam — *bannnng*. That's the sound of my hand connecting with the latch on the window frame. Females don't slam, but I'm slamming now.

I thought...I thought I could do this. I've been training for this my whole life. Igmora showed me pictures of every manner of being over the rotations and my body was *prepared* to accommodate them. I thought my mind was too, but it isn't. It really isn't.

The Egama was *so* much taller than I thought he'd be. He was terrifying and worse, Igmora let him touch me despite Tyto's protests and the Egama's grip was rough, cruelly so. I know that Igmora isn't my mother and I know that Tyto isn't my father — they've made that exceptionally clear my entire life to this point — but I still mistakenly thought that they'd want to protect me better than this.

Tyto especially. I haven't forgotten what he whispered in my ear when we disembarked. He told me

I shouldn't worry. That no male here would be able to match the price Igmora wants for me. He told me that soon, I'd be back in the safety of his nest, though I didn't understand why he used the word *back* considering that Igmora had never let him take me there before. I asked him and he told me that soon, what Igmora thought wouldn't matter at all. Then, he touched my back, touched my neck in ways that Igmora discouraged — that they'd fought over...

"Tyto, with your claws and your barbed tail, you'll ruin the merchandise. She isn't meant for you."

This time though, she was too distracted to see it, already working her schemes to give me to the one male she said she'd planned for me all along and, in her absence, Tyto let his forked tongue trace my shoulder up to my ear. He shuddered and let his wandering claws cup my rear through my dress and I let him because I thought that it would be the last time and that my new master would treat me at least *decently* and that he would take me away from Tyto and his frightening stare and, more importantly, away from a life of captivity.

But then Igmora introduced the potential masters, with their wandering hands and violent eyes.

The only other bidders that offered enough to compete with the Egama were a clan of Oosa and, seeing them in the flesh, I'm revolted by the idea of letting their slippery blue skin enter me in between my legs — *perhaps even more revolted than at the thought of spending a lifetime in Tyto's nest, though I'm not fully sure yet.*

The Oosas' collective touch might not have been hard, but it was no less cruel than the Egama warlord's. They touched everywhere, caring nothing for communication between us. Between themselves, the bright lights that illuminate their translucent bodies is communication enough. But my physiology doesn't allow for that. Perhaps if there were some sort of translator…

"Oh! What are you saying?" I whisper out loud to myself in Lemoran, the language I've come to speak best over the rotations. "That you'd *like* to bed an Oosa? Nob, you wouldn't. They're slimy and wet and Igmora said…" I wince dramatically, like I've been hit. It sort of feels like I have been.

Igmora made promises, showing me pictures of males with warriors' builds, bulky arms and massive legs, horns shooting up into the sky in defiance of the stars, and rough, gruff faces built to intimidate, more than charm. I'd liked the look of those males, the Lemoran ones in particular. Perhaps, only because I'd been trained to, but I can't deny the arousal I feel at the sight of their images.

But I was also trained to like the Egama… Niahhorru, too, and so far, my reality was all tentacles and gelatin, eyes as big as my torso, fins in alarming colors…mouths without tongues or teeth or worse, mouths with too many tongues *and* teeth…

I shudder and beat my hand harder against the window. "This isn't working."

I quickly turn around and find a hideous statue on top of a monstrously decorated table. The statue is of a Quadrant One prince and was cast in a most unusual and, um, *flattering* way. The little prince's cock is as long as his two legs.

"Even this prince would have been better than the males who came to view me," I snort — an unattractive sound Igmora didn't manage to train out of me. All she did manage to instill in me was, at the involuntary sound, an immediate sense of shame to follow it.

I wince again and try to refocus. I lift the gold statue of the boy with limbs like mine and the same amount of eyes and teeth and ears, but skin that's colored in gold and hair that's every color found under this planet's three suns. I'd have been fine with a golden rainbow for a mate so long as his voice was a *little* kind and his touch was a *little* gentle.

"Essmira, you don't have time for this!" I can hear footsteps in the hall — either real or imagined, they're terrifying. The latch on the golden window won't come loose, so I focus on the glass and crack the prince's golden head against it. A splinter appears in the bright pink glass and then shivers outward, like a spiderweb. I thump the statue against it again. My arm is shaking. The back of my neck is covered in sweat. *What will Tyto do when he finds me?* Tyto with his reptilian skin and barbed tail. *He's used that tail on me more than once, against Igmora's wishes even, and it hurt badly every time. He wants me to run, just so Igmora will give me up to him and so that he can spend his lifetime punishing me...*

"No. Don't think like that. *If*...if he finds you. And he won't. You can't be found if you escape. I mean, when...when..." I snort again as my panic builds. My arm gets jerky but, as I bring the statue against the window pane a fourth time, it shatters.

I return the statue to its proper place on the hideous table, then grab the ottoman beside it and drag it below the window. I lift my heavy skirt and step up onto the thing, which is a little alarming because it's green and very furry and possibly *alive*. It rolls beneath me and I squeal, my hands reaching out to catch hold of something to keep myself upright. The first thing in my vicinity? The jagged window. I grab onto it and pain lances my palm immediately.

Nob. Nob nob nobnobnobnobnobnob. What have I done?

I stare down at the blood on my hands and the cuts slashing horizontally across them. "Essmira, you have to escape now. You don't have any other choice. If Igmora sees you like this...if Tyto sees you..." And just as the first breath of fresh air caresses my face and neck, the doorknob behind me twists and the door swings inward and open.

I turn, jaw working, eyes growing wide and round in my face. Nob. Nobnobnobnobnobnobnob. "Essmira, this is it," I snort in terror.

But when my gaze swings around and connects with the being who just stepped into the room, my breath gathers in my stomach like a series of knots I can't free for an entirely new reason. This being isn't Igmora or Tyto, but one whose picture Igmora showed me often. This is the Lemoran she said would buy me.

I exhale shakily, suddenly so relieved I could cry, and then I remember that I'm supposed to be making a good impression so that he *does* actually buy me. If he doesn't, there's a possibility I might still be sold to the Egama or the Oosa or maybe a surprise species Igmora's prepared for me in secret and that's even more gruesome than the ones who've spent the solar pawing at me.

"Calm down, Essmira," I whisper quietly under my breath. I pray he can't hear it. I don't want him to think I do this often, though I do, or that I'm crazy, which...after a lifetime in captivity, I might be.

I stiffen and straighten and carefully fold my fingers over the fresh cuts in my hands and offer him a bow, rather than the Lemoran greeting, which would require me to show him my injured hand. He might not want me if he sees the cut on my hand. Tyto always hated the few times I got scrapes. *He liked licking them clean, though.*

Hinging at the waist, I bow deeply, but when I try to step one foot in front of the other, the furry thing under my feet decides to keep rolling, this time, straight out from under me. …

I go flying across the furry carpet, landing hard on my right shoulder. My head hits the floor, springing painlessly off of the plush blue and yellow carpet. A strangled grunt hits my ears and I groan instead of reassuring it. *A female must always reassure the male, even when he is wrong. It's very important for his pride and this fragile beast should be protected above all things. It is your duty as his pleasurer to bolster it, even at the expense of your own.*

I wonder distantly if this is what Tyto taught Igmora, what Igmora taught Tyto, or what they taught one another. She always seemed like the Alpha between the two of them and if Tyto ever frightened her, she did not let it show.

"I'm fine, truly," I say, but the breath has been knocked out of me and my heart is hammering in my lungs now, making my words unintelligible. Tears come to my eyes as I fight for my next breath and then gulp it in greedily, making unattractive sounds in the back of my throat.

"Ohr! Stay where you are," an angry voice grumbles before hands that are just as rough, just as angry as the voice they belong to, fit to my shoulders and pick me up like a grain sack.

Dooth. That's the sound my feet make when he sets me down and, though the room spins, I force myself to remain upright. *A female must always be graceful. It helps reassure the male, providing him with essential comfort.* I force a smile. *A female must always smile, it...*

I open my eyes and have a tough time keeping my smile in place. This male, he is *much* bigger than he appeared in the holo images Igmora showed me though I doubt, looking at him now, that an image would have ever done him justice.

He carries a history with him written in the rings of his eyes. There are so many of them. White on the outside, like mine, but then black and blue and purple and grey and orange and yellow and pink and in the very center, an iridescent green that flashes blue when the light strikes it.

His eyes are, in a word, beautiful. Even if the rest of him is too rough to use such a descriptor.

He has the same rough skin the Egama have, only his shoulders are blockier, almost stone-like in their roughness. His cheeks are high and his lips are full and a pale brown against his medium-brown skin. He doesn't seem to have hair anywhere because his pate gleams bald between twin horns that loop so huge past his cheeks and then up above the top of his head that it's a wonder he can see out of his peripheries.

His chest is even deeper than my shoulders are wide and appears to be completely solid...as solid as stone. I have a hard time processing whether this being before me is truly made out of the same blood and bone I am or if he's just rock all the way through. I have to fight the urge to lift a hand and touch his arm to see for myself, but then I recognize that the temperature around me has increased with his presence, so I must assume that, if he is stone, it's at least got a pulse.

I stay my touch and remind myself that even though males like to be touched by females, it should be on the male's command at the time of their choosing. This is what females do. *Females who don't want to end up on their backs in pleasure houses*. If I play my tokens correctly, this male could be the *only* male I have to pleasure.

And it would not be a tragedy.

So far, he has not touched me inappropriately or done me any harm. He hasn't even shot me a lascivious leer. He's just watching me like I'm a…like I'm any other member of the delegation outside, even though these are the Quadrants' most esteemed leaders and traders and I'm but a thing to be traded.

He looks at me like I'm real.

My cheeks warm at the thought and a sudden burst of nerves wash over me. I could mess this up. He could decide not to bid and I could go home with the Egama, at best, and that's only if he wants me now that I've been so foolish as to cut myself. *Males like unblemished females. Your skin should and will be perfect for me.* That's what Tyto always used to tell me though, in Igmora's presence he'd amend himself to say that I'd need to be perfect for when they *sell* me.

Pushing thankfully away from thoughts of Tyto, I lift my gaze from his chest, past the worn out collar of his cream-colored tunic with the frayed olive stitching around the neck, up over his chin which is hard and smooth, his mouth, wide-set nose, back up to his eyes. My heart beats faster. His eyes are so pretty. I could pleasure this male, I think quite suddenly. My mouth opens and I realize with horror that my next words are going to be to tell him just that.

I clamp my mouth shut and am aghast when he's the one to speak first. *It is the female's job to speak first and smooth out the conversation. The male does not need to trouble himself with this.*

"Are you hurt?" He speaks to me in Meero, but I can tell it is not his native language. Nob, his native tongue is the same one that was bred into me from the start.

I offer him another deferential bow before making the quick switch into Lemoran. "I am perfectly fine, thank you so much for asking. You're very kind."

I stand and meet his gaze and attempt a smile. It's strange how much more difficult this is out from in front of a mirror. I've practiced this smile with a thousand different subtleties — perfected it, even — but faced with his scowl, it's a little hard to remain confident in it. I've practiced that smile, sure, but this is the first time it's been tested. *And I cannot afford to fail now.*

He narrows his gaze and takes a half step back. His own gaze wanders over my face, offering no critique or assessment. The other bidders were quite vocal in what they liked about me, but he is...silent. His flinty gaze passes to the window and then drops to the floor, like he's searching for something.

Evidently unable to find it, his mouth puckers and his forehead wrinkles and his prominent yet hairless brows scrunch together over his nose. "What did you smash the window with?"

He cannot know that I tried to run. *A female does not run. Not from Tyto.* Not if she fears punishment. "I..." I swallow. *A female is always elegant.* "Pardon me?"

His scowl becomes more severe — so severe, it's like he's trying to squish all of the features of his face into as small an area as possible. It would be funny if his ire weren't targeted at me because I know that if he chooses to act on it, it is my duty to accept his anger in any and all of its forms.

"What did you use to break the window?" He says again and, when I don't do anything but stutter foolishly, he prompts, "Was it your hand?"

"Nob, it was the statue." I indicate with my chin.

He doesn't look away from my face. "What statue?"

"The one on the lovely little side table just to your right."

"I don't see it."

"But you…" *Never contradict the male. He is always correct.* I have to fight a frown because Igmora didn't prepare me for this. My instinct is to disagree with him, because I *know* he did not look, but I also know that I need to help him along and make the answer to his question quite clear.

I swallow. "Of course. It's just over here."

I walk sideways to stand beside the statue so I don't have to remove my wrists from behind my back where they're safely hidden away.

His shoulders slump forward. He rubs his face and sighs, as if he's exasperated with me. Panic surges in my lungs. I almost snort, but manage to disguise it beneath a delicate sneeze. When I look up he grunts, "We both know I don't give an ohr about the statue. Let me see your hands, female."

The female must obey the male's commands. His every command. She must be gracious and do whatever he says. But if I show him my hands, then I'll…

"Pagh! I don't have all lunar!" His voice is so loud it booms through the room and through me, like I'm nothing but air.

I jump and quickly hold my fists out in front of me, cautious to only show him the backs of my hands. It has the desired effect because his own fingers halt as they circle my wrists and I hear him suck in a very subtle, yet reverent breath.

"Your markings..." he says softly, his thumb rubbing over the bright red pattern that curls across my dark brown skin. "Tevbarannos didn't mention markings. You're not the female he's looking for."

"Nob, I'm not," I say, confirming his words. The kind pirate male had looked so sullen when Igmora had given him a glimpse of me from the door. He hadn't been allowed to touch, like the others. "He said so himself."

"Good," the male grumbles to himself. He makes the word sound like a curse, distracted as he is by the colors clashing over my arms. "That's good."

The red skin-toned markings extend over the backs of my palms, circling both arms. On the right side, they slide past my shoulder and unfold over my neck before curling around my right ear. On the left, the markings extend up my arm and spread over my shoulder blade to form one enormous swirl on my back. Though he cannot see them, my breasts are also red and so is my stomach, abdomen and groin. There are also red swirls on both my feet and ankles and my left leg, but strangely none at all on the right one.

Abruptly, he clears his throat and when he speaks again, his interest seemingly evaporates. He's dispassionate surliness once more. "I haven't seen your markings before. Are you from Quadrant One?"

My heart summersaults. My stomach dives. My lungs float. *He doesn't know who I am. He isn't here to buy me at all.* I gasp and rip my wrists out of his overwhelming and rough fingers. "Stars!" I stumble back, running into the moving chair and causing it to scurry away from me again.

Because if he isn't going to be my master, then all of my talk of having *one* master has flown out of that broken window. Because no one will want me if I've been tainted by another male and maintaining my purity is the most important commandment I've been given. *A female must be untouched, except by her master. If she is, then she will end up on her back with not just one master, but hundreds of them.* If I'm tainted, Igmora might just give me to Tyto freely then for him to torture with his pronged tail and his cutting claws before voiding me into space, like trash, as it's rumored he's done to other pleasurers before.

"Who are you? What are you doing here?" I shout again when he says nothing.

His shoulders jolt, as if stunned. He glances around like he's confused, then reaches up and touches the base of his left horn in what appears to be an absent gesture. "I thought this was the way out."

"Nob...nob nob nob..." I'm suddenly furious. So furious that I do the unthinkable. I rush to the small side table, grab the statue and turn... Before I know what's come over me, I chuck the statue at his head and, in a split instance of pure horror, I realize my aim was true. The gold connects.

The little alien prince's penis clunks against the center of this mighty male's forehead before bouncing off and onto the carpet. The huge male canters back a step, like I just blasted him with a cannon instead of a dinky little thing, barely a trinket in his oversized paws.

"Off!" He scoffs, moving the hand on his horn to the space between his eyes, so large and lovely. "What was that for?"

Honestly, it's a good question. I should be angry that he came in and touched me or that he saw me and that no one is supposed to see me except for the bidders. I should even be angry that he came in and stole precious moments from me that I should have been using to escape. But I'm mostly, irrationally, overwhelmingly angry because in those precious seconds when I thought he was here to purchase me, I felt something I haven't felt in a very long time. Maybe, even...ever.

I felt hope.

And now, just as quickly, he's stolen away this shriveled, desiccated dream that he never knew he gave me at all.

"You are not supposed to be here!" I point at him and a droplet of blood slashes from the end of my finger and onto his tunic, making my hand feel like a blade.

"Your ohring hand," he growls, touching his horn again — nob, grabbing onto it like he's worried it'll fly away. Then he reaches up with his other hand and grabs both horns at once. He looks rather...*ridiculous* like this, but I don't have the adequate time to appreciate it as I scramble once again for the window. "I told you, you were injured."

"You didn't tell me I was injured, I *was* injured and right now you're in my way," I snap. I've never snapped at anybody before and my momentary thrill at how good it feels is quickly doused by shame.

I open my mouth to apologize until he grunts, "Your way?"

"Yeffa," I huff, annoyed all over again. "You're Lemoran. You're supposed to be one of the clever ones, but right now you sound about as dense as an Egama." *Wait. Essmira, did you just insult the male?*

"I...you...an Egama!" He shouts and suddenly he's right up against me. I know I should be panicked, but my need to escape is too large and unwieldy to fear being alone in a room with a male who has no intention of purchasing me and, evidently, too great to stop me from insulting him.

"I'm clearly trying to escape, now would you hand me that fuzzy chair over there so I can reach the window?" I reach for the shattered frame again, not caring about the jagged edges, but he snatches my wrist from the air.

"You cut your hands the first time and now you're trying again and you have the gall to call *me* an Egama?"

I try to yank my arm away from him, but the point is futile. He could have broken every bone in my body with likely very little effort on his part, but I couldn't really care less at the moment. I shove his chest with my other hand, smearing my own bright red blood across his no longer pristine tunic. *How many zaps of electricity would this have won me from Tyto's eager claws? Many. Hundreds, spaced out over solars.*

I nearly scream, "Don't you see I'm trying to escape?"

His lips mouth the word *escape* as his eyes dart from my hands to the window back to my hands back to the window before finally dropping to my face. He gasps — *gasps* — and suddenly staggers away from me, dropping my arm like it's a rotten log teeming with flesh-burrowing insects.

"Ohr!" He hisses. He grabs onto his left horn again, only this time, when my gaze follows, his hand twitches and his face does this horrible twisting thing, like he's in a world of pain.

I jolt, startled by such a sight and the training beaten into me from birth kicks in. "Are you alright?" I reach for him, intending to soothe, only to be arrested by the soft clearing of a throat on the other side of the room.

I glance up and all the blood drains out of my body. My soul abandons my bones and floats up and out through that jagged patch of window. *Bye bye.* The dark hole where I'm going, I won't need it anyway. Standing in the open doorway is Igmora.

She steps forward and I know her black eyes well enough by now to sense that she's neither surprised nor horrified though she appears to be both. On the contrary, the false breathiness to her voice is well rehearsed and the outrage she levels towards me is something completely contrived. No one else can see it though. And my concern isn't for Igmora anyway, but for Tyto, an Egama giant, and the Oosa delegation crowding the space behind her.

Continue reading in ebook or hardback on Amazon and in paperback anywhere online books are sold

All Books by Elizabeth

Xiveri Mates: SciFi Alien and Shifter Romance
Taken to Voraxia, Book 1 (Miari and Raku)
Taken to Nobu, Book 2 (Kiki and Va'Raku)
Taken to Sasor, Book 3 (Mian and Neheyuu) *standalone
Taken to Heimo, Book 4 (Svera and Krisxox)
Taken to Kor, Book 5 (Deena and Rhork)
Taken to Lemora, Book 6 (Essmira and Raingar)
Taken by the Pikosa Warlord, Book 7 (Halima and Ero)
*standalone
Taken to Evernor, Book 8 (Nalia and Herannathon)
Taken to Sky, Book 9 (Ashmara and Jerrock)
Taken to Revatu, A Xiveri Mates Novella (Jewel and
Gorak)

Population: Post-Apocalyptic SciFi Romance
Population, Book 1 (Abel and Kane)
Saltlands, Book 2 (Abel and Kane)
Generation One, Book 3 (Diego and Pia)
Brianna, Book 4 (Lahve and Candy)
more to come!

Brothers: Interracial Dark Mafia Romantic Suspense
The Hunting Town, Book 1 (Knox and Mer, Dixon and Sara)
The Hunted Rise, Book 2 (Aiden and Alina, Gavriil and Ify)
The Hunt, Book 3 (Anatoly and Candy, Charlie and Molly)

Made in the USA
Middletown, DE
31 December 2021